Sugar Island

WHERE VERONIKA LAKE VANISHED INTO THIN AIR...

A KAREN BLACKSTONE THRILLER - VOLUME 1

NINO S. THEVENY

SEBASTIEN THEVENY

Translated from French to English

By Jacquie Bridonneau

Original Title : *La disparition de Veronika Lake*

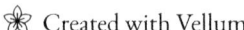 Created with Vellum

Prologue

SUGAR ISLAND, SUMMER OF 2017

"CYNTHIA? Ah! There you are. You know where the hell Veronika is?"

Tom Malone, holding a bottle of beer in his left hand, nervously pushed away the greasy strand of hair on his forehead, while running up to Cynthia Favor.

"Haven't seen her for a good half an hour," she replied to the visibly drunk young man. "How come? I thought she was with you."

"She was. But she took off."

Cynthia shook her head.

"Now what?" she asked.

"Nothing. I mean nothing worse than usual."

"You guys had another fight, didn't you?"

"What's it to you?"

"Hey! Quit talking to me like that! You just asked me if I saw your girlfriend and a second later you're getting aggressive. Fuck off, Tom. You don't even realize that you're half drunk, like each time we get together and after that you're astonished when your girl takes off. Just look at yourself, with your can of beer hanging on the tips of your fingers like a continuation of your arm. Like you had a graft when you were born. Veronika must have simply had enough of your alcoholic delusions and decided to get some fresh air."

Behind them, in the sumptuous villa of the Lake family, music was blaring. A couple of minutes ago Cynthia felt she wanted to escape the frenzy for a short while. She walked down to the little isolated creek across from Lily Bay and looked out on the lights of the rare cottages there, a quarter of a mile from the bay.

Tom groaned trying to arrange his hair.

"Shit. Fuck that bitch!" he said without knowing if he was referring to Cynthia or Veronika who wasn't there.

In a large circular gesture, he tossed his can of beer over the young lady's head, looking at it land in the lake with a deaf *ploc* before filling with water and sinking.

Above them they could see a rising half-moon in the star-filled sky.

Then the young man turned around and rushed up to the villa where a handful of dancers were on the patio, next to a large swimming pool lit by colored spotlights.

. . .

Cynthia was alone again, sitting right on the pebbles by the beach, her bare feet in the dark waters of Lake Moosehead. She circled her knees with her arms, putting her head in the hollow created by this nearly fetal position and sighed deeply while closing her eyes.

What a crazy summer, she thought to herself. A summer that's over, like an unreal interlude for their group of friends. A summer that none of them would forget. No one would never forget this summer. They'd have good or bad memories of it, who cares, but would never forget it.

The summer of 2017, for Cynthia, Tom, Veronika, and the others, would always be the cornerstone of their youth.

After a few minutes of reflection, the young lady got up, dusted off her shorts and walked up to the villa.

When she got there, she noticed that the atmosphere wasn't the same. The music was still playing in the speakers on each corner of the pool, but no one was dancing anymore. Veronika Lake's guests were all rushing around now. Each of them seemed to be looking for their hostess who'd vanished. Some were looking in the huge yard surrounding the property whereas others were looking in the rooms, including the outbuildings. Tom, amongst them, was now nearly hysterical.

"Fuck! I'm too old to play hide-and-go-seek!" he shouted.

He rushed down the wooden staircase into the living room right when Cynthia walked in.

"You didn't find her?" she asked, looking at the big clock on the wall above the fireplace where six-feet long logs could fit.

Three a.m. Sunday August 27, 2017.

No, no one had found Veronika. Not at three, not at five, not even at seven when the sun came up, making it easier to see.

No one had found Veronika in the villa, in the yard, on the huge Sugar Island beach, in the dense forests surrounding it, nor in the waters of Lake Moosehead.

On the shoreline, the inflatable boat that had been used to bring the party-goers from the continent to the island, was docked in the same place where it had been attached to the pontoon, about six p.m. on Saturday, August 26th.

So where was Veronika?

Why had no one seen her? Her or her corpse, floating on the surface of the dark lake, swollen, or stuck on the branches of some dead trees?

No, no one had found Veronika, despite the search in Sugar Island Forest, despite having dredged the dark waters of Lake Moosehead, despite helicopters flying over the huge area in Piscataquis County surrounding the lake.

. . .

This Sunday, August 27, 2017, has remained the mysterious and unsolved day when Veronika Lake vanished from the face of the earth.

CHAPTER 1
Piscataquis

WHEN MYRTILLE FAIRBANKS, the greatest boss in the world, asked me to write an article on the disappearance of a young lady in Greenville, I immediately thought about South Carolina.

But when I got to Greenville, Maine, I quickly understood we weren't talking about the same city.

One thousand five hundred souls max, according to the official census, a long way from the sixty thousand that its homologue - much more well known - in South Carolina.

Here, in Piscataquis Country, the least populated one in Maine, no need for a satnav to get around in town. The easiest way to know where you are is to situate the little port on Lake Moosehead and then look out at the town that spread - maybe I'm exaggerating here - around it. People apparently make their living by fishing or the timber industry, omnipresent in this little town.

Don't bother looking for three-story buildings; the tallest building is the town hall, one of the rare buildings made from brick, and all the other dwellings look like big wooden cabins. No need of course to say that delinquency must hover around zero percent, as there are no fences anywhere. Makes you wonder what the police force does all day long.

Anyway, they sure didn't find Veronika Lake, the seventeen-year-old kid who disappeared five years ago now and who was never found dead or alive.

I WAS STAYING at Grenville Inn, a stately residence overlooking the lake, on East Cove. As my boss had been quite generous for my expense package and there weren't too many hotels in this neck of the woods, I was shown to a charming room with elegant woodwork and a bit dated decoration, including the choice of wallpaper that seemed to date back to when this hotel had been built. The advantage of this place? It would be calm, meaning that I'd be able to carry out my investigation on the Veronika Lake affair with peace of mind.

At least that was the plan.

What was to follow though would prove that sticking my nose in the troubled affairs of a miniscule town in one of the most remote places in Maine wasn't a piece of cake.

Stirring up Lake Moosehead's still waters wasn't a good idea either. Same thing about waking up a moose[*], king of the forest, and the animal that this lake and the little mountain you could make out from the west bank were named after.

On the other hand, my boss could have chosen another season rather than October to send me to freeze my butt off here. But still, I was going to *make the best of it*.

I walked into my room, thanking the charming hostess who handed me my keys. She told me that breakfast was served in the dining room from six thirty to ten every morning. As for lunch and dinner, she said she was sorry, they weren't served here but gave me a couple of addresses "in town" where I could find something to eat that was "not too expensive and not too bad." I was just hoping they didn't serve moose steak...

I checked the time on my cell phone, which confirmed what my stomach had been trying to tell me: I was hungry. The three-hour drive - including breaks - from Portland had whetted my appetite. I went back to my car in the parking lot and drove to the center of town, called Greenville Village.

I took the long way around so I could drive through "downtown" as well as the roads on the lakeshore, as much as to appreciate the scenery as to find a place to eat.

I finally decided to stop at the Dockside Tavern, where they served all sorts of pizzas, burgers and hot-dogs, but decided to try a *handwich*, as they called it

---

[*] Moose, the largest living cervid in North America.

here to differentiate it from other sandwiches, made from fried fish, obviously.

"On vacation here?" the waitress mechanically asked me while chewing gum as she brought me my order.

"No. For work," I replied.

"What field? Water or forestry? 'Cuz here you know…"

"Not at all, Charlene," I answered, seeing her name on her apron.

The waitress didn't budge. She seemed to be waiting for me to tell her more about my presence here. Probably one of those people who like to shoot the breeze with customers to kill time. I hesitated to inform her why I was here in Greenville, but when I looked at her, I said to myself that she must be in her early twenties, twenty-five at the most, and that she'd certainly have known Veronika Lake, as they were about the same age. I decided to throw my bottle in the lake water…

"I'm a journalist," I finally said.

"From the Portland Press Herald? We get it every morning and our customers like to leaf through it while having a coffee."

"No, not at all. I work for TCM."

"What's that?"

"True Crime Mysteries."

"Really? One of those magazines specialized in criminal affairs? Good Lord, I can't read things like that. They scare the daylight out of me! Tell me,

Ma'am, is it true all those awful things they write in magazines like that? Excuse me, if I'm offending you."

I gave her a conciliant smile.

"No problem Charlene, I know what a lot of people think about magazines like mine. But a lot of people read them, that's for sure. They read them without daring to tell others. Crimes have always sparked curiosity, maybe unhealthy, but real. Plus we don't just write about serial killers or pedophiles who should be thrown into jail. Me for example, I'm specialized in cold cases about unsolved disappearances."

When I said that, I saw the waitress make a face while looking at me, worried.

"Have a nice meal then, Ma'am. I have to go back to the kitchens."

She wiped her hands on the front of her apron and turned around, leaving me with my fish handwich.

I had to admit though that Dockside Tavern made a decent burger. With tartar sauce and home-made fries, it was delicious. A good omen for my stay here?

"Some dessert?" asked Charlene a few minutes later, clearing my empty plate.

"I'm full, but I do want to try the gluten-free chocolate cake."

She brought it to me, and I spoke before she could leave again.

"Did you know someone called Veronika Lake?"

She froze. I could tell she had something to say but was hesitating. She turned around.

"Enjoy your dessert, Ma'am."

And I did enjoy it looking out at the sunset over the hills on the western side of Lake Moosehead. Magnificent scenery, peaceful, a calm little town. Seemingly...

While gobbling down the last spoonful of my chocolate cake, I was wondering if my presence here wasn't going to make a few waves on the surface of this too calm lake. But a job is a job. And not just to make money. I must admit that I've always loved solving the mysteries I work on. For me, shedding light on an unexplained disappearance is bringing justice to the missing person. Resuscitating their souvenir, at least.

But when the first person I met didn't want to talk to me, I said to myself that this one might be a tough one.

That was why I didn't believe my eyes when Charlene put the bill on the table, attached to a saucer. On the piece of paper, above the total amount to be paid, she wrote "*Thanks for coming, Charlene,*" something all waitresses do, except that right after her name there was a little arrow telling me to turn the bill around.

She'd written something on the back.

"I finish at nine. Meet me at the Stress-Free Moose Pub, half a block on your right when you leave."

CHAPTER 2
In the middle of nowhere

AFTER HAVING FINISHED EATING, as it was late, I decided to have some herbal tea rather than one of the many beers on tap at the pub. I sat down at a small round table in a corner. It smelled like hops and fries here; the TV screens were showing a baseball game with the Boston Red Sox, one of the teams closest to Maine and one of the Major League's most famous ones.

Ten p.m. I was chomping at the bit as the minutes went by, heating my hands around my warm cup, wondering if Charlene would actually come as expected from her message.

I heard the bell ring as the door opened and looked into her eyes as she walked in, swinging by the bar to order a drink.

"I was afraid you wouldn't show," I said.

"Sorry. Couldn't get off sooner. But I'm here now."

She was still chewing her sempiternal gum. I wondered if it was the same one the whole day or if like a rodent, all she did was chomp with an empty mouth. I got my answer when she took the gum out of her mouth and stuck it in a little napkin, then put it in the ashtray when the waiter brought her beer to her.

"Here you go Charlie. Haven't seen you in a while."

"Too much work, Jamie," she said, apologizing.

"Cheers!" I said, raising my now nearly cold glass of tea.

I let her savor a long amber swallow.

"Thanks for coming. So I can conclude that the name of Veronika Lake must be familiar to you. Did you know her?"

She put her beer down and licked the white foam from her lips.

"A little. You know. We were about the same age, us two. We went to the same schools. But we didn't really hang out together."

"Yet you seemed a bit troubled in the restaurant when I mentioned her name and disappearance. How come?"

Charlene winced.

"Let's say... like it's a sensitive subject here."

"What do you mean by sensitive?"

"Quasi taboo. I'm sure you noticed, Greenville is a little village, a little fishing village. Anyway it's in the middle of nowhere in the huge forests in Maine, at the end of the continent. You know, you could say we live in a little lost place where nothing ever happens, see what I mean?"

"Another facet of the American dream? But lots of people like Maine, don't they? Like I'm thinking of Stephan King."

"Sure, he likes Bangor, but he wouldn't like Greenville. I guess that's all I had to say, Ma'am."

"Please call me Karen.

"So, Karen, what you have to understand here is that people like living in this little place where nothing happens, and they all want to forget this story that's already five years old and that dug up enough dirt back then. Now, the waters in the lake are calm, and we don't want you to stir things up. Got it?"

I nodded.

"Sure, I understand. But my job consists in stirring up the mud, lifting rocks where fish are hiding under, so I can tell our readers the truth."

Charlene sighed.

"Readers looking for excitement, they're peeping Toms who lick their chops when they read about how others suffer in your despicable magazine."

"That's not how I see it."

"Of course, it's your job. I understand, you have to make a living. Flipping burgers or rummaging around in other people's garbage…"

Now it was my turn to sigh. I was trying to figure out why this young lady said she'd help while criticizing my intensions and my work.

"Charlene, you never wanted to know what really

happened to this young lady from Greenville? This is something that's never bothered you?"

"I told you; we weren't besties or anything."

"But still, it was a local drama and I'm sure it impacted a lot of people here. Do you know what happened?"

She finished her beer and put her glass down a bit too loudly on the table.

"No idea. Nobody knows! One day she was there and the next day she'd vanished. We never saw her again. That's it. Do people often disappear in thin air? In your job, you must know that."

"There weren't any early warning signs before she disappeared?"

"I don't know. The only thing I'm sure of is that she disappeared one night during a big party at her parents' house on Sugar Island."

I'd already heard that name, having read some articles about this in the papers.

"And uninhabited island in the middle of Lake Moosehead, right?"

"Right."

"Uninhabited except for the villa the Lake family had… Were you invited?"

"No! Like I said, I wasn't a part of their Clique."

"The Clique?"

"Yeah, the clique of her good friends, rich people like the Lake family. Not in the same world as me."

"I understand," I said, nodding, seeing how tired she was after working all day at the diner. "Would you be able to tell me if I could meet some of the people who were there?"

"Um, in my opinion, most of those who were at the party left here ages ago. When you're rich, you don't stay in Greenville for a long time. You go to Bangor, Portland, Boston, or New York. There's just nobodies like me, people who didn't go to school, who stick around. Maybe her boyfriend at that time, a guy named Tom, who wasn't really in the upper class like her, I think he might still be here."

"You know where I could find him?"

"I think he works as a carpenter or a lumberjack. Tom Malone, that's his name. You'll find him. I gotta go, I start early tomorrow."

Charlene got up, I thanked her, and she nodded once more.

"Try not to make too many waves. Think of it as advice from a friend."

She left and I paid for her beer.

When I got back to my room at Greenville Inn, I plopped down on my bed, exhausted before even having started my investigation. With a huge effort, I got up and went to the bathroom, making a face when I saw myself in the mirror. I brushed my teeth, got undressed, and because I needed them, it's not my fault, I grabbed the three plaquettes of pills that I never go anywhere without.

I know that after I swallow the three pills, I'll sleep better.

I don't have the choice.

I must continue, or else… I'll die.

CHAPTER 3
A white lie

I WOKE up to a blinding light filtering through the shutters that made me blink. I turned on my side so it wouldn't bother me and remembered that evening. Meeting up with Charlene, her warnings, her info that would help me progress in my investigation about what happened to Veronika Lake.

I had to meet that Tom Malone guy, who was her boyfriend when she vanished. They were together that evening on Sugar Island, the night she disappeared. I was sure he'd have lots of stuff to tell me. Unless it was "taboo" for him too.

I got dressed and went downstairs for breakfast.

When I got into the dining room, I smelled some delicious coffee. I would have killed for some caffeine to start off my day. The hostess walked up to me.

"Good morning Mrs. Blackstone. I hope you slept well. Sit down anyplace. Coffee or tea?"

"Thanks, I did sleep well. The mattress is great. A black coffee, please. No sugar, no milk."

I had to find out where Tom was working. I looked at her.

"Do you know someone named Tom Malone? I think he works in a lumber company."

"No, I don't, sorry."

"Is there a book somewhere listing all the local companies?"

"In the town hall, I'm sure there is."

While mentally noting that I had to hop over to Greenville town hall, I enjoyed my coffee and breakfast of scrambled eggs, smoked haring, and a bowl of fresh fruit. I went on the internet to see what companies were located here. One of them popped up: *The Haymond Lumber Company*. Visibly one of the most important lumber companies in Maine, with about twenty branches, including one in Greenville. And the site said they even won the 2021 Award for the Best Company to Work for in Maine. Maybe I'd find a Tom Malone who was happy to be working there? Happy to see me?

AT THE WHEEL of my 1967 Ford Ranchero, a faded beige pickup that my father had left me when he drove off to see the Pearly Gates, I headed to the office of the company hoping to find Tom Malone there.

It was both an outlet where customers could shop or order plus the administrative department of the company, recently built, out of wood of course, sporting an aluminum and glass sign. I walked into the lobby and saw a young lady with a smile at the front desk. We greeted each other.

"What can I do for you, Ma'am?"

"It's sort of special. I'd like to talk to someone named Tom Malone, who I think works for you."

"Tom Malone? Doesn't ring a bell. What do you want to talk to him about?"

I was hovering between playing it straight or inventing a pretext. I decided to play it almost straight.

"I'm a journalist and I'm doing a feature article on the timber industry in Maine."

"Vast subject," the young lady said with a smile. "Maybe you should meet our logging supervisor. Or I could talk to you about my own experience," she said with a wink.

"Good idea," I said to butter her up. "Thanks for the offer, but I want to start by hearing the story from someone who works in logging, a young man like this Tom Malone who was recommended to me. Can you help me? After that, I'll come back and interview you and the supervisor."

"Of course. Let me check the list of our employees. I don't know everyone. Even here in Greenville there's at least a hundred of us, from my little job up to the site manager."

I could tell she bought my story and let her check her employee data base.

"Got him!" she said triumphantly. "Tom. C.

Malone is one of our employees. He works as a lumberjack. Right now his team is working in the north-east, after Big Spencer."

"Big Spencer?"

"The hill you see overlooking Lily Bay. Just a sec, I can print out where they're cutting trees today, that'll help you find them."

She printed out a sheet of paper with topographical lines, cut lines and arrows all over. Then she circled the sector and handed it to me.

"All that's left to do is hop in your car and ask around when you get there. Have a nice hike and see you soon!"

"Thanks. Will do."

What a beautiful drive! Driving from Greenville to Big Spencer was an opportunity for me to discover the country, driving on the eastern side of Lake Moosehead through Lily Bay and Spencer Bay. The scenery was breathtaking. Maine is the state with the most forests in the whole United States, and everywhere I looked I saw trees with yellow, orange, and red leaves, ready to fall. On the right hand, woods, and the calm waters of the lake on my left. In front of me and behind me a nearly deserted road snaking through this pristine landscape. After having checked my route several times, I arrived at the spot the young lady had circled for me. I parked my Ranchero in an earthen parking lot that seemed to be the limitation before going into the cut zone. I saw lumber machines and equipment that I'd never even imagined.

I walked up to a guy wearing a hard-hat and smoking a cigarette he'd just rolled. He was wearing a florescent yellow jacket with the name *Haymond Lumber Company* on it. I was hoping he'd pay attention to where he'd toss his butt.

"Hi. I'd like to talk to Tom Malone. Do you know where I can find him?"

He turned around and looked me up and down. Noticing I wasn't wearing protective clothing, he warned me.

"Who are you? What do you want to talk to him about? You can't stay here like that, Ma'am."

"Oh, sorry. I work for a notarial firm, and I have to see Mr. Malone as soon as possible."

Another white lie, but one that seemed to unlock the door for this old, bearded guy. Just wave the flag of an official body and it's open sesame.

"What a way to work," the bearish man growled. "Let me see what I can do."

He took out the walkie-talkie on his belt.

"Michael? Aaron here. Tommy's working for you this morning? Okay. Tell him to come to the parking lot, there's a lady dressed in civilian clothing who wants to see him. Okay, I'll tell her."

The guy with the long white beard put his walkie-talkie back on his belt and summed up what I'd make out in their crackling conversation.

"You gotta wait till break time. Tommy'll be here in half an hour. In the meantime, move away from here. You can go mushroom picking across from here if you want."

"Thank you, Aaron," I said walking away.

Asshole, though is what I said to myself.

Forty-five minutes later a tall guy with strong shoulders, wearing a lumberjack shirt beneath his florescent jacket, walked up. He stopped to talk to Aaron, who pointed at me, standing by my car. Tom, as it must have been him, nodded and walked up to me slowly. His craggy and sun-chiseled face, probably because of this job, looked worried. He was holding a cellophane-wrapped sandwich.

"I'm Tom Malone. What's up? Did I inherit from some old uncle?"

I extended my hand, that he shook with his callous lumberjack hands. When I finally got my fingers back, I had the unpleasant feeling that he'd confused them with some branches.

"Karen Blackstone. I have to tell you the truth. I don't work for a notary, but that's all I found so that you'd talk to me."

The lumberjack glared at me, his eyes as dark as the humus in an oak forest.

"What the hell? So who are you?

This time tell me the truth."

"I'm a journalist. I'm writing about someone you knew well a couple of years ago. I'd like to talk to you about her."

"And you traveled all the way to this forest just to talk to me? I don't believe it! What could I tell a journalist? And who the hell is this person you say I know?"

"Veronika Lake."

Tom Malone's eyes opened wide, surprised, and a vein popped out on his craggy forehead. He turned around.

"I don't got nothing to say about that bitch!"

CHAPTER 4
There's always hope

I STOOD there in the undergrowth where Tom and I had spoken, my mouth hanging open. For a couple of seconds I watched him walk away with furious long steps, before getting out of the torpidity that his brusque reaction had triggered.

"Mr. Malone, wait. Please..."

Without turning around he waved a hand in the air with exasperation.

"Just leave me alone. I don't got nothing to say to you."

"Tom," I said, running after him, "this will only take a minute. Just a couple of questions and then I'll go."

"I'd like you to go now. And not come back."

I joined him fifty feet farther on, went in front of him and stood facing him, blocking the large lumberjack's path with my skinny body.

"Just while you're having your sandwich," I

begged. "I need to know just as much as you what happened five years ago."

"I don't need nothing," he answered roughly. "I didn't ask you for anything. You show up here, without any warning, to talk about old news that I couldn't give a damn about anymore and you want me to spoil my lunch break for that? What have you been smoking lady? This story is over. It hurt me enough."

I had to say I understood the guy. In his shoes I'd be just as surprised and shocked if an unknown person showed up in person in my workplace, to talk about a horrible story of someone who had disappeared without a trace. Yet I heard a breech in his voice and went into my professional mode, jumping in. The keywords spilled from my mouth automatically.

"You should never leave a wound unattended. It could become infected and impact you for your whole life. Trust me, with my help, you'll cauterize your pain."

Tom Malone sighed deeply. He seemed to lighten up slightly.

"What do you know about this affair?"

"What the media at that time wrote, which wasn't much. But I'm specialized in cold cases. There's always hope, even years later. At least that's what I always hope. Please, just a few minutes."

"The time it takes for me to eat my sandwich, not a minute more. I got a real job."

"Deal."

. . .

We sat down at a picnic table on the edge of the clearing. Tom unwrapped his sandwich, which I think was slices of pork between two layers of mayonnaise. I looked at him take huge bites out of it, like the famished lumberjack he was. I let him enjoy his meal for a couple of minutes.

"So, my sources told me that in the summer of 2017, you and Veronika Lake were an item?

"You got good info," he said, his mouth full and a dab of mayonnaise on the corner of his lips.

He wiped his mouth with the sleeve of his checkered jacket.

"Were you together for quite a while?"

The lumberjack squinted as he thought back.

"I guess so if you boil that down to how old we were. We started going out in our first year of high school so that must have been about two years then. We were serious about each other."

"In love, you mean."

"I suppose you could say that. At least I was."

"And she wasn't?"

"No idea. Yeah, sure, she must have been in love too, though I was aware that I was more of her bad boy than an ideal boyfriend."

"Why do you say that?"

"It's easy to see you don't know the Lake family. To make things easy for you, the Lakes and the Malones were from two different worlds. Veronika and me we weren't from the same caste. There's the rich and the poor. You see what category I'm in…"

And with a circular gesture of his arm, he included his lumberjack clothing, his sandwich, and the surrounding forest.

"That didn't stop you from having a relationship with her."

"No, it didn't," he admitted, taking a few sips of water – or something else, what did I know – from a metal flask. "But it wouldn't have lasted forever."

"Why?"

"I don't know, an intuition. Let's just say I knew that the day would come when she'd return to her own people. I was just a brief fling between us. You know, sometimes those rich girls from the right side of the tracks like to scare themselves by going out with bad boys from the wrong side of the tracks."

"You think you're a bad boy?"

"Maybe more of a mad dog. Not someone you want your daughter to go out with, especially in Veronika's parents' eyes."

"That's what they made you feel?"

"I couldn't have cared less," he admitted with a wry smile. "I had a crush on their daughter and that was enough for me. I didn't need the approval of those old farts."

"No love lost between you, apparently."

"For sure. It was reciprocal, of course. So like I said, it only lasted for a while, and that summer I could feel that Veronika was distancing herself from me, little by little."

"What makes you say that?"

Tom Malone smiled ironically, exhaling with a short breath.

"You never been in love, lady?"

"Joker... We're not talking about me. But I see what you're getting at. Little things that add up to a lot. The way you look at each other, natural gestures at the beginning of a relationship, that slip away as time goes by or become more artificial."

Tom Malone laughed out loud. The first time he relaxed in this interview.

"Karen, you said it much better than I could have," he admitted. "I don't have all those words in my head, but yeah, it was sort of like that. Anyway, that summer, I could feel that our relationship was going to end."

"The end of your relationship then?"

"The end of a lot of things. Something I brutally became aware of that night in Sugar Island."

CHAPTER 5
A hell of a weekend

I COULD FEEL that Tom Malone was starting to trust me. As he'd almost finished his sandwich, I quickly continued.

"So what happened that night?"

The young lumberjack shook his head.

"It should have been a hell of a weekend on the Lake family's island..."

SUMMER OF 2017, Sugar Island.

In Maine, this was beginning to be old news: hotter and longer summers and this one obeyed this new rule. The heatwave began the week before, including in Piscataquis County and in the many lakes around Greenville, where you normally would have had much cooler weather around Lake Moosehead's peaceful waters.

Because of, or perhaps thanks to this dry heat, the group of young high school students were planning on staying in Veronika Lake's parents' sumptuous villa for the weekend, the only property still remaining on Sugar Island. They were hoping for some cooler weather to have a big party.

The island, nearly four miles long and about two miles wide, had been occupied for three generations by a few families and friends for their vacation. But for the 2000 official census, it was listed as uninhabited. Since then, Sugar Island was officially an island where no one lived.

Nonetheless, like whims that rich people have, Mason Lake, Veronika's father, who had been born into money but had also made a fortune in the financial field, was able to acquire the abandoned island. He had a villa constructed there, which, fifteen years later, would be the place where his daughter had mysteriously disappeared.

That Saturday, August 26th, the Lake family's Zodiac was moored at Greenville's port, and everything needed for a party between young adults was being loaded. Packages of potato chips, hotdogs, nachos, pizzas, and frozen burritos were next to coolers stocked with beer, bottles of rum, vodka and soda. They were planning on having a barbecue with slices of bacon, dozens of sausages, burgers and brats. That was going to be a hell of a party, at least for those kids from Greenville.

But not all the kids from Greenville had been invited to the fiesta. Only a handful of privileged people – the small "*Clique*" of Veronika's friends – had been invited. A handful of participants, whose parents were rich or belonged to the movers and shakers in the local economy.

Everyone except for one person.

Tom Malone, that mad dog who didn't have a pedigree like other Clique members. He wasn't one of them and had only been invited because he was Veronika Lake's boyfriend. A quality to be proud of, but some of the others were still suspicious of him. He was a part of the Clique, but not an integrated member.

On the other hand, when it came to loading the Zodiac, Tom was the only hard worker who had volunteered. Wasn't he the Mr. Muscles of the gang, the guy with a lumberjack's broad shoulders?

"Come on guys, help me out here! I'm not going to do this all alone," he complained, loading one of the alcohol filled coolers onto the back of the pneumatic boat.

"Tommy dear," replied Veronika, "I thought you like physical labor, that it was good for your muscles. Now's the time to prove it."

The young lady, turning talk into action, put a box full of brats and hotdogs into her chum's arms, as they said a few miles north in Canada, and gave him a little kiss.

"So what are those other wankers doing? Carlos, Alvin, and Paul?" asked Tom, putting the box into the boat.

HALF AN HOUR LATER, they were ready to cast off. Plenty of room for all of them in the *Zodiac Medline*, a twenty-seven-foot-long boat that could hold up to twenty people. Two seats on the bolster behind the steering wheel, a double square behind and in front, and a three-hundred-fifty horsepower motor that Tommy had revved up. As Veronika had obtained her boating license a couple of months ago, she manned the helm to slowly take the zodiac out of the Greenville docks. Heading north-north-east, cruising on the right of Lake Moosehead up to Lily Bay where she changed tack to head north-west to Sugar Island. A good half an hour later they'd arrived at Mason and Janet Lake's private island.

Ideal conditions. No waves, a wind of less than five knots, a blue sky and sunshine. The boat gave the teens a pleasant cool feeling, something they didn't have on the land, with drops of water sprinkling on their swimsuit-clad bodies, better than a mineral water spray would have. Just for this, Veronika would have liked to continue around the lake before docking at Sugar Island.

But they soon saw the wild coastline at the boat's

bow and the guests were eager to kick off their party. They were composed of three official couples and two single people, equitably broken down into four girls and four boys. The six bedrooms in the villa would be enough to sleep everyone, should they want to sleep of course! But you could say that they didn't lack imagination nor hormones to use these rooms dedicated to resting…

Sugar Island was an impenetrable island, full of different types of conifers and trees, one that was very nice to look at but difficult to dock a boat at as the roots of the trees went directly from the rocks to the lake. Without hesitating, Veronika steered the dinghy directly to a pontoon hidden in a small creek and slowed down to allow Tommy and Alvin moor the Zodiac.

This time everyone helped unload their cargo, eager to begin the festivities. The villa was about a hundred and fifty feet from the pontoon, in the middle of a large clearing. Two or three round trips were enough to unload.

To celebrate the beginning of their weekend, when they'd put everything away, the guys and Cynthia opened a cool bottle of beer.

Paul Tennent was sitting on the villa's wooden patio, with a smile on his face.

"This is the life guys! Don't you agree?"

This sentence had a wave of approval, and they all raised their bottles.

"Make sure you thank your father again for having

lent the villa to us," added Alvin Brown. "Anything goes?"

"What happens in Sugar Island stays in Sugar Island," she answered.

"Let the party begin then!" shouted Carlos Iglesias.

The others all joined in.

"See what I'm saying, Karen?" asked Tom Malone finishing up his sandwich. "We were ready for a fantastic weekend."

I looked at the lumberjack who was now frowning.

"What happened then? What changed this perfect weekend into a nightmare?"

Tom Malone thought things over.

"I don't know. Probably a bunch of little things. Things happened, were said, were discovered or revealed during these two days. Our solitude, the heat, fatigue, alcoholic beverages, a few drugs and couples fighting, who knows... '*What happens in Sugar Island stays in Sugar Island*,' like Veronika said that Saturday. For the past five years that sentence has haunted me, Karen."

CHAPTER 6
Death at the bottom

HE GOT up from the picnic table, but I couldn't imagine letting Tom Malone leave me like this in his story of the summer of 2017 at Sugar Island. He had whetted my appetite, had tipped me off, or whatever expression you use, but I needed to know more.

"What happened that was so bad that weekend on the island? Tell me what you remember, Tom."

The lumberjack balled up his cellophane paper and threw it into the bin, like a basketball player.

"I gotta go back to work, Ma'am. If I sit here twiddling my fingers any longer, the boss ain't gonna be happy. Sorry. I gotta go," he said, glancing at his watch.

"You can't leave me like that."

"That's what I'm gonna do though."

"Can we continue this conversation later? After you finish work? We could have a drink in Greenville, my treat. Here's my phone number."

I ripped a page out of the little notebook I always

have with me and quickly wrote my phone number. He started back off into the forest. I handed him the piece of paper.

"Please."

He stopped, his shoulders low.

"You never give up, do you? What do you care about how this ended? You think you'll know the truth? That's not gonna make Veronika come back..."

He reluctantly took the piece of paper and put it in his pocket.

"Why do you say that? Sometimes people who have disappeared come back."

"Not when they're six feet under or attached to a stone at the bottom of a lake."

Veronika Lake's former boyfriend left me there, in the middle of the Big Spencer Mount clearing, with this terrible sentence that had left me speechless.

I SPENT the rest of the day at Lily Bay. I needed to go to Sugar Island.

From the tiny Lily Bay beach, you could see make out the banks of this now uninhabited island, its earth covered with vegetation, the place where Veronika Lake had disappeared five years ago. Maybe a mile from the port where I was standing was where the young lady had last been seen.

I shivered with the idea that her body – as Tom Malone suggested this morning – could be at the bottom of the peaceful waters surrounding Sugar Island. The lake where kids go swimming, where people go fishing, where yachtsmen show off their wealth, where families go waterskiing, where there's life you could say.

Life on the surface, death on the bottom.

What could be left of a body that had been submerged for five years and that had never come back up?

Bones maybe, as the abundant marine wildlife must have eaten all the flesh.

"Veronika, what's left of you?" I said to myself, looking at the lake.

I thought of the young lady who'd vanished, but not just her. Hundreds of faces were swimming around in my brain, all those lost souls, sometimes lost forever. I thought of the four hundred and sixty thousand children who disappear every year in the United States. A huge number, one that must be qualified. Luckily for most of them, it's just kids who ran away or were kidnapped by their parents.

Amongst the hundreds of thousands of cases, only 0.5% of them have a criminal origin. A very small figure, but if you bring that to individual persons, it does represent two thousand three hundred people who were kidnapped, confined, killed, buried, burnt alive...

"Is everything alright Ma'am?"

The voice ended my morbid thoughts. I shook myself and realized that while thinking I had neared the lake. My shoes and bottoms of my jeans were already wet.

I turned around to see who the voice belonged to. A white-haired lady who was carefully standing six feet behind me.

"Miss? Are you okay?"

"Thank you, yes. I was daydreaming."

"Your jeans are all wet."

"Don't worry, they'll dry. I was just trying to see the Sugar Island coast."

"The cursed island?"

My eyes popped wide open.

"Excuse me?"

"That's what folks around here call it. At least those who know what happened?"

"So what happened?" I asked innocently.

"You're not from here then. The girl who disappeared. You never heard of that? The daughter of the Lake family, the owners of this uninhabited island. No one lives there anymore."

Since I'd arrived, I noticed that talking about Veronika Lake directly wasn't a good idea and I was so glad that I'd run into this old lady who seemed to want to talk about it. I just had to keep on asking questions.

"Someone disappeared then on that uninhabited island? How could that have happened?"

"Well, here we don't really like talking about it, but five years ago, a young lady disappeared during a weekend she'd spent there," - she pointed to the island with her chin - "in her parents' villa. They weren't there of course. Such irresponsible parents. Leaving a bunch of young kids totally alone to do who knows what on that island…"

"Do you know her parents?"

"Of course, everyone here knows the Lakes. Even more since that happened."

"Maybe I could meet them? Where do they live?"

"If you have a plane, you might meet them."

"They don't live around here?"

"No, hun, they left Piscataquis County when their daughter disappeared. Rumor has it that they're in Florida someplace. But you know rich people, they got houses all over, no one knows where they are. A month here, next month someplace else. The Bahamas, then Europe. All I can tell you now is that they deserted both Greenville and their private island. Too many bad memories here, I imagine."

I wouldn't get much more info from the old lady, but now I knew that the Lakes wouldn't be as easy to talk to as I'd imagined. I tried one more question.

"I'd like to go to this island. It doesn't seem very far. Is there a ferry or a boat service that goes there from here?"

The old lady smiled ironically, allowing me to appreciate her missing teeth.

"A ferry to Sugar Island? There's nothing to see there! No, there's no way you can get there," she concluded with another movement of her chin.

"A fisherman or a private boater maybe?"

"Ha! I dare you to find someone who wants to dock at Sugar. Or if they do, they're not from around here. No one ever goes closer than a nautical mile to that cursed island."

Words...

I'm not strong enough to continue like this.

Lying to myself for so long. Lying to others at the same time.

It's a fantasy to want the past to lead to a more serene present, then a future in which I finally will be able to find some peace of mind.

To find the peace I'm seeking without ever reaching, all I can do is advance, keep on going.

Step by step, stage after stage.

But I have to be quick as time is my biggest enemy.

The challenge I'm facing is huge, but I must delve into the deepest part of me to find the strength to bounce back.

Get better.

Not sink. Quit following ghosts and fantasies.

Live my life to the fullest and forget my heavy past.

I've made my decision and I'll be unwavering.

CHAPTER 7
Carte blanche and full credit

THE RINGING of the phone startled me while I was taking notes. I immediately recognized Myrtille's number, my boss at *True Crime Mysteries*. I instinctively looked at the clock on my cell phone - ten p.m. - and wondered when she left the office.

She's quirky and always impatient and I heard her quick voice start talking without even greeting me.

"So sweetie, you solve the Veronika Lake enigma yet?"

"Myrtille," I sighed, "like I've only been here a bit over twenty-four hours. You really think I can solve a five-year-old mystery just by snapping my fingers?"

"Karen, you can do anything you want, I keep on repeating myself, month after month, investigation after investigation. You're a first-class muckraker and that's why I hired you."

"Thanks for the compliments, I'm really touched. And hello, by the way. How have things been? As long as you asked, things are fine. If I don't mention the cold reception I get every time I mention the Lakes around here."

"What were you expecting? That they'd roll out the red carpet or bring you the solution on a seafood platter? If I sent you there, it's because you're good. In the past you accomplished miracles, remember the Lacassagne affair.

"Sure do. Three months of total immersion in the charming *Teletubbies'* world of pharmaceuticals. I thought I'd overdose."

"See! So what you bitching about? Today you're basking in pristine waters in Maine, all expenses paid, well, I'm the one paying them, in the middle of peaceful forests... Better than Boston, isn't it?"

"Right in the middle of October though," I said looking out my window where I saw the tops of the trees dancing in the north-eastern wind that had picked up in the evening, making me think that the next day wasn't going to be all that peaceful.

"You would have preferred a heatwave? Lighten up Karen. Your welcome is as cold as the lake? I trust you; you'll break the ice."

"Let's just say that as soon as I mention her, everyone gets tongue-tied. I've already been told a couple of times that it would be better not to stir this mud."

"Threats? So soon? You never cease to amaze me Karen, in just two days there's already animosity."

"No threats. Just people telling me to be careful. Here this is an incident they want to forget."

"An incident? Nice euphemism. We're talking about a seventeen-year-old girl who disappeared at the bottom of a lake or something like that. Those people from Maine make me laugh. No blood, no crime. We're not going to make any money at *True Crimes* with a philosophy like that. I have to go now. I'm counting on you to unearth something juicy, sensational, heavyweight! Oh. I almost forgot. Of course you've got a *carte blanche* and full credit. *Ciao*, sweetie."

And she hung up like she called, without saying goodbye to me. Yet the *carte blanche* and the full credit didn't fall on deaf ears, and I was ready to use both. She'd soon be receiving my expense slips, Miss Myrtille Fairbanks.

ONE OF MY first expenses wouldn't be listed though. The next morning bright and early after breakfast, though the wind was still blowing over the lake and making tiny whitecaps, I walked down to Greenville's cute little marina. At this time of the year it wasn't busy. There were only a few pleasure boats moored there before being placed in winter storage. I could see some fishermen's boats across from me. Some of them were manned, and I walked up playing "tourist," sniffing the sea breeze and squinting over the ocean while turning the collar of my coat up to keep my neck warm.

I spotted my prey.

And decided to attack the one who seemed the friendliest. A man with a huge beard, wearing a gray wool cap coming down right over his generous eyebrows, with pearl gray eyes and who seemed kind to me.

I walked up to him, my arms around my coat to keep warm.

"Hello. You sure are brave to go fishing in this weather."

"Ma'am. Oh! You get used to it. Whether it rains, snows or the wind blows, I go out. I love to fish. Once I get to the middle of the lake, I cast my nets and listen to the silence. You know that the sound of silence is beautiful? So what brings you out with weather like this?"

I thought back on what I'd invented this morning at breakfast, so I wouldn't have to mention the taboo subject.

"I'm studying the flora and the fauna of lakes in Maine and comparing it with those in Canada. Especially in insular habitats."

"Sounds interesting."

Maybe he was being ironic here, but I decided to ignore it. After all, it was a white lie I'd fed him.

"It is. And Lake Moosehead seems ideal for my thesis. I heard that there are unique varieties of softwood on one of the islands. I think it was Sugar Island."

"If you say so. No one lives there anymore."

I hopped right in.

"That's exactly what I'm looking for: uninhabited islands. But there's a little problem, you could say a technical issue. From what I heard there's no way to get to Sugar Island except by a private boat."

"Correct."

And silence, that he loved so much, followed this laconic response. My turn. This time I dove right in.

"If I asked you as a favor, would you take me there with your boat?"

The fisherman seemed to be weighing the pros and cons silently while finishing his preparation. It looked like with the movements his big gray beard was having that he was ruminating the question, digesting it before regurgitating an answer.

"Of course I'd pay you," I added.

"That's not the sticking point," he mumbled in his beard.

"So? What's the problem? If we can't do it today, it's no big deal. We can go another time."

"Well, today or tomorrow, it's the same thing. I don't really like navigating around there."

"Why?"

"Not a lot of fish there, that's all. And I don't like the courants."

I tried my trump card.

"Maybe a little exception for a hundred dollars round trip?"

The old man with his well-worn cap lifted his head. He looked me right in the eyes, as if he were trying to guess my true motivations. He finally decided to answer.

"No. For a hundred bucks, it's only one way."

"So how do I get back?"

"You swim," he laughed uncovered yellowed teeth caused by decades of smoking.

"Okay. Two hundred."

"Two hundred? What about waiting? Three hundred and I'll take you there now and pick you up this afternoon when I've finished my day. Hope it's a good day," he added with a malicious smile that looked just as good on him as a tutu on a rugby man.

That guy knew how to bargain. I thought about my expense note that I'd have to give Myrtille thinking he'd never sign a paper for this. She'd have to believe me. To force my reluctant fisherman to decide, I took a roll of dollars out from my jacket, pretending to count them. Seeing hard cash is always more convincing than abstract numbers.

"Two fifty?"

He proffered a hand as calloused as a sharp rock.

"Welcome aboard!"

CHAPTER 8
Down below our feet

TEN MINUTES after we'd left the Greenville Marina, I already was regretting having succeeded in convincing Herman – as that was the fisherman's first name – to have taken me to Sugar Island in his antique boat.

There was a strong wind on the lake and waves on its surface, generating an uncomfortable feeling in the pit of my stomach. The old guy noticed I was a bit green at the gull.

"You don't have sea legs, Karen," he laughed looking at me. "It's not the best day to be out here, but you're the one who wanted to go."

"Is it going to be long?" I asked, trying to distinguish the side of the island I was interested in.

"Another half an hour, little lady," he shouted out over the noise made by the outboard that he also used as a rudder.

Herman steered his motorboat well, just using a

long handle he called a tiller. I admired how at ease he was with his equipment. I tried to understand the principle and ran into a problem of logic: when I saw him push the bar to one side, the boat headed to the opposite side. Was it port or starboard? I always get those two mixed up.

"You must have done this your whole life. It doesn't look that easy to me."

"It is. Child's play. Wanna try?"

"No, thanks. I don't want us to sink!"

Just then there was a gust of wind, and I pulled the cover that Herman had given me when we left around me.

"Karen, did you take anything for seasickness?"

"I guess I didn't plan ahead."

"Have a look in the metallic box under your seat. There should be a package of lemon candy. Take one and you'll feel better."

I followed his advice though I didn't want to put my hand in the package in question, one that seemed to date back to Methuselah. The paper stuck to the candy, but I made the best of it and put it in my mouth. But I quickly felt better, and my stomach relaxed, as did I.

I let myself rock in the boat in silence for a few minutes. I just looked at Sugar Island. I couldn't wait to walk where the *drama* had taken place back in the summer of 2017.

The motor suddenly stopped, cutting this line of thought off.

"There's a problem?"

"Shh," said Herman, an arthritic finger raised in front of his lips, or should I say his beard. "Listen to the silence, Karen. The sound of silence that I told you about earlier. Can you hear this deafening silence? That's what I like when my boat drifts by itself, smack in the middle of this big lake, far from any land. Let it rock you, Karen. Appreciate it."

I closed my eyes. His boat swayed slightly. My thoughts drifted too. I was thinking not only of this soothing silence, but of a more eerie one at the bottom of the lake. I wondered how deep it was but didn't want to break this moment of silence. Fifteen, thirty, a hundred and fifty feet? How many millions of gallons of water had the body of a seventeen-year-old girl swallowed? Did Veronika Lake finish her existence somewhere below, in that immense lake?

I shivered and Herman noticed it. Without saying a word, he pulled the cord to start the motor, and we headed off again to Sugar Island. Twenty minutes later, he turned the motor off when we were nearing a pontoon at the back of a creek, just like Tom Malone had described the day before.

"Milady has arrived," said Herman. "What time should I pick you up?"

We agreed that he'd come and get me at three o'clock, so we'd be back before it got dark, which was quite early at this time of the year. I thanked him and made him promise not to forget me as I didn't want to play Robinson Crusoe. Plus I wasn't equipped.

Neither from a logistics point of view or from a psychological one.

I stepped out onto the wooden pontoon with its rusty nails.

Herman waved goodbye to me, and I responded by raising my thumb, though inside I was shaking. I was suddenly aware that I was alone on an uninhabited island without any way of getting back to the town, though it didn't seem that far as I could make out Lily Bay vaguely.

I CAREFULLY WALKED to the end of the pontoon and then started down a small path surrounded by weeds. It was easy to see that no upkeep had been done for months, maybe years. Without hard work and nimble fingers, nature quickly goes wild. I didn't think this place had been lived in since Veronika Lake disappeared, five years ago.

The wind picked up, making the foliage dance. There was a type of mist on the highest branches. I could make out the gray sky above the leaves that now in October, had already turned and were beginning to fall. I suddenly felt like I was in a thriller novel, like those I was a fan of when I was a teen. *What's at the End of the Path?* could have been the title of it, I thought.

At the end of the path was the Lake family's famous or should I say now infamous, villa. I don't know why I'd imagined a sort of colonial house with white stones, columns leading to a huge patio and a balcony surrounding the entire building. Instead of that, it was an immense log cabin.

A majestic two-story cabin made from tree trunks. It did have a patio surrounding the house, but no columns, and no balcony in the front. Even though it had been abandoned, I could still feel an intimidating splendor emanating from it. I wondered how many people had worked on it and how long it took them to build this cabin on an island. But nothing surprises me anymore with whims of *nouveaux riches* and the Lake family was one of the best representatives of their species.

Watching my steps and twisting so I wouldn't be scratched from all the thorn bushes, I decided to walk all around it. I wanted to get a feeling of the premises, appreciate how big it was, see what it smelled like and what noise it made. The shutters were closed, probably by the owners after what happened. I couldn't see inside, so I kept on going till I got to the back of the building, where the pool Tom Malone had described to me was located.

Or could you really call a pool what I was looking at: a rectangular hole filled with filthy, almost black water and dead leaves and algae? When I got closer an odor of putrefaction hit my nostrils. An animal must have died there, in the pool, and was decomposing at the bottom of it.

I plugged my nose and walked up to the cabin. The

backyard patio was huge, made from some rot-proof exotic wood. It must have been so great in the summer to dive into the pool and then walk barefoot on the patio before lying down for a suntan. The Lake family must have enjoyed the freedom so much, taking advantage of their private piece of heaven where no one except for themselves and their guests could go!

Did Veronika and her friends have unforgettable moments that weekend in August of 2017?

Or was this merely the place where drama had unfolded?

This was what I was thinking about as I walked around the villa.

Now I wanted to go in. I knew this was against the law. Violation of private property, something I could do time for. But you know I was already on private property as the whole island belonged to the Lakes. But there's probably a difference between walking on private property and visiting inside a home. Trying to get in, even more so when the villa is locked, is an infraction. Breaking and entering. I'd be breaking and entering, according to the law.

But that was what I was here for, right? I had an investigation to solve, and I had to do what I had to do to find out everything I could about the Lakes. If that included not quite legal activities and taking risks, I assumed. That was something that has already happened to me in the past, so it wouldn't have been the first time.

To make me feel good I told myself that at least

here there wouldn't be any nosy neighbors. Alone on an island.

So I started quite logically by trying to open the front door. From experience I've learned that often the simplest and most direct way is the best. But that wasn't the case here as the door didn't open.

I tried to open the shutters but didn't find a way in either. I was starting to get discouraged when I saw another door at the end of the back patio, which must have been their summer kitchen. There was just a mosquito net on it. Right behind it, there was a wooden door that didn't look very thick. I shook it and it moved a bit. I was sure that if I insisted it would open.

I mechanically looked around so see if anyone was there before trying to open it with my shoulder.

And it finally did open, with squeaky hinges.

I'd broken into the Lake family's villa and at the same time, into a part of their private lives.

What I'd discover in the next couple of minutes would overwhelm me and change my investigation.

CHAPTER 9
The walls have ears

THE ROOM HAD AN END-OF-THE-SUMMER ATMOSPHERE, but you could tell that time was frozen, not last summer, but many years before. Only a bit of palish light was able to make it through the gaps in slats of the wooden shutters and the lighting was thus subdued in the Lake family's cabin.

The furniture and floor were covered with a layer of dust proving, if still needed, that no one had been in this place for ages. Yet there were some footprints still visible, as if someone had recently been there.

I carefully walked into the open and central living room that seemed to be used as an office as well. A smoking room too, with two leather armchairs facing one another and a large ashtray with a half-smoked cigar in it.

Though the house gave me an impression of peace,

you could tell that it was used to a lot of action. Bottles were on the floor between the armchairs. I bent down and picked one of them up with my fingertips. A nice Chivas Regal 18 years of age, uncorked, with a bit that hadn't spilled out contrary to the rest that had turned into a dark stain on the rug. A big *fiesta* had taken place with a lot of negligence.

No one had cleaned this joint since 2017?

They'd simply closed the shutters and door and forgotten about the past?

Abandoning the building and its souvenirs?

I put the bottle on the table between the two armchairs, an ancient reflex of someone who likes things put away. Which was far from being the case here. If what people told me was correct, the last people to have stayed here were some boys and girls who were still teens with no adult surveillance. Kids of rich or powerful people taking advantage of a luxurious cabin to have a good time. *Sex, drugs and rock-'n'roll*, like Ian Dury said in his song? Or *cigarettes, whisky and girls* like Eddie Constantine? In any case, I'm sure no one got bored here that last weekend of August 2017.

I continued inspecting the first floor, discovering vestiges that probably dated back five years. Like a dried-up rubber hanging like an old sock on the angle of a cornered tub in the bathroom. Yuk. Even with gloves I wouldn't touch that. It was musty and stunk of a backed-up sewer in the bathroom, as is often the case when the water hasn't been turned on for ages.

Whiffs of standing water coming from the pipework made the whole room reek. There were toiletries on the edge of the sink below the mirror. A tube of opened toothpaste, two toothbrushes, makeup, and a hairbrush.

As if their owners had had to flee, without being able to gather up their belongings.

What was the rush? Were they all looking for their friend who had vanished? Or were they afraid of something?

I tried to imagine what the group of friends had done between these walls for two days. I was wavering between a peaceful, playful, and happy picture or scenes of debauchery, noise and quarrels before the tragic ending.

"Tell me what happened here," I said aloud, speaking to the walls. "Come on, tell me!"

Doesn't the old saying go that walls have ears? But have they got eyes to see and a mouth to relate it? Can a house retain souvenirs of events that took place within it, especially tragic ones? I wanted to believe it. I wanted to talk to the building, interpret the traces that it still had.

I consequently kept on looking. I walked from room to room, taking the wooden stairs without risers or balustrades that took me to the second floor. There were five bedrooms and a new bathroom there, in the same state as the previous one, with the same toiletries for a handful of people.

The beds were unmade, and the sheets were wrinkled, damp and moldy. Bottles and cans of beer, soda and alcohol were scattered on the floor. It was darker upstairs than down, so I wanted to turn the lights on, but to no avail. Either they had had a short circuit after a storm, or the owners had simply terminated their contract.

I could open the shutters to get some light in, but I don't know why, I still felt an irrational anxiety, probably caused by my intrusion and the fear of being found out though I knew quite well I was the only person on the island.

Or was I trying to persuade myself of that? Was I actually alone?

I turned the light on my phone on, and looked right and left, and under the beds. Sometimes you can find all sorts of things there. Children with a good imagination know that.

But here, only ordinary stuff. Dust bunnies, used Kleenex, the top of a pen, rubber bands and a pair of lace panties.

I inspected each bedroom. Outside I could hear the wind picking up, the branches swaying, and I thought that the kitchen door where I came in had started to slam. I had probably not closed it well. There was grim whistling coming from downstairs. In an empty house and in the dark, sounds are always eerie.

I suddenly jumped. A sharp noise from downstairs. I stood up, my heart racing. I thought I could hear the floors creak or maybe it was the stairs. I felt so stupid, trapped. My brain was working in fifth gear and my pulse must have been approaching two hundred beats per minute.

Had someone followed me?

I didn't know what to do. Hide? Go downstairs and see? I tried to calm down and convince myself that no one knew I was here except for Herman, the inoffensive fisherman.

I plucked up my courage and decided to go down. I couldn't stay in this bedroom forever anyway. Very carefully, trying to weigh as little as possible on the hardwood floor, I left the bedroom, went down the hall and looked out at the stairwell before taking it.

I couldn't see anyone downstairs. I put a foot on the first stair, which made a cracking noise. I froze for a second, took a deep breath and continued going down, stair after stair.

I finally identified the noise that I'd heard upstairs when I noticed the bottle of Chivas I'd put on the pedestal table wasn't there anymore. It was on the floor, next to one of the armchairs. A gust of wind must have blown it off.

Just to be sure, I put on my big girl panties and walked all around the first floor, closing the door that had blown open in the wind.

I was getting ready to leave the villa when I remembered that because of the noise I'd heard, I hadn't gone into the last room upstairs. I went back up and down the hall to the last door that was closed, contrary to the others that had been opened.

I turned the knob and opened the door.

. . .

WHAT I SAW there made me think that I luckily had not left before exploring this room.

I nonetheless regretted my decision as soon as I walked in...

CHAPTER 10
Scenes of debauchery

SOMETIMES CURIOSITY CAN BE an excellent quality. Especially when you're a private detective or a journalist investigating cold cases, like I was.

When I walked into the last room of the Lake family's villa, I had a strange feeling. I certainly wasn't expecting to find a child's room here.

A young child, too, as there was a crib in one of the corners of the room, not far from the window where light was shining in through the half-closed shutters.

The way the furniture was placed, and the type of it, as well as the room's decoration, made me think a young child had slept here. And when I looked at the colors and the bedding, without forgetting the toys, the child must have been a little boy.

Despite all the research I'd done on the Veronika Lake affair, I hadn't seen a thing about a male child at the Lake's. Of course, all the documentation about this subject, in the local papers or in the obituaries, concerned the drama of the disappearance of the young lady.

Which is why I thought that Veronika was Mason and Janet Lake's only child. The unsettling loss of their daughter was like the end of an era for them, the end of the time they'd lived in Maine, either in Greenville or in Sugar Island. Which caused *de facto* their departure for Florida, putting enough milage between the cursed island and the Florida peninsula, about two thousand miles away, a large enough distance to forget the past.

At least that is what I'd believed up till now. But when I went into this little boy's room, all my assumptions shattered. There was another Lake in the family!

I went inside slowly, troubled by my confused thoughts. For some unknown reason I was uncomfortable in this room. Paradoxical scenes were entwined in my mind. Superposed upon the scenes of drunk teens and their debauchery were peaceful ones of a child asleep in his crib. A mixture of scenes of disorder and pictures by Norman Rockwell of a wealthy family on vacation in their log cabin on their private island. Two parents, two children, a boy, and a girl.

The king's choice.

In this room, in contrast to the others, everything was in place and neat. As if it had been spared from the drunken orgy that had taken place elsewhere. Preserved, like a forbidden sanctuary.

I wondered about something else then. How much time did the Lake family spend on their island? I imagined that this was a place where they only came occasionally, a weekend or maybe a week in summer, so why did they have an infant's room fitted out? Wouldn't a folding baby's bed have been enough?

But then again, maybe it would have been much easier to have everything for a young child right in the cabin. Much more than a mere summer home, the Sugar Island villa was a second main home.

I noted to try to get more information on this point and continued my inspection.

There was one detail that I noticed: something that didn't go with the rest of the room.

A poster that shouldn't have been in a child's room.

On the wall across from the crib there was a poster about a foot and a half high and a good foot wide. The image vaguely reminded me of something, but I was too far away to be sure. I walked to it to see the details.

Then it all came back to me, like a flash. When I saw this poster, I remembered both a song and its lyrics.

Don't cry, don't raise your eye
 It's only a teenage wasteland

Got it! *The Who*. Their *Who's next* album. Beginning of the 70s, I thought.

That poster was on the front of the album. My

parents had it and I sometimes listened to it. An image of desolation where the four members of that British group were standing around a sort of concrete gray monolith standing in the middle of a charcoal gray wasteland, like the end of the world. Or like a sterile volcanic earth after lava had flown on it.

You could read *Who's next* without a question mark in small letters above the monolith. A simple and unsettling cover.

What was this poster of one of the most iconic groups of alternative rock doing here? It wasn't fitting for a child's room.

But what was even stranger was what had been added to the poster...

Someone had modified the *Who's next* title on top of the poster, above the monolith. Or should I say completed it. A permanent red marker had added the question mark that was initially missing.

Who's next?

Then, below it, a quickly handwritten sentence had been added.

A terrible sentence that nearly made me gag.

Who killed Brandon?

CHAPTER 11
In the backwaters

WHO KILLED BRANDON?

The next question that came to mind was: who is - or should I say who was, if he was dead - the person named Brandon?

Was it his room?

Brandon Lake?

Mason and Janet Lake's son, making him Veronika's brother?

I was feeling uneasy. Disgust and primeval fear just thinking about what this sentence scribbled on with a marker implied.

The horrifying notion of infanticide was making me sick. Just wanting to hurt a child was something I couldn't accept. Couldn't even understand wanting to kill an innocent being.

The premises were suddenly different. This abandoned villa, built on an isolated and uninhabited island, which was in the middle of a large lake with dense forests surrounding it - this whole decor impressed and oppressed me. I felt like I was in an inexorable *mise en abyme*, an infernal whirlpool whose epicenter was this child's room frozen in mothballs, this terrible warning written on a poster in this place.

Yes, a warning. *Who's next? I didn't want to be that person.*

I swallowed painfully; my throat was dry. What list? A list of victims where Brandon was the first one - or not?

I quickly thought of something. If Brandon, let's call him Brandon Lake, was killed, as this sentence written with a permanent marker said, was the following victim already known? His sister, Veronika Lake?

As no one had seen her since Sunday, August 27, 2017 and the poster invoked another victim, could I conclude that the young lady had been assassinated?

Or was I imagining things?

Certainly one of my flaws. Thinking of the worst-case scenario first. Because the worst is often the most direct path to the truth. By professional experience - but not just that - I'd often witnessed what human nature is capable of. Sometimes the best, often the worst.

Before leaving this room where I now was finding it hard to breathe, I took a couple of pictures of the poster, the crib, and the half-open shutter. Just to be sure, I walked up to the window and found out that it was not locked, just shut.

Questions bouncing about in my mind, I ran down the stairs, out of the cabin. I'd seen enough for today. Now I needed to find the answers to too many questions.

Who was Brandon? Who killed him? Who was the next victim on the list? Who added the sentence in red? And when? During the August 2017 weekend? Before or after Veronika Lake officially disappeared?

I glanced at my phone, and it was nearly two, something my stomach confirmed by growling loudly. I hadn't even brought a thing to eat nor a bottle of water with me. You could tell I was a city slicker trying to be a wannabe Robinson Crusoe. Time flew by and I saw I just had about forty-five minutes before I was to meet Herman at the pontoon, my fisherman-taxi. I mentally prayed that he hadn't had the fantastic idea of forgetting me here on this island, the place where so many tragic events had taken place.

When I went to Greenville, I thought I'd be stepping into backwaters but had no idea that they'd be this deep. Nor this black and scummy.

I took advantage of the time I had left to explore the yard, seeing what was near the cabin. I noticed quite quickly that the Lake family's limits were quite vague. No fences anyplace. But why would they need any if the whole island belonged to them? I had to admit that the limits of their lot were the coasts of the island.

A bit farther away from the cabin I saw a little pond where there was a rowboat that had water in it but was attached to the trunk of a dead tree with moss-covered rope. The *mise en abyme* thus continued to this pond in the middle of the island. There were dark water lilies floating on the surface. How deep was it? What could be lying on the bottom of the sludge? I would imagine that back in 2017 research teams must have explored the pond.

I now had a vague idea of the place where Veronika had disappeared, was never seen again, and this despite everyone searching for her.

Walking up to the pontoon I thought about what I'd accomplished. I'd set foot on Sugar Island with tons of questions, I'd be leaving with tons of additional ones.

Leaving the cabin behind me, I went into the little woods taking me to the pontoon and relieved, saw Herman waiting for me. He was sitting in his boat smoking a nicely sculpted ivory pipe, looking towards Lily Bay on the continent. He heard me but didn't turn around.

"Miss Karen, I was waiting," he said with his rough voice.

Yes, I was fifteen minutes late.

"Thanks so much for waiting, Herman," I said carefully getting into his little boat.

"The wind's going to pick up, we better get going. Ready?"

And he pulled on the starter of his outboard which began to hum obediently.

When Sugar Island was behind us, Herman turned towards me and surprised me.

"You see a ghost or what?"

"Excuse me?"

"You're as white as a sheet. Even worse than this morning when you were seasick. You want a piece of candy? I still got some left."

"Actually, I haven't had a bite to eat since this morning," I admitted shamefully.

"Oh. Should have said so. Take a look in the trunk below the bench, you'll see a loaf of bread, some salami, and some sardines. Help yourself. I don't want you to faint in my boat. So how was your little trip? You see lotsa nice plants?"

I hesitated for a second then finally decided not to lie any longer. To tell him everything. You never know, maybe he could tell me something useful.

"Did you know the Lake family?"

He glared at me.

"You're not a fauna and flora researcher, are you? Or else you're only interested in one sort of flora: rich families with tragic fates. I thought that a lady like you wouldn't have much to do on Sugar Island except to approach that cursed villa."

"Sorry to have lied. It's true though that I am a journalist. I work for a specialized magazine and I'm investigating Veronika Lake's disappearance. Had I told you that this morning, would you have let me into your boat? Because up till now, I've noticed that this wasn't a subject the inhabitants of Greenville wanted to talk about."

"And rightfully so," Herman mumbled.

"Meaning?"

"Let's say they didn't only leave good memories here in town. Without even talking about the trauma when their oldest daughter disappeared."

A light bulb went on in my head.

"Oldest? Like they had other children?"

"I think so. I didn't hang out with high-class people like them, but I think they also had a little boy. But the poor kid died young. One day we just saw them with her when they were in Greenville. We never knew – at least I didn't – what happened to him."

"Another dramatic event before their daughter went missing?"

"Well, you know, like they say *money doesn't buy happiness...* nor does it prevent misfortune."

"I didn't know the second part of that old saying."

"Not surprising, I just invented it," laughed the fisherman biting down on his pipe.

I didn't want to continue with this subject and wanted to keep what I'd found in the little boy's room a secret. A few minutes later, Herman dropped me off at the Greenville Marina and I got out and thanked him for his help.

I knew who I could ask for more details about Brandon Lake. Tom Malone, the lumberjack and Veronika's boyfriend in 2017. They must have talked about it at some time or another. The only problem though was that he didn't seem too willing to work with me. As I'd given him my phone number, I nonetheless hoped he'd use it, or else I'd have to go back to his workplace again.

In the meanwhile, I decided to learn more about Brandon Lake, the little boy who also disappeared too early. Disappeared? Or was killed?

I decided to look for official documents.

They were not going to disappoint me...

CHAPTER 12
Greenville cemetery

THE SLICE of bread and the sardines that old Herman had given me hadn't really filled me up because I just nibbled on them. Though I was starving when I got back in his boat, I couldn't stand the stench of fish. And no way was I going to touch the sausage that I would have devoured a couple of years ago.

Which is why, though it was too late for lunch and too early for dinner, I went straight to the Dockside Tavern, which had been *unanimously elected with my sole voice* as my headquarters. Charlene was there, the waitress who I saw the first time.

"Hey!" she said, still chewing gum. "Karen, right? So? How's your research going?"

"Ups and downs," I admitted, looking out over the waves on the lake. "Just like the waves you see here on the surface of Lake Moosehead!"

"Yeah, the wind had changed. It's probably gonna rain. What can I get you?"

"I know it's not really the right time, but I'm hungry. What would you have that's light and quick?"

"Don't worry, the kitchens never close here. I'll ask them to make you a serving of onion rings, okay?"

"Sounds great. With plenty of coffee please too, Charlene."

"Consider it done."

A few minutes later she came back with my order.

"You ever heard of Brandon Lake?"

Charlene seemed to be thinking.

"Should I have? Except for him having Veronika's last name, it doesn't ring a bell. Is he from her family?"

"I think they're brother and sister."

"That's strange."

"Why?"

"Because I never heard she had a brother. But then again, Veronika and me weren't besties. We just knew each other. That was it. She could have had a brother I didn't know about. Did you ask Tom Malone?"

"Not yet. Speaking of which, the ex-boyfriend isn't very cooperative. I hope he'll get back to me because I've still got loads of questions."

"If you want to talk to him, just stop over at the *Stress-Free Moose Pub* at the end of the day. He and his colleagues usually have a beer there after work. There are lots of vehicles from the Haymond Lumber Company there."

"Will do," I said with a smile. "Thanks, Charlene."

"No problem. Enjoy!"

And she walked away, leaving me with my onion

rings. There was hardly anyone in the restaurant at this time of day. Background music, where it smelled like French fries and coffee, cleaning products and onions: a typical American diner.

While I was eating, I logged into the web on my phone. I looked for the name Brandon Lake, but it was slim pickings. I added the words Greenville, Sugar Island, Lake Moosehead, and other ideas, but didn't find anything either. No data, neither administrative nor journalistic, that popped out.

As if this little boy had never officially existed. Yet, if he was dead – and who knows, maybe even killed – that meant that he had been alive before. An elementary truism. Nonetheless, there was no information about him. It seemed like the Lake family were expert in conjuring tricks; they disappeared even better than Houdini...

Finally filled up, I felt ready to go out despite the drizzling rain in Greenville. The wind was blowing the small drops of rain almost horizontally, and I had to put the collar of my coat up so I wouldn't freeze.

Then I had an idea. Rather than trying to find the trace of Brandon Lake on the web, why not go to a place where dead people are generally resting in peace.

To the Greenville cemetery.

LOCATED in the south of the little town, with the railroad on one side and the forest on the three others, there was only one road that led there. This was a good place for eternal rest. There were four paths cutting through the grass on which I could see white tombstones. I was sure what I was looking for would be easy to find. I was trying to imagine what kind of grave little Brandon would have. I hesitated. Would it be a grave in the area dedicated to little angels who'd left too early or rather in a family plot with dimensions matching the Lake family's fortune?

There was no one else in the cemetery. Only a crazy lady like me walking up and down in gusts of wind and drizzle, her coat buttoned up to her chin, which was hanging down on her chest and hands in her pockets. I scrupulously looked for the Lake name on the plaques or crosses.

Brandon wasn't mentioned in the children's section.

And finally, in the place the farthest away from the entrance, right before the railroad tracks, I found a family vault where three generations of Lakes seemed to be resting.

Benjamin M. Lake
  Melina B. Lake née Horton
  Georges T. Lake
  Suzanne V. Lake née Martineau
  John C. Lake
  Patricia D. Lake née King

. . .

Three generations who, if I looked at the dates, must have been Mason Lake's parents, grandparents, and great-grandparents.

But no Brandon Lake.

Perhaps he died after the family went to Florida? And was buried there, in the shade of the palm trees, under the Miami sun?

Yet if I believe the Who's poster that was tacked onto the wall in the infant's room in Sugar Island, everything led me to believe that he had passed away at an age when he still slept in a crib.

But after all, I couldn't date the moment when the poster had been tagged.

I left the cemetery soaked to the bones, freezing and my mind fogged up with all those mysteries.

It was time to go back to the Greenville Inn. I could see the huge slate roof from the cemetery, on the side of the hill. A hot shower would be just what the doctor had ordered after this mysterious day.

This morning, I'd set off to find Veronika Lake.

This evening, I was looking for Brandon Lake, supposedly her brother.

Two Lakes for the price of one! Myrtille was going to love this!

... to help...

Change scenery.

Physically distance myself to better near my dream. Even though the word is strong, perhaps improper.

A dream? Undoubtedly, reality is cruel, relentless.

This is what I must do, what we've decided, my conscience and I, and I must follow this path whatever it takes.

And it's going to take a lot, that's for sure. My decision implies some voluntary renunciation, but at the end of the tunnel, maybe I'll find light.

Never regret a decision like this. If you lose on one side, you win on the other, that's life.

I lost a lot before...

Now I hope to win...

CHAPTER 13
Smelling blood miles away

"THAT'S FANTASTIC, HUN!"

I just had time to dry my hair before Myrtille Fairbanks called, late at night as usual.

This exclamation followed what I'd told her about the life and death of Brandon Lake. As soon as she can smell another mystery, she jumps with joy and begins imagining the number of pages she'll be able to devote to the subject. At the same time, she thinks of the number of readers that will increase in the next edition of *True Crime Mysteries*, and subsequently, the number of dollars she'll have in the bank.

In a nutshell: a new death equals new dollars.

That's why I do this job. I'm not complaining though, far from it. I let her manage the money side of the deal and I focus on *in situ* research.

"If you say so. For me, it's another headache."

"But Karen, you love that, admit it. It excites you. Like a shark that can smell blood miles away."

"I confess. Not to the point of getting excited though. Interested maybe. Tomorrow I'll try to see what I can get from the authorities in town. We'll see. And... by the way... I had an unexpected expense this morning..."

I told her about the bribe given to Herman and then about my visit to the abandoned cabin on Sugar Island. Without forgetting the poster with its *Who's next* tag, and I sent her the photo of it.

"That smells good," said Myrtille, overjoyed. "Love it! And I bet there's lots of stuff behind the story of the Lake family. I'll let you sniff it out, my little cocker with a wet nose."

As usual, she hung up on what she thought of as being witty or friendly and that always left me uneasy. I loved my boss, but sometimes I just wished she'd shut up. I know, I'm paradoxical. Like everyone, right?

AFTER HAVING TAKEN my favorite pills and slept like a log for a whole night, I felt like getting out and getting going right after breakfast at the Inn. The sizzling bacon caught my eye as did the scrambled eggs, but I didn't allow myself to be tempted. That was finished! I had some poached eggs, yogurt, and some fresh fruit instead. I looked out the window of the dining room and was relieved to notice it was no longer raining and that the wind had died down too. Leaves had fallen from the trees since yesterday and only a few beautiful orange or red ones were left. In October, Maine is so very beautiful. A show that even the natives never get tired of.

I dressed warmly before leaving the inn, having decided to walk to the Town Office in Greenville. It wasn't even eight yet and the town was slowly waking up. Before leaving, I checked the Town Office's opening hours. They were open from seven till four, sunrise till sunset at this time of the year.

I went in and walked to the front desk. A young lady named Jocelyne asked if she could help me.

"I'd like to have a look at the Greenville civil registries, please. Would that be possible?"

"Do you have an appointment?"

"Um, no, I'm sorry, I didn't know you had to..."

"Would you like to consult the original registries or the copies?"

"Whatever. I just need to look at the death certificates."

"In that case you can just have a look at the digital data online. They start from the beginning of the 20th century, because it takes a lot of time for our volunteers..."

"That will be fine," I said, cutting her off. "I just need to look at the past twenty years or so."

"No problem. Just a minute, I'll give you the link."

She went to her computer.

"There you go," she said two minutes later. "Do you want me to mail it to you, so you don't have to type it in? It's a hard one."

I gave her my email and decided to go to the *Dockside Tavern*, my unofficial head office, where Charlene wasn't working this morning. Nancy, Charlene's clone, welcomed me. Same blond hair in a ponytail, same apron, same gum she was mechanically chewing – well I do hope it was not really the same gum they shared shift after shift... and sadly the same weariness and fatigue.

I ordered coffee and a glass of water and logged into Piscataquis County's data base.

IT WAS NOT an intuitive system and didn't have a search engine that used keywords, which would have saved me a lot of time. I had to go through the death certificates year by year. Of course, to make things more fun, they hadn't been scanned in alphabetical order, that would have been too easy. They were *implemented* by date.

I was starting to have sore eyes looking at the screen already, especially as I didn't know what date to start with. Should I use 2017 as the closest date? When Veronika vanished, her so-called brother must have already been dead as no one remembered him then.

2017, nothing at all.
2016, *nada*.
2015, *rien*.
2014, *niente*.
I asked for more coffee.
2013, *nichts*.

2012, *nič*.

2011, diddly squat.

2011, zilch.

I was exhausted. I luckily discovered an index by decades! With, per year, the names of the deceased. I started hoping again.

Except…

Except that I kept going backwards and didn't find anyone named Brandon Lake who died in Greenville, Maine.

People were starting to come into the restaurant. And I still hadn't found a thing. I had gone back to 2000, which was when Veronika was born, as she was seventeen when she went missing. Was her so-called brother already dead when she was born? I didn't think so, without being able to put my finger on why I thought so.

How much older was she? If I had the answer to this question, I would have been able to progress.

But as I didn't, I had to continue my investigations.

I ordered a vegetarian salad with a glass of iced tea, while continuing.

When I reached the dessert, a brownie with pecans, I was in 1990 and there still was no Brandon Lake in the database.

As if he had never died…

CHAPTER 14
Totally disgusting stuff

OR HAD NEVER BEEN BORN?

Except for the child's room in the cabin in Sugar Island, what proof did I have that Brandon Lake actually existed?

Maybe it was a fantasy. Or a ghost. I kept on thinking of those two words as I went back to the Town Office. I needed some confirmations.

The same Jocelyne was there at the front desk.

"Any joy in your research?" she asked, recognizing me.

"I wouldn't use the word 'joy.' It was more of a headache, but maybe you can help me."

"My pleasure. What can I do for you?"

"I'd like to know if you know or knew the Lake family."

That question surprised Jocelyne.

"Of course, everyone knows the Lakes around

here. A family that lived in Greenville for several generations."

"That was what I understood at the cemetery. But I'm not really interested in their genealogy, but rather in the current members of their family. Mason and Janet, the parents. Then Veronika and Brandon, the children."

"Sweet Jesus, I know, those poor children," said Jocelyne. "What a story!"

"That's the story I'm interested in. When their daughter disappeared in 2017 and then when their son died."

"Their son died too? Really? That's awful. They lost their son too?"

"You didn't know? That's actually my problem. Some things lead me to think that he passed, but I can't find his death certificate in any of the registries. Nor in the data base, to tell the truth."

"That could mean he wasn't born in Maine," suggested Jocelyne. "They don't use the same registries. Maybe you could expand your search to a federal level. Or perhaps he was born abroad, who knows. The Lakes travel all the time."

"Thanks, I'll see what I can find. And in the meanwhile, can you tell me where they lived in Greenville?"

"Sure, just a second. I think their house was in West Cove Point. Yes, there it is, the last house on the road with the same name, right on the end. But the system says they no longer own this residence. I don't know if you know this, but they still have Sugar Island.

Mason Lake purchased it. Stirred people all over the county up at that time. Just imagine, someone who buys a whole island for himself."

"It was uninhabited, wasn't it?"

"Of course, otherwise it wouldn't have been available for purchase. But people here gossiped, you know, that it was really *snobby*..."

"And they didn't like the Lake family?"

"Let's just say they were influential. And people often don't like that. They were people that you fear more than admire. You know, money spoils everything."

"Would you happen to know where they live now? Someone told me they moved to Florida."

"I'm sorry," Jocelyne said sincerely. "I don't have that information. But you could ask Mr. Martineau, our mayor. He knew them well."

"When can I meet him?"

"He's been on a trip to Bangor since yesterday, but if you want, I can fit you in tomorrow."

"Thanks so much."

I thanked the helpful employee and left the building. And if I drove out to West Cove Point? See what the Lake family's old house looked like. I wouldn't learn much, but why not, it wasn't far at all.

I DROVE OUT OF GREENVILLE, with the lake on my right, then I turned onto the road in the peninsula. A narrow road that snaked through spruce trees, balsam firs and larch trees, a spectrum of brightly colored leaves. The ground, covered with needles and dead leaves, hugged the old road. As the weather was better, I was able to enjoy the drive and scenery. The farther I got to the end of the peninsula, the farther the houses were apart. A nice place to live, in the middle of the forest with Lake Moosehead on both sides. I could easily imagine the Lake family enjoying it here. A half mile down the road I could see what I assumed to be the last house.

It was a beautifully built one, with a slate gray roof and white walls and a large yard overlooking the point of the peninsula. I estimated it to be at least 1,500 square feet and it was two stories high. A perfectly mowed lawn surrounded the house, and you could see the lake on each side of it. I was sure they had a private pontoon behind it. No fences here either, which was the case for most houses in Greenville.

A calm town, now that the Lake family, with their ambiguous reputation, no longer lived here?

I glanced at the mailbox which told me I was at the Kissinger's. Maggie and Liam Kissinger. I heard the noise of an electric lawnmower coming from behind the house. I came closer and saw an overweight nearly bald man mowing the lawn. Hard to tell if he was pushing the lawnmower or of the lawnmower was pulling him. But together they were doing a good job. I saw him and raised my hand, signaling I'd like to talk to him. He slowly finished the line he was cutting and turned the mower off.

"Can I help you, Miss? Are you lost?"

"Hello. No, no I'm not lost, thanks. My name is Karen Blackstone and I'm a real estate agent. I'm prospecting in the county looking for a villa like yours, one that has direct lake access. Such a beautiful lot. And so nicely kept up."

"Thanks. We do what we can. It's always so much nicer to live in a nice clean place. I'm just hoping this is the last time I have to mow this year. As for your research though, I wouldn't know if there are houses up for sale. Not in West Cove Point anyway. At least not that I know of. Have you asked in the Town Office? I would imagine they've got a list of vacant properties."

"Yes, I did, but they don't have this info, outside of people they actually know. Have you lived here for a long time?"

"I'd say five years. Yup, we moved in in November 2017, I remember the weather was just awful that whole week."

"That's too bad. But could you tell me - I know the neighborhood a bit, and wasn't it the Lake family who lived here before you? I think I remember they had a residence on the point."

The bald mower's eyes squinted, and his forehead wrinkled, just like the lines in his mowing pattern.

"Don't even talk about those slobs," he said, annoyed.

"Excuse me. What happened if it's not too indiscreet?"

"You should have seen the house. I bet they must have been Mr. and Mrs. Perfect in public. Money and all. But at home, let me tell you, it wasn't the same song. I don't know what the hell they did between their four walls but... it's none of my business."

"I would imagine you purchased the house from an agency?"

"We did. And we lowered the price, that I guarantee you. Luckily, I never met those sons of bitches, otherwise there would have been quite the discussion, believe me."

"You really don't like them, that's for sure. I feel bad for you. It's always terrible to see damage in a home you're buying."

"Oh! It wasn't really the damage. To tell you the truth, anything that's material can be repaired. It's more stuff we found after we moved in. When we redid a couple of rooms."

My instinct was kicking in now. I could feel that the owner was about to give me something juicy. I didn't let the occasion pass.

"What kind of stuff?"

Liam Kissinger looked around to be sure nobody could hear us.

"When we wanted to redo the flooring of one of the rooms upstairs, for me I'd say it was their office – see that balcony over there – we had to move a heavy wardrobe that the Lake family didn't take with them.

We found a USB flash drive that that must have been dropped on the floor and was hidden beneath the wardrobe, between two blades of flooring."

"You looked at the flash drive, I imagine?"

"I did, or else I wouldn't be telling you all this. I hesitated for a while before inserting the flash drive into my computer and opening the files. You never know, all the viruses and Trojan horses, you know things like that. And, God forgive me, we found photos that made me and my wife sick to our stomachs."

"Photos of what?"

"Absolutely disgusting things."

CHAPTER 15
Not very kosher methods

YOU COULD ALMOST SMELL the sulfur in what the new owner of the former Lake family residence in West Cove Point had said. I was loving it. I was all excited to be announcing a scoop to Myrtille Fairbanks, my boss. I had no idea if the guy trusted me because I looked honest or if he was merely angry. I continued.

"What do you mean by 'disgusting?'"

"I don't know why I'm telling you this. I have no idea who you are. But just talking about it makes me madder than hell, that I can say. You know I'm a respectable person, nothing to hide. I've always been a member of the Lion's Club, I go to mass every Sunday, and I teach my children about respect, generosity, and all that. So when I stumbled upon those photos, I went crazy."

"Why?"

"Because they were photos you wouldn't want your children to see, get me?"

No, I didn't really get him, but I could imagine what kind of disgusting stuff he was implying. I insisted.

"Were there children on the pictures?"

Liam nodded his head, without adding anything. I continued, to avoid him any uneasiness linked to this confession given to an unknown person who just showed up and – I was proud of this – and who was able to get a non-loquacious person to talk. An art!

"Adults too?" I asked, fearing the answer.

"Yeah. Adults too."

"Did you know anyone? Members of the Lake family?"

"No one. We're not from here. We're from Oregon. We didn't know a soul here."

"You never met the Lakes?"

"Never. Like I said, only a real estate agency in Greenville."

"If I show you some photos of them, would you be able to tell me if they're on the USB flash drive?"

"No idea. Like I said, all this dates back to nearly five years ago."

I felt like trying anyway. I got my phone out and looked for portraits of Veronika and her parents, Mason, and Janet Lake, on the internet.

While I was peering at the results, Liam frowned and looked at me suspiciously.

"You're not more of a real estate agent than I am."

"Excuse me," I gulped, caught in the trap of my lie.

"I been around the block a couple of times lady. When you came, you were in real estate mode, but now I'm thinking you're trying to get info from me about a subject that you love more than selling houses. I think you're here to get info about the Lake family. Am I wrong?"

I looked down and he continued.

"I'm going to ask you to beat it or I'm gonna call the cops! I wasted enough time with you. It's going to rain, and I haven't finished mowing my lawn."

He walked back to his lawnmower.

"Wait! Please. I confess. I'm not a real estate agent. And yes, I am interested in the Lake family. I'm a journalist for *True Crime Mysteries* magazine. You must know what happened five years ago in Greenville, just before you moved in."

"Yeah, I heard about that. But it's none of my business."

"But you discovered an element concerning them right in this house... That sort of links you to the affair."

"What affair? When the girl went missing? I have nothing to do with that. So quit your bullshit and get the hell out of here. I never should have told you that. I don't know why I did."

I raised my hands, surrendering.

"Okay, okay, I'm sorry to have taken so much of your time. But I think you discovered something that will help my investigation, in one way or another."

"And find the missing girl?"

"Maybe, but not just that."

"What do you mean?"

"Let's just say there are other unsettling facts about the Lake family members."

"Like what?" he asked, now interested.

So without going into details, I told him about what I already called the Brandon Lake affair. Then I asked him another question.

"On the photos on the USB flash drive, do you remember having seen any very young children?"

Kissinger closed his eyes to concentrate.

"My memory isn't really clear, but no, I don't think so."

I sighed internally in relief.

"Can I show you the Lake family portraits now?"

"Go ahead, but after that forget about me. Understand?"

"*Cross my heart and hope to die.*"

"Don't talk about dying."

I pointed my phone towards him after having found a picture of the Lakes that was taken in 2016 in Greenville for a charity event.

"Were these people on the flash drive?"

He looked closely at them.

"No idea. Frankly. I could say yes like I could say no. But you gotta admit that it's not easy to recognize people on photos when they're wearing a tux in one photo and they're nude in another one…"

"I understand. What did you do with the USB flash drive, Mr. Kissinger?"

"What should I have done with it? I couldn't keep it here. There were kids in the pictures. My Catholic principles wouldn't let me do nothing. I gave it to the police in Greenville."

"What did they do?"

"Got me. Go ask them. Listen, I gotta go, this lawn isn't going to mow itself."

"Sorry again to have bothered you and thanks for answering my questions. And sorry for the not too kosher methods I used."

"No hard feelings. If that can help solve a missing person mystery."

And he started his lawnmower up again.

As for me, I noted to myself that I had to have a friendly visit with the Greenville police.

CHAPTER 16
Dwelling on the past

AS NIGHT WAS FALLING on Greenville, I remembered what Charlene, my waitress friend from the *Dockside* told me: that I might stumble upon Tom Malone at the *Stress-Free* when he'd finishing working.

I went to the pub and noticed that a *Haymond Lumber Company* pickup was already parked there.

I went into the thick and musty masculine bar. Odors of grease, tap beer, fried onions and rancid sweat from lumberjacks and fishermen after work. The smell clobbered me, but I saw the lumberjacks, including Tom Malone, at a table in the back of the pub. At this time of night, ladies weren't a very common sight, and all eyes turned towards me. Veronika Lake's former boyfriend recognized me. Easy to see with the face he was making... and he wasn't happy to see me again. Resigned, at the very most.

I sat down at a round table not too far from the guys and with an upward motion of my chin, signaled

Malone that I'd like to talk to him. He turned to his colleagues, said something that made them all laugh – undoubtedly some macho pride thing, – picked up his glass of beer and came over. But wasn't happy about it.

"You decided to follow me like my shadow or what? If so, I can't wait till the sun sets."

"Glad to see you too," I said ironically. "Have a seat."

"I'm not gonna be long, I'm almost finished," he said sitting down anyway and showing me his glass of beer. "Now what do you want? I told you I didn't want to dwell on the past."

"Tom, I appreciate your help. Right now you're the only person to be able to tell me about 2017. You had a front row seat, could I say. I've been really busy since we last spoke, and I've got a couple of other questions that I'm sure you'll be able to answer for me."

"We'll see. Shoot."

"I went to Sugar Island," I admitted pointblank.

"Hell, you don't waste any time lady. You know what you want! You know it's private property."

"I do. And yet I even went inside the house. But that's between you and me, okay?"

"Karen, you a one *loco* lady," he smiled, shaking his head. "But I like that. Cheers!"

We raised our glasses, a Coke for me and a beer for him.

"Veronika wasn't an only child, was she?"

"Sort of. How come you're asking me that?"

I told him what I'd seen in the child's room in the

villa. A baby boy's room. I didn't mention the tagged poster.

"Is that right? A kid named Brandon. You must have seen his room too."

"I saw it, yeah. But no brother."

"Never? But you must have talked about him with her. You couldn't have gone steady for months without having mentioned the brothers and sisters theme. That's important when you're getting to know one another."

"It's true. I wanted to know. I asked her at the beginning of our relationship, but quickly understood by her answer that she didn't want to talk about it."

"What do you mean?"

"Um, I don't really know. She just didn't want to talk about him. She just told me that yeah, she had had an older brother, but she never knew him. That he died before she was born."

I thought about the Greenville cemetery, where Brandon should have been buried.

"He must have died young then."

"I don't know, probably. Veronika's parents weren't that old, so I imagined that her brother hadn't been that much older than her. Maybe two or three years."

"That's what I thought too, looking at the bedroom and the crib. Did you also go to their house in West Cove Point?"

"Of course. I spent a couple of nights there and had dinner there quite often. Why?"

"Did Brandon have a room there too?"

"Got me. All I knew was the kitchen, living room and Veronika's room. Her parents were always there when I went there. But I did see that one of the rooms was always locked. I was curious and tried to open it. Like a forbidden room. I knew I thought that it was the dead boy's room."

"Like a forbidden and impenetrable sanctuary?"

"I don't really know what all that means, but why not."

"What I mean by that is a room that's forbidden, intimate, one that has secrets that you don't want to unveil to people who are not members of the family."

"Yeah, right, it was something like that."

With an association of ideas, I thought about the photos Kissinger, the current owner, had found on the USB flash drive. And what if the same room had other secrets? For now, I didn't want to talk about that with Tom. I bounced back to Sugar Island.

"Can you remember having seen a strange poster tacked onto the wall in the child's room on the island? A poster that didn't fit in with that type of room?"

"Can you be more precise? I didn't go there yesterday you know."

"A poster of the jacket of a famous album of the Who, *Who's next*."

"Oh. That one? With the granite monolith right in the middle? Now that you speak about it, yes, I do remember that. But... Like everyone knows that cover so well, I really couldn't tell you if I remember having seen it there or somewhere else, like on TV or in a store, for example."

"Try to remember. Remember that evening in August, 2017."

Tom Malone thought back while finishing his beer.

"Could be. I can see the poster. But, and here I'm sure of myself, it wasn't in the little boy's room, like you say."

"Really? Where was it?"

"I don't know anymore, but I'm sure that it wasn't in the dead kid's room. For the pure and simple reason that we didn't go in there, that weekend."

"You're sure?"

"Yup. Sure. Now that I think back, like you asked me to, I remember that that room was locked. And that was one of the reasons that Veronika and I argued that night."

CHAPTER 17
The forbidden room

I REFORMULATED my question after what Tom Malone had just said.

"You guys had a spat that night?"

"Yeah," he sighed. "Isn't that ridiculous? Knowing that one of the last things we shared, Veronika and me, before she disappeared forever, was a fucking fight."

∽

SUMMER OF 2017, *Sugar Island.*

EMBERS WERE BURNING in the barbecue next to the swimming pool, supervised by Paul who had proclaimed himself the barbecue king. The brats were nearly done, "grilled but not burned," as the good-looking young man with his blond hair in a ponytail had promised. Each time they organized a getaway in

Sugar Island - they called it their *Sugar Plan* - he was in charge of the barbecue. The others thought that was just fine. While the meal was cooking, they had time to have a beer or a cocktail or fool around in the pool or in the yard. Paul didn't mind. He didn't have a girlfriend. That didn't stop him though from appreciating Cynthia's generous bosom as he turned the brats over. Who knows, maybe one day they could do it together...

Cynthia was floating around on an air mattress in the pool. It was dark outside, but the spotlights on the pool converged in the same direction as Paul's eyes: on the top of the young lady's swimsuit. He couldn't keep his eyes off her. He even thought of leaving the brats cook by themselves and jumping in the water to join Cynthia, covering her body with his. He shook his head though, saying, and rightly so, that they'd both fall in.

So he kept an eye on the grill and the other on Cynthia's breasts while listening to *Don't You Know* by the Kung blasting out from the speakers.

"*Your beating, breathing heart is keeping me from dying...*

I'm gonna rock your body."

Cynthia's eyes were closed, Paul was flipping the brats while wondering where everyone else had gone.

There they were. Carlos and Dorothy were lying on the grass, Dorothy had her hand in Carlos' swimming trunks... and just a couple of minutes ago he saw Becky and Alvin cutting some tomatoes in the kitchen.

But where the heck were Veronika and Tom? Another ten minutes and the brats would be too done.

"Come on Veronika, over here," whispered Tom in his girlfriend's ear and grabbing her elbow. "There's no one here, they're all outside. Can you smell those brats that Paul's cooking?"

"No, Tom, stop it, I don't want to," the young lady replied once again. "Is that all you can think of?"

"We're here to have fun, aren't we? Like alone in the world, wow!"

Tom was trying to take Veronika to the bedroom they'd chosen when they arrived.

"Just leave me alone, Tommy. We'd better go back down, everyone else will be wondering what we're up to. Plus you stink of beer, that makes me want to puke."

"Come on, they couldn't care less about us. Look at them," he said looking out one of the windows. "Your best friend is floating around in the pool, Paul is cooking brats, and the two others are making out on the grass. And us? We can't have fun? Everyone knows what happens in Sugar Island stays in Sugar Island. We're not here to read books."

Tom tried to steal a kiss from Veronika, hoping that would thaw her out. But she turned her head away.

"Quit trying to escape like that," he said laughing and running after her in the hall.

The two lovebirds had a race, Veronika was ahead and suddenly Tom couldn't see her. She must have gone around a corner and hid in one of the closets. The young man opened the doors one by one, looking in each room after having turned on the lights, calling his sweetie and promising her a seventh heaven if she let herself be caught.

Then he came to the last door, the only one he hadn't yet tried to open.

And the only one that was locked, unlike the others. Tom remembered that each time he'd come to Sugar, the room had been inaccessible.

"Hey! You in there?" he shouted, shaking the doorknob several times.

No answer.

"Veronika, if you don't answer me, I'm gonna break down this fucking door!"

With his lumberjack's shoulders - the job he was planning on doing - Tom Malone could do something like this.

"I'm gonna count to three. One... Two..."

Still no answer on the other side of the door if Veronika was there.

"Three!"

Tom slammed his shoulder into the door. It trembled but didn't open. He reiterated the maneuver when he heard Veronika behind him.

"Stop that right now dammit!"

The shrill sound of Veronika's angry voice interrupted his movement. He turned around and saw his girlfriend, her eyes wide open with furor he'd never seen before.

"What's wrong?"

"Never try to open that door again, Tom. Understand?"

He walked up to her.

"Why? You gonna stop me? With your little chickenshit biceps? Huh? What's in this forbidden room? A skeleton in the closet?"

Veronika was now staring at the door, her lips pursed to the point they were starting to turn blue, the arteries in her neck throbbing. Tears welled up in her eyes.

"Veronika, what's wrong? Tell me what's happening. What's going on? If you don't tell me, I'm going to knock the door down. That way I'll know once and for all. Each time we come here this door is locked. What's in there?"

An interminable followed this question; the music was playing outside. The young lady finally spoke.

"My brother."

CHAPTER 18
Fly, Winnie!

I MOTIONED to the waitress and ordered another round of beer and soda.

"My treat," I said to Tom Malone, sitting across from me. "That's really what she said? That her brother was behind this forbidden door in Sugar Island?"

The lumberjack nodded.

"Those were her exact words, and you can believe me when I tell you that my eyes popped wide open. I asked her to tell me what she meant by that, and she said...

∽

SUMMER OF 2017, *Sugar Island.*

...WITH TEARS IN HER EYES:"

"It's not really my brother behind the door," Veronika said, sniffling. "It's his souvenir."

"He's dead, right?"

"That's right. But I never knew him. We already talked about this."

"I remember now. But still, why keep a room locked up with the *souvenir* of your dead brother? That's sort of creepy, like *Under Wraps*. Fuck Vero, don't tell me that your brother's mummy is in that room?"

"You're an idiot Tom. You don't respect anything. Nothing. You know what? Forget it and I never want to talk to you about that again, okay?"

She turned around towards the wooden stairs and joined the rest of the group, drying her tears.

"Yeah, sure," muttered Tom, still looking at the door.

Not at all resigned, he tried the handle once again, with the same lack of success. Then like a wannabe Arsene Lupin, he took the pocketknife from his jeans and tried to pick the lock, turning the narrow blade around in the hole. It didn't work. Curious, he glanced through the eyecup.

What he saw petrified him.

Without a doubt there was an infant's crib, the bed was still made. In the middle of the mattress, a teddy bear, its round eyes staring, as if it was waiting for the dead child to come back. It made him think of Winnie the Pooh.

But Winnie could wait forever, little Brandon would never again hold him in his chubby little arms.

But, perhaps because of the alcoholic beverages he'd had, Tom Malone wouldn't admit defeat. He had a stroke of genius and ran to one of the other doors upstairs.

He came back with a standard key that he put into the locked door.

And turned it.

The mechanism didn't protest.

The door opened.

Tom went in.

Just goes to show that the easiest solutions are sometimes hard to find, he thought as he walked into the sanctuary.

He looked at the strange room for a while, frozen, as if the child would be coming to bed any moment now. A dresser with a stack of well-folded pajamas, a bedside lamp shaped like a mushroom, new sheets, and a Micky Mouse rug on the floor. On the wall there were posters from Disney films at the end of the 90s: *Tarzan, Toy Story 2, The Tigger Movie.*

That was when he made his first mistake of the evening.

He bent down over the crib and grabbed the teddy bear.

Then he left, slowly went downstairs towards the back of the house where the pool and guests were.

He walked to the edge of the pool.

"Fly, Winnie!" he shouted out, as if he were crazy. "And swim!"

With a large circular gesture, he threw the stuffed animal into the pool.

Everyone surrounding him froze, in total incomprehension. Paul raised his arms, a brat on a fork in one of them, gaping.

Veronika was petrified, staring at the surface of the pool where Brandon Lake's teddy bear was floating. Her brother, the one who'd died before she was born, the brother she never got to know.

Alvin, understanding that something serious had taken place, dove in to get the teddy bear back. When he got back out of the pool, the entire group of friends was silent.

Had there not been any music coming from the speakers, you could have thought time was standing still. Each person understood that something unusual had happened, without realizing the whys and wherefores of it. This silence was interrupted by Veronika, addressing Tom.

"You're really a fucking asshole, Tommy."

The others silently nodded, without really understanding this verbal bomb.

The young lady then ran off towards the pond with the water lilies.

"Wait!" shouted Tom, running after her.

He caught up with her on the pond's pontoon, from which she was going to jump into the black water.

The young man hugged her, preventing her from committing that act.

"You're right, Veronika. I'm a fucking idiot. Forgive me. I don't know what made me do that."

They dropped to the ground, hugging each other, both crying.

They finally calmed down enough for Veronika to speak calmly.

"No, I'm the one who has a problem with that. But it's not my fault. All that is my parents' fault. Ever since I was little, they always repeated the same thing. I grew up with his death on my conscience. It's hard, you know."

"What did they say?" Tom wanted to know.

Veronika wiped her nose on her sleeve, took a deep breath and began, with emotions mixed with a tad of bitterness.

"As soon as I understood that there was another child in the family - meaning when I saw his room - everything went belly up. My parents made me understand that never, and they meant never, was I to speak of that subject. Neither at home nor outside. Neither at school, nor to my friends. Never. It was taboo. I insisted, you know how kids are. When they're not satisfied with the answer they get, they continue. So I insisted. I wanted to know. They said there was a baby boy before me, that his name was Brandon, and that he was dead. I asked them why. They just repeated he'd died. I was stubborn though. And too bad for the spankings I got because of my insistence. Up till the day that my mother gave in and said it was a terrible accident. And without explaining it, she said it happened when she was pregnant with me. Ever since then, you understand, in my little girl's brain, I had the idea that it was all my fault. And I grew up with his death on my conscience. That's why Tommy, and I'm begging you here, never talk to me about my dead brother, never talk to me about his crib, never mention that forbidden room. We're going to lock it and throw away the key. Promise?"

"I promise," he said, calming her and kissing the last tear on her cheek. "Come on, let's forget all that and relax. Have fun with our friends."

"It's not easy for me to forget you know. Sometimes Tommy, there are moments when I'd like to disappear too…"

CHAPTER 19
Without a trace

I COULD TELL by Tom's voice how stirred he was by this episode. By telling me it, he relived it, and I was also overwhelmed. But one word flashed in my brain, and I asked him to confirm it.

"Did Veronika explicitly say she wanted to *disappear*?"

"She did. I remember those words. But I don't know what she really meant by them. Disappearing in the sense of going someplace else or in the sense of committing suicide, get it?"

"Perfectly. And in the light of what we now know, I'm wondering too about her intensions."

"Me too. But hell, how can someone disappear like that without a trace? Stuff like that only happens in books or in movies. Not in real life."

"Unfortunately it does. I'm well placed to know that," I said pensively. "That's my job. Each day I try to find traces that people left, when, in one way or another, they wanted to end their life or just end the life they had."

"What's the difference?"

"It's not just a linguistic nuance, Tom. When you end your life, you commit suicide, kill yourself, or help someone else do it. But when you end the life you have, you don't accept it anymore, you want to become someone else, something else, you want to be different. You reject your past. You erase your own identity; you invent a new one. Elsewhere. It's not a myth. Here in the US there are even federal services officially in charge of recreating lives, new identities to protect witnesses in some very sensitive affairs."

"Well, I'll be damned... Really?"

"Really!"

"And you think that could have been the case for Veronika? That she might have witnessed something horrible and that someone had taken her out of the life she had to protect her from something or someone?"

I raised my hands helplessly.

"At this stage I have no idea. But I'm working on it, trying to make sense of this affair, Tom. That's why I need your help."

Tom and I decided to have some local tapas to accompany us with our drinks. A beer for him and an herbal tea for myself. The waitress brought us a plate of onion rings, cheddar balls, fish and chips and a bowl of tartar sauce with pickles on the side. While grabbing some, I continued my investigations and gave Tom some additional information.

"I went to Greenville Cemetery. And you know what? Brandon Lake isn't buried there. If it's true that he died when Janet was expecting Veronika, I'd deduce that he must have died in 2000. Can you confirm this, Tom?"

"Yeah, in 2000 or 1999 as Veronika was born in February, 2000. But maybe he just died someplace else than in Piscataquis County. The Lakes travelled all the time. They had houses all over. Here, in Sugar Island, in Florida, in California, and Texas too, I think. Plus probably an apartment in New York, Paris, London... Maybe if he died there, he was buried there? What do you think?"

I mentally weighed up the question. It was not impossible.

"But several generations of Lakes are buried here. Why wouldn't they have brought their son home to be with them?"

"Because... there's no body...?" suggested Tom, eating some meatballs (something I would never touch).

I considered that a minute, but that was what I had seen in the archives: no body, no death.

Yet, there was a baby, there was a room, and there had been a death! What a headache! And for the Lakes, what a pain in the butt, to be polite! They couldn't do stuff like everyone else? Be born, live, and die normally?

No, they had to disappear, one after another. And

leave bad memories, bitterness, dirt, and sourness behind them. That's what I told Tom.

There was a moment of silence while we finished our tapas and drinks. Then Tom looked at his watch.

"I gotta be going. My colleagues are getting impatient. It's late and we start early tomorrow."

I also realized that time had gone by and that this morning I'd walked into town. And now it was dark out and I didn't have a car.

"Could you drop me off at the Greenville Inn?"

"If you don't mind riding in a truck that's not clean, between two lumberjacks in their work gear, we don't mind either," joked Tom.

"I'll be fine, thanks."

We all left. In the parking lot I asked Tom Malone another question.

"Do you have any contacts with the others? I'd like to talk to them too."

"Like I told you, I wasn't really a part of their clique. Just accepted in it. They were Veronika's friends, not mine. So I didn't stay in touch with them, and I think they all left Greenville. If you don't work as a fisherman or a lumberjack, it's not a *dream location* here. But I can tell you where Alvin Brown is, you know the guy who was with Becky back in the day. We ran into each other this summer at the marina, and he told me he works in Boston. He's a lawyer. You should be able to find his cabinet easily. That's all I can tell you, sorry."

"No problem. You already really helped me, Tom.

If you think of something, even something you think is insignificant or ridiculous, you've got my number."

"Will do, Karen," he said, pulling my business card out of his pocket. "See, it never leaves me."

Tom and his colleagues moved so I could fit in, and they dropped me off at the inn. I thanked them warmly and went in, plopping down on my bed.

A BRIEF MENTAL list of the day - two missing persons, shocking photos, taboos in the family - and I fell asleep after having taken my daily medication.

Indispensable.

I couldn't wait to meet the mayor of Greenville the next day, mayor of this little town full of secrets.

CHAPTER 20
Upper class

I DECIDED TO SLEEP IN. After all, as Veronika Lake had gone missing five years ago, a couple of hours wouldn't make any difference.

While I was having breakfast, scrambled eggs, and smoked trout, just before the cut-off time at ten, I consulted the Yellow Pages for lawyers in Boston. The list was as long as a month of Sundays, and there were several Browns exercising this honorable profession. Pretty soon there'd be more lawyers than delinquents in our country. I finally found him at Neyman & Bernstein & Brown. When I clicked on the link for the site, I found Alvin Brown's face, a junior lawyer specialized in family affairs - divorces, child custody, child protection, alimony, adoption, things like that. A good-looking black man with close-cut hair, an engaging smile, white teeth, sparkling eyes. A lawyer who inspired confidence, no doubt about that. If his fees were proportional to his plastic, his clients must be really upper class!

I keyed the number into my phone. I'd call Alvin Brown sometime during the day. For the moment, I had an appointment with the mayor of Greenville.

This time I thought ahead, and I drove to town, just in case like yesterday, I wouldn't have a way back at night. Moreover, the weather was morose today, as was I. Drizzle, mist, and the temperature had fallen once again.

Jocelyne recognized me and smiled.

"Mr. Martineau is expecting you in his office. Follow me."

I followed her upstairs. She opened the door and showed me in after her boss had shouted out:

"Come on in Jocelyne. Thank you."

Victor Martineau was in his sixties, with short cut gray hair. A nearly military cut, but a face with reddish jowls that devoured a mouth hidden amid a well-cut beard. A stout man, who walked towards me, holding out his hand.

"Mrs. Blackstone, is that it?"

"It is. Thanks for having me Mr. Martineau."

"Sit down, please. So, what can I do for you? Jocelyne told me you were interested in genealogy and our civil registries?"

"Amongst other things."

"As well as what happened in our peaceful little town five years ago."

"That's it. To be frank with you Mr. Martineau, I'm a journalist and specialist of unsolved missing persons cases."

When he heard that, his mouth twisted in the middle of his beard. As if he was ruminating words that didn't want to or couldn't be pronounced.

"Hum, I see. Like I said, this unfortunate affair dates back five years and I don't think you'll be able to shed any light on it now. Plus, I don't see how I'd be able to help you."

"You never know. By experience, I know that the tiniest detail can be important. Sometimes people aren't aware they know something that could help make progress in a case. Plus, as mayor, I would imagine that you're the first person to know what is happening in your town, aren't you?"

"You know, people always exaggerate the supposed powers of mayors. In reality, we're just officers of the government. For private affairs, like when poor Veronika Lake went missing, that's not something we really deal with."

I nodded my head, showing I understood, even if I didn't believe a word of his newspeak.

"Let me be the judge of that. Could you answer a few questions, Mr. Martineau?"

"Of course, if I can. Go ahead. What would you like to know?"

"An easy question to begin with. How long have you been mayor?"

I could tell he was flattered by my question and proud to answer it.

"I began my third mandate two years ago, which brings me to a total of ten years as mayor of Greenville. I think I must be doing a good job if I'm reelected."

The man then laughed nervously, making his heavy potbelly jiggle.

"I'm sure of that too," I said cajoling him. "Plus I imagine it's not an easy job. So many responsibilities."

"You're preaching to the choir there! So many more problems than advantages. The tiniest problem in town, and people call me. A waterpipe that burst, keys to the tennis courts that someone lost, the circuit-breaker in the town hall that tripped... See what I mean?"

"Totally. It seems to me that Greenville is a nice little town if those are the only problems. So when something happens like when Veronika Lake disappeared, that must be exceptional. You were already mayor back in 2017."

"It sure was exceptional. An earthquake you could say. Trauma for many inhabitants. Including myself. I can guarantee you that with the help of Bob Patterson, the head of our police force, we did everything that was possible to try to find her. But it was as if she had simply vanished. One day she was there and the next day she'd disappeared. Without a trace. I couldn't sleep for days. I felt like I was responsible for that, do you understand? Something like that happening in my town."

"Not really in *your town*, Mr. Martineau. From what I understand, the disappearance took place on Sugar Island. Or at least that was where she was seen for the last time. And unless I'm mistaken, Sugar Island is a private island."

"You're right. But the Lakes lived in Greenville. In West Cove Point."

"I know," I said, thinking about my conversation with Kissinger, the day before, wondering if I should bring up the subject of the USB flash drive the new owner had found.

I decided not to at this point.

"Did you know the Lake family well?"

Martineau squirmed, his prominent abdomen and his rear were a bit too big to fit in the armchair. I wondered if there was a shoehorn someplace. Maybe he could use it. I smiled.

"Yes, you could say so. Let's say we often had the same circles of activities. The Lakes were very pleasant people. They contributed to various associations in town, sometimes to help schools, the firefighters, and the library. They were always there for charitable institutions and gave their time and their money. They went to church on Sundays, they helped finance the renovation of our football stadium. Yes, really very good and very appreciated people."

Hmm, I thought, not really what I'd heard before about them. That being said, I was well aware that a mayor was always going to tout the best side of his town and its inhabitants in general. Victor Martineau continued.

"You understand, Mrs. Blackstone, that the tragedy that struck them also struck us, all the people in Greenville, city employees like inhabitants."

"I can imagine that."

I also could imagine that a mayor would not publicize this type of event, one that would give his town a bad reputation. A little town nestled in the middle of lakes and forests where it should be a pleasant place to live... and not to disappear. A town that wants to attract tourists, boaters, and yachtsmen and all their money.

I hopped right on the bandwagon here.

"Especially as the Lake family already had an unfortunate event in the past, or so I was told," alluding to the death of Veronika's brother.

Martineau sighed and sat up.

"Goes to show that a family can be a respectable one and be struck by the will of the Lord several times."

"What exactly happened to the young Brandon Lake?"

"That's *really* old history. It happened over twenty years ago, before I was mayor, so I didn't really pay attention."

"But he's not buried in Greenville Cemetery."

"He must have passed elsewhere. Did you check the archives?"

"I did, unsuccessfully though".

"You'll have to go on a federal level then. Listen Mrs. Blackstone, I'm afraid this is all the time I have for you today, because I've got an appointment with the architects for a multi-purpose room project. I hope I was able to answer your questions."

He got up, inviting me to do the same, and walked me to the door.

"One last question. Do you have the current address for the Lakes?"

"Sorry, no I don't. I just know that they preferred sunny and busy Florida to our misty and peaceful Maine. You can't account for people's choices…"

CHAPTER 21
Electric and nervous

WHEN I LEFT the Town Hall, I decided to call the lawyer's office in Boston where Alvin Brown was an associate. The switchboard operator told me that he had an appointment.

"Are you one of his clients? Can I leave a message?"

This time I didn't lie. Told the truth. I know that it's better to be honest with lawyers. Then they can sort things out. My call wasn't really a professional one, but I nonetheless was frank.

"No, I'm not a client. My name is Karen Blackstone and I'm a journalist for True Crime Mysteries, a magazine that specializes in unsolved cold cases. Could you just tell him that I'm in Greenville right now and that I'm investigating the Veronika Lake affair. He'll understand. And that I need his help."

"Consider it done. Can he reach you on this number?"

"Yes, he can. As soon as possible, it's important. Thank you so much."

Alvin Brown called me back about an hour later, probably during his lunch break.

"Mrs. Blackstone? This is Alvin Brown. Do you need a lawyer? Is the Greenville Town Hall suing you for rummaging around in their affairs?"

"Thanks for calling back Mr. Brown. I can see we're on the same wavelength. But I'm not really trying to join Mr. Brown, a lawyer in Boston, but rather the young Alvin who lived in 2017 in Greenville. A summer on Sugar Island, does that ring a bell?"

There was a silence.

"Good Lord, no one's talked about that terrible summer for ages. Why the sudden interest from a scandal magazine journalist in this subject?"

"Not a *scandal* magazine, we prefer *sensations*. Everything we publish is authentically checked and true. That's what I'm trying to do with the Veronika Lake affair. And as you called me back, I can deduce that you'd be willing to talk to me about it. You were on Sugar Island August 26 and 27, 2017 when Veronika went missing?"

"You're quite well informed. How did you find that out?"

"Someone named Tom Malone."

"Hum, I see... Tommy. He's a great talker."

"Not great enough. At least not enough for me. That's why I wanted to also hear what you had to say about that dramatic weekend. Would you have a moment, Mr. Brown?"

"What can I say about it? It's so long ago. So vague."

"Anything you remember, even the most insignificant details. Plus, you can be reassured that I've got tons of questions that will help stimulate your memory."

There was a new silence showing he was thinking things over, the guy from the Clique, as Tom Malone called his group of friends, that small group of kids of rich people gravitating around Veronika Lake.

"Are you still there?"

"Yes... Well, listen Mrs. Blackstone. I don't know who you are, where you're from really and your true motivations, but it's okay. I accept. But not on the phone."

"No problem. What would you like to do then?"

"You're in Greenville now, aren't you?"

"I am. On the traces of an unexplainable past."

"That's only four hours from Boston. If you can leave now, I'll see you at six tonight at Fenway Park. Do you like baseball?"

I looked at my watch, it was doable.

"See you there. Why baseball?"

"Come on Mrs. Blackstone, you've never heard of the Boston Red Sox? One of the best teams in the

United States. They're playing in Fenway Park tonight. I've got a pair of VIP tickets; you can have one. One of my friends had to cancel. And as I wouldn't like to miss this match for anything, we can talk while watching the first Play-Off match. I'll be at Door A, on Brookline Avenue."

"Perfect. Thank you, Mr. Brown."

As soon as I'd hung up, I jumped into my Ford Ranchero, which, though it was getting up there in age, was reliable for long distances. Cars like those love to take their time. Greenville to Boston was a four-hour drive, taking the I95 on the east via Augusta, Portland and Portsmouth, an opportunity for me to get some fresh air.

The sun was beginning to set and on my left I could see the Atlantic with its brilliant colors. Traffic was fluid and I took a break to buy myself a vegetable salad and a donut. I also bought a CD and inserted it into my antique auto radio. The electric and nervous notes of The Who made me nod my head in rhythm. Just what you needed when driving and at the same time I thought back on the Lake affair. I did mean the Lake affair and no longer the Veronika Lake affair, because the names of Brandon, Mason and Janet were also in my mind. Plus what Kissinger told me about on the USB flash drive, the Greenville Cemetery family plot, and the mayor. I thought about Sugar Island,

West Cove Point, and Florida. When I reached the outskirts of Boston, I could see the city all lit up. It was nighttime in Massachusetts when I pulled into the Fenway Park parking lot.

There was a crowd in front of Door A, so I had to look to find my rendezvous. I knew what Alvin looked like as I'd seen his photo in the lawyer's directory, but how would he recognize me? I called.

"I'm here, Mr. Brown."

"Me too! I'm right under the blue 1914 banner, easy to find."

I looked there and saw him waving at me. He'd changed his lawyer's costume for jeans and a leather jacket. We shook hands.

"Thanks for agreeing to see me."

"And welcome to Fenway Park. Is this your first match here?"

"It is."

"You'll love it. Let's get in line."

Half an hour later, we sat down in the VIP lodge, right behind the home plate, while the players were warming up with spots that lit the whole enormous playing field up.

In the aisles, you could smell fries, beer, and churros. It was a friendly atmosphere and for myself, who'd never set foot on a baseball field, I felt immediately at ease.

"So, your magazine is interested in the Veronika Lake case?" asked Alvin Brown. "Crazy, don't you think so? Are you making any progress?"

"No, I feel like I'm staying in the same place. Each time there's a new revelation, it gives me an additional mystery to solve. Like a multi-layered cake made from hidden secrets. Each time you cut it, there's another secret that pops out. I'm hoping you can help me. You were a part of the Clique, weren't you?"

Alvin Brown smiled.

"The Clique, yup, our little nickname. Stuff foolish teens do."

"And Tom Malone said he wasn't a part of it."

"True. Tommy didn't have the same background as we did. He lived in Greenville like us, but his parents didn't have the same social and economic category, as we say now being politically correct. For us, he was a mere peasant, a guy with calloused hands."

"You didn't like him?"

"He wasn't always very... likeable. Like a loud-mouth who never knew when to shut up. Sometimes he pretended to be a thug in front of Veronika, his girlfriend. To impress her I imagine."

The loudspeakers announced the beginning of the match. Alvin quickly explained the rules to me. He was using words like *batter, catcher, mound, diamond, first base, strike zone, foul and line drive.* I really liked the name of *Green Monster*, the mythical wall 37 feet high that surrounded the playing field.

"Did Malone impress you?"

"Not at all, but I think he thought he did. I remember that night however, he was nervous. More than usual. You have to remember that we'd all had quite a bit to drink, and some had smoked grass too."

"A bunch of friends alone on a deserted private island, I'm not surprised at all."

"Sea, sex and sun."

"A nice cocktail."

"True. Totally letting go. Like *when the cat's away, the mice will play*!"

"Do you remember any details that would explain why Tom Malone was really nervous that night, as you said?"

Alvin Brown was watching what was going on in the playing field, especially the pitcher warming up by circling his throwing arm on the mound.

"Details, I don't know anymore. It was a long time ago. I just remember one scene that was strange and could have explained why Tommy was so agitated and jittery that night. If we saw the same thing…"

"So what did you see Mr. Brown?"

The young lawyer bit his lip and sighed. He was hesitating but decided to drop the bomb anyway.

"It must have been about one or two in the morning. Anyway, in the middle of the night. The others were still at the poolside, and I had to pee, so I went up to the room I was sharing with Becky. In the hall, going in front of the doors, I heard people groaning and sheets being moved in one of the other rooms. I admit that excited me and made me curious. The door was ajar, and I was able to look in. I saw Veronika wearing next to nothing, and in a position that was quite suggestive, with a partner who, and I'm sure of this because he was still at the pool with me, and anyway, who wasn't Tom Malone."

CHAPTER 22
Caught red-handed

THE RED SOX batter hit the ball over the Green Monster, for a home run and the crowd went wild. I had to wait until Alvin sat down again after whistling loudly to reformulate my question.

"So you're telling me that you saw Veronika having sex with someone other than Tom that night in Sugar Island?"

"I am. That's what I meant."

"You're sure? It was her? Like you couldn't have been a victim of hallucinations because of drugs or alcohol?"

"I did have a few beers and smoked a couple of joints, I confess. But I'm sure of what I saw. Plus Veronika was a good-looking gal, if I do say so myself. So I did have quite an eyeful, I admit. And the show was worth it..."

Summer of 2017, *Sugar Island*.

The embers at the bottom of the barbecue began to turn into gray ashes. Their stomachs full of brats, and yummy burgers, it was now time for the teens to get serious: drinking and smoking, at the poolside, while appreciating the music coming from the speakers hidden in pots of succulents. There weren't any neighbors to disturb here in Sugar Island! They could turn up the sound as loud as they wanted without being heard from Lily Bay, the peninsula that was the closest to the island. For Veronika, Tom, and the others, it was heaven on earth.

At this time of night, the evening was finished, and the wee hours of the morning had not yet arrived, bottles of beer were being opened with their characteristic *pschitt* and no one turned down the joints that were circulating from hand to hand. After having taken a long puff, Alvin suddenly had to go, and now.

"Hey guys, that ain't all but I gotta drain the dragon."

The tall black man awkwardly got up from the sunbed where he was lying and zigzagged his way to the villa, going through the kitchen. He began to look for the bathroom but couldn't remember exactly where it was. As his bladder was informing him he'd better find a solution and fast, he ran up the stairs to his bedroom suite.

When he got to the hall, he didn't know which

door it was. Which suite was theirs? The second or third one? Ah no, that was last summer. This time they'd given Becky the first one unless it was the fourth.

"Shit, I'm gonna burst, I'm not going to pee in the hall. Shake a leg Alvin," he said to himself.

Right then he heard loud sighs and the easily identifiable noise of sheets and bedding. A young lady, he was sure of that. In just a few seconds his hypothalamus addressed primary signals to him, arousing him. In a nutshell, these feminine *ahs* and *ohs* gave rise to an honorable erection for him, one that stuck out of his swimsuit and attracted him to the door that was just pushed shut.

By a leverage effect, his erection instantly stopped his urgent need to pee, and when he looked inside the room with dimmed lighting from the bedside light with a lampshade, he didn't believe his eyes.

Not at all what he'd been expecting.

Yet, and despite his advanced alcoholic state, Alvin recognized the beautiful Veronika Lake, who was just wearing the bottom of her bikini. The young lady was lying on another body whose face he was unable to see, as it was hidden by Veronika's long curly hair. The couple's attitude though left no doubts about what was going on: they were kissing each other passionately, their nude bodies rubbing against each other.

Alvin squinted to try to see who the second person was while trying to mentally remember who had been with him at the poolside when he left. He remembered that Tom had given him a joint, which he then passed to Becky. He recalled that Carlos and Dorothy were necking at the poolside, their feet in the water. But he couldn't remember having seen Paul Tennent. Could this be possible?

"Fuck me then. Paulo and Veronika?"

He was so surprised he stumbled against the door. It squeaked when he touched it, and the noise made him skedaddle before they accused him of being a Peeping Tom. His erection disappeared immediately and the need to pee like a racehorse returned. He rushed to the toilet in his room and peed to his heart's content, evacuating all the beer he'd had.

When he finished, he went out to the hall, past the door that had been open, but it now was closed.

They must have seen or heard him. Alvin didn't dare continue his investigation by knocking on the door.

He ran down the stairs like a robber caught red-handed. All his other friends were still there, Paul and Veronika were still absent.

"Hey, where were you?" asked Tom Malone, handing him a cool beer.

"Taking a leak," Alvin replied.

The young black man didn't know what to do. Should he tell Tom what he had just seen, or leave it? He finally decided that it wasn't his role to tattle and throw a monkey wrench into their couple. Stories like that never end well. Plus... *what happens in Sugar Island...* was their group's leitmotiv, wasn't it.

"You didn't see Veronika, did you?" asked Tom, raising his beer to his.

"Um, no," Alvin hesitated. "How come?"

"She pisses me off always running away like that. What the heck though, we can still have fun without her."

Alvin Brown's inner self said that Veronika could also have fun without him…

CHAPTER 23
Who's the ninth?

I WAS FINDING it hard to concentrate on the Fenway Park playing field. Whether the Red Sox won or lost was less important to me than what had happened to Veronika Lake in the summer of 2017. The young lawyer had a new element in his tale which I wrote down in my little mental notebook, the one that never leaves me, the one I can't lose, contrary to my former techniques where I would constantly misplace my pieces of paper and notebooks. Good memory training!

"Do you think Veronika's infidelity to Tom could have caused her to disappear?"

Alvin Brown nodded, pensive, his lips pursed.

"I wouldn't say that wasn't important, but I'm not sure. After all, I didn't say a word about it, so it remained a secret. At least, I suppose so."

"Tom couldn't have noticed? Or someone else, at a different time that night, who would have spilled the beans?"

"I frankly have no idea."

"And you're sure it was Paul with Veronika on the bed that night?"

The young lawyer's eyes opened wide, surprised.

"What do you mean? Of course it was."

"But you told me that you were unable to affirm who the person was with Veronika that night. You said her hair masked the identity of the person below her."

"Yes, you could be right. Plus, the lights were dim. Outside of Veronika's silhouette, I couldn't make out anything else. Plus I'd been drinking and had smoked a few joints. So, I guess you're right Karen, I can't affirm that Paul Tennent was on the bed with Veronika that night. I just proceeded by elimination at that time."

"So you just presumed that then."

But now Alvin was paying more attention to the Red Sox who'd tied when one of their batters was able to score with the bases loaded.

"I guess so. Now that you say this, maybe I've always imagined things that perhaps weren't true. And like they say in my line of work, every person is presumed innocent if they've not been proved to be guilty. And it's true that I can't categorically say that Paul Tennent was guilty of having had sex with Veronika that night. I don't have any proof. Just a simple conviction that he wasn't sitting at the pool with us that night when I went upstairs to take a leak."

"Right. So if he wasn't at the pool with you, he must have been the one who was with Veronika that night in her room. That's your deduction. What if he was elsewhere than in the bedroom *and* the poolside?"

"In that case, who was with Veronika? Now that I think about it, Paul with Veronika, that would be strange."

"How come?"

"Because Paul, even though he was single that summer, had a crush on Cynthia."

"But in parties like that, with lots of alcohol and drugs, maybe he changed horses?" I said jokingly.

Alvin was munching on a fry when he suddenly stopped chewing.

"Wait a sec. I got it. I just realized something else that I'd overlooked all along, probably because I never paid attention to her. I don't think I'm wrong in saying that at that time, Cynthia wasn't with us at the pool. So that must be it!"

"What?"

"It wasn't Paul with Veronika in the bedroom. Because he went off with Cynthia a bit earlier. That's what must have happened. Paulie finally scored with Cynthia, and they went off to make out somewhere else in the yard."

In my head things were going a hundred miles an hour, first names and images of the protagonists.

"And what if, let's say, in your not so normal state, you'd confused Veronika with Cynthia? Maybe those two were together in the bedroom. Cynthia was lying on Paul..."

Alvin shook his head.

"No. I'm almost sure that wasn't it. Cynthia had really short hair. Impossible to mix her up with Veronika who had long hair almost down to her butt. It was so sexy incidentally... Wow!"

I let him reminisce back on this souvenir that was visibly a nice one and decided to resume things to be clearer.

"Alvin, can you count now who was where and with who when you left the pool?"

He closed his eyes and counted, using his fingers.

"Okay. That night there were eight of us at Sugar Island. At the poolside: Becky and me, Carlos and Dorothy, and Tom, alone. Which is five. Then Paul and Cynthia left to make out someplace, which makes seven. And Veronika was inside, which makes eight. Got everyone."

"Except that Veronika wasn't alone in the bedroom. Which makes nine!

Who was the ninth, Alvin?"

CHAPTER 24
Keeping the strings taut

THOUGH IT WAS cold at Fenway Park, the atmosphere in the stadium was sizzling. Alvin Brown and I were surrounded by noisy fans, but they didn't stop us from thinking about the affair.

"Wait Karen, maybe I miscounted. Otherwise it's not possible."

The young lawyer thought back but arrived at the same conclusion. But then changed his mind.

"Or maybe it was Paul in the bedroom with Veronika. But now I don't believe that anymore. It's not logical considering the feelings he had and who he was attracted to. Paul dreamed of Cynthia; he really did. He wanted to score with her that summer, I remember hearing him say that."

"So here we are back to who that ninth person could have been. Who was he? You're sure you guys were only eight that weekend on Sugar?"

"I am. I can still see us in the Zodiac leaving Greenville. Eight, not one more."

"Maybe someone else could have snuck in with you that evening? Or at least joined Veronika in her bedroom without the others knowing."

"If we're right, we can't dismiss this eventuality," Brown said. "But then we've got a bunch of other questions. Like: how did he get to the villa without anyone seeing him? But no one heard a motor."

"The music was really loud."

"That's true. But still, it wasn't like there were a hundred of us at that party, and no one could have crashed it to sneak a glass of champagne or some appetizers without being seen, you know like in a party where no one knows everyone, including the host! We would have seen the extra person."

"Unless Veronika was the one who wanted him to come to see her on Sugar Island?"

"She'd have been taking a big risk there. Like throwing herself into the lion's den or handing someone a stick to beat her with, don't you think? If Veronika and him wanted to see each other, they could have done it elsewhere, like in Greenville or who knows. But not in the villa on Sugar, at a small private party. Or they liked to take risks?"

"They wanted to be caught red-handed cheating? To end a travesty that had been festering for weeks? Or Veronika was unhappy? Speaking of which, was she in a good mood that weekend? I mean, like did you see a lack of enthusiasm, uneasiness, or did she want to... en it all?"

"End it all?" Alvin asked, surprised. "You mean kill herself? Commit suicide? You want to know if her disappearance was voluntary and definitive? Actually Karen, I think that weekend in August Veronika was a bit depressed. In general she was a joyful girl, though she didn't always show it. Like not exuberant I mean. But now that you mention it, I think she'd changed, something that had started a few months back. She seemed to be moodier, sometimes not paying attention to us, like she was lost in her thoughts."

"Thoughts that could have led her to commit something irreparable that night? Firstly cheating on Tom with her 'lover' and then disappearing with him and thanks to him," I mused.

The visitors scored a home run, bringing the score five to five. The crowd was completely silent, leaving Alvin and I time to think that possibility over. Veronika couldn't have left alone.

After having considered that for a minute, as the crowd began to get noisier now, Alvin Brown had a whole different idea.

"There's another option," he said with a muted voice. "What if that unknown person in Sugar Island - let's call him that - was the one who kidnapped Veronika? Or even worse, killed her? Killed her - we don't know why - and threw her into the lake? Or buried her someplace on the island?"

"I thought that they had dredged Lake Moosehead and searched the island?"

"Not completely, that would have been materially impossible. The lake is huge and deep in places. Unless the body comes back to the surface because of fermentation gases, no one could have found the body. As for Sugar Island, it's about seven thousand square acres, wild, covered with a dense forest, marshlands, and a rocky coastline with difficult access. Lots of places to hide a body..."

Though I used this term often during my career, and it's already been a long one, the word *body* always leaves a bitter taste in my mouth. But that's the most probable explanation when someone disappears. The family hopes for a long time. Hours, weeks, months, years. Then one day they must admit that the person who went missing will never come back. So friends and family as well as the investigators, finally must mourn, even when there's no body. Psychological mourning.

In the Veronika Lake case - as in many others - my work consists in tightening the string that had come loose at each end: on one side, a missing person, and on the other, the hope, even though it may be just slightly larger than a nylon fishing line, to find the person who went missing voluntarily, or ... their body.

My goal was to keep the strings taut.

INCLUDING those in my own life...

CHAPTER 25
All kinds of fantasies

THE MATCH HAD ENDED, Boston had won, and the tens of thousands of spectators were elated when the Red Sox pitcher was able to strike the third and last batter out.

Alvin Brown and I left the stadium. Two anonymous people in the middle of the fans and their comments on the game.

"Did you stay in touch with the other members of your Clique?"

"From time to time. I think except for Tommy, we all left Greenville to do bigger things. Greenville is a nice little town for retired people or when you're on vacation. But to work there, unless you love lumberjacking or fishing, it's not the place to be. It's bucolic, not dynamic."

"What about Becky, your girlfriend at that time?"

"We broke up the year later. I came to Boston to study law, and she went to New York. I think she wanted to study medicine. I don't know if she did. We lost touch with each other."

"Anyone else I could talk to then?"

"I can give you Paul Tennent's Facebook page, we're still virtual friends. Paul's now a gamer."

"What does he play?"

"A gamer, he's a video gamer! His work consists of playing video games. He tests them for companies that create them. And he also develops scenarios for them. So his job is much more fun than mine!"

I opened the Facebook app on my phone and looked up Alvin's profile, which led me to Paul Tennent's profile and sent him a friend request.

"I'll send him a direct message later to let him know who I am. But if you could introduce me to him, that would be great."

"Sure," said the lawyer.

We finally got out of the stadium and Alvin walked me to my car.

"Hey! Nice wheels!" he said when he saw my Ranchero. "Hard to imagine you in that."

"That's a stereotype, Mr. Brown," I said teasing him. "What did you think I'd be driving? A pink Suzuki for girls?"

"I didn't think anything. Just that I'd imagine a Texan rancher driving this magnificent Ford rather than you, Karen. No offence though."

I laughed out loud.

"I inherited this car from my dad. But he wasn't a

rancher either. One more thing Alvin," I said, opening the door.

"Sure."

"I'm also investigating another case for the Lake family. A family that seems to have more than one issue. When you hung out with Veronika and her friends, did you ever hear that she had an older brother named Brandon, who would have passed before she was born?"

The friendly atmosphere suddenly got colder. Alvin Brown's jaw imperceptibly tensed up. I saw him hemming and hawing before answering.

"Did Tommy tell you about the child's room in Sugar Island?"

I nodded.

"Quite the mystery. And about the teddy bear he threw into the pool?"

"That too."

"When I told you he was pretty agitated that night... I couldn't tell you if that crazy act came before or after I'd discovered that Veronika was cheating on him. Or even if he found out. Anyway, that forbidden room was a fucking mystery for us, a morbid sanctuary in my opinion. How can someone keep a mausoleum like that after the death of a child, even though their grieving process may have been difficult. Plus how can you grieve when you've got a material trace that dates back like that?"

"Do you know what the infant died of?"

"I don't think we never knew. It was a taboo in the

Lake family. Veronika wouldn't answer a single question about the death of her older brother."

I showed my hand here.

"I discovered a poster in that room."

"You went to Sugar?" asked Alvin, surprised.

I told him about my solitary excursion onto the island, how I broke into the house and the room that was no longer locked, with the poster of the Who that was tacked onto the wall and...

tagged with a terrible question: *Who killed Brandon?*

Putting his hand over his mouth to hide a shout or surprised swearing, Alvin was astonished.

"Fuck Karen, that's really what you saw?"

I showed him the photo I'd taken there.

People were all driving away and soon the lawyer and I were the only ones left in the parking lot.

Silent.

Pensive.

"I have no idea who could have written that,' admitted Alvin. "But Jesus Christ, that confirms the suspicions that some of us had about that subject."

"What do you mean? You thought Brandon hadn't died naturally?"

"If not, why so much mystery about his death?"

Then I told him everything else I'd recently found out, including the absence of a tombstone, the administrative vagueness about when he was born and when he died, all the shadows surrounding the fate of this poor kid.

"One more reason," he said. "Karen, you have to look into that. And what if I told you that when we were kids, then teens, what we thought."

He was hooked now.

"About Brandon Lake?"

"That's right. You know, mysteries like that fatally generate all sorts of fantasies. Tales, whispering, rumors. Legends and extrapolations. Kids have an unlimited imagination which paradoxically, is often not too far from the truth.

"Alvin, you either told me too much or not enough. Spit it out."

"I see that up till now, no one ever told you about the Sugar Island Cemetery.

...healing...

What can be worse than the loss of someone you love?

Especially when that person is just a child, a baby. A tiny little man who hasn't yet had the time to enjoy the tastes of existence.

I was still so young and innocent that I was forced to grieve.

I cried so much.

I regretted so much.

I suffered so much because of him and for him...

Where is he now?

Is he still alive even?

I made a decision and it's unwavering: find him wherever he is.

Go to him.

I'm coming, I promise.

Dear angel, I'm coming to see you...

CHAPTER 26
Like a dog

I WAS TOSSING and turning in the bed of the hotel where I found a vacancy near Boston, after having left Fenway Park.

The discussion I'd had with Alvin Brown felt like it was unfinished, a can of worms in my brain.

The junior lawyer, formerly one of Greenville Clique's members, had thrown a rock in a pond that was as big as all the mysteries that surrounded the troubled past of the Lake family. A rock thrown into Lake Moosehead, whose waves made bigger and bigger concentric circles, just like the secrets surrounding the past of the Lake family.

I couldn't get the Sugar Island Cemetery story out of my mind.

Open eyes, staring at the ceiling, the conversation we had in the stadium parking lot was running in a loop in my head.

"The Sugar Island Cemetery?" I repeated after Alvin, my hand on my Ford Ranchero in the stadium parking lot. "There are tombstones there?"

"Not really," he said. "In reality, like I said, that was a fantasy of kids who liked to play being scared. Something kids whisper to each other, in summer sitting around a campfire, toasting marshmallows. See what I mean? Like stories of poorly closed tombstones or will-o'-the-wisps dancing around the graves at night."

"Yes, I do," I nodded, thinking back about when I was a kid over twenty-five years ago. "I'm all ears."

"For the Brandon Lake mystery, that kid that no one seems to remember nor even be able to affirm if he's dead or alive, the kid whose room is always locked, and as you noticed, the kid who's not buried in the Greenville cemetery, of course, people have a lot of questions. If he is dead, his body must be buried someplace?"

"At the bottom of the like, like his sister years later?" I asked.

"That's not what the legend says. Rumors have it that Brandon Lake died when he was at Sugar Island. No one knows why, everything is only guesswork, but people invent things, adding details each time, always more sensational, sordid, creepy. Up to when they insinuate that Janet and Mason's son was buried clandestinely some place on the Island."

"Which would explain why he isn't in any official

records. That's awful Alvin. Does this rumor have any proof?"

The lawyer shook his head, the word *proof* echoing in his professional mind.

"None. Like I said, stories dumb kids invented. But we didn't let that stop us. To try to find out the truth in the Brandon Lake affair."

"So, what did you do?"

"Something I'd been thinking about for months, each time we had a party at Sugar. Each time we saw that damn door that was locked. And then, that night of August 26th to 27th, after Tommy had fucked up by going into the room and throwing the teddy bear into the pool, screaming out '*Fly, Winnie*!' Paul and I decided to do something about it."

"What did you do?"

"Like I said, we'd had a lot to drink, we had no idea what we were doing. So Paulo and I decided to go find Brandon Lake's legendary tombstone that night on Sugar. We lit the lamps on our phones and set off into the woods behind the villa..."

Summer of 2017, *Sugar Island*.

They looked at their phones and it was after midnight. Saturday was finished, and it was now

Sunday August 27, a tragic day no one would ever forget.

Paul Tannent and Alvin Brown, both wearing their swimsuits and sandals timidly progressed in the dark forest surrounding the villa. A can of beer in one hand for courage, in just a couple of seconds they'd decided to investigate themselves, after Tommy Malone's unfortunate act. Tommy had gone to see Veronika who was furious, to apologize.

"Fuck!" swore Paul when a bramble scratched his leg, "who had this stupid idea?"

"You did," replied Alvin. "Only an idiot like you would have dumb ideas like this. Where do you think we're going to find his grave? This cursed island is just as big as all of Greenville. Like looking for a needle in a haystack."

"Gimme a break, Alvin, you believe in it too. It's too big not to be true. We'll find it."

"We don't even know where to look. It could be anywhere. Plus he was buried years ago, as Veronika told us she never knew him. Think of that. Almost twenty years, who knows. Come on, we're busting our balls for nothing. Let's turn back. It wasn't a good idea."

Paul stopped in his tracks.

"No, we're not gonna turn around, think!"

"Coz you're able to think drunk like you are? How many beers did you have?"

"A few, it's hot when you're manning the barbecue. Listen. If you want to bury your kid – fuck, just saying that is crazy – are you going to dig a hole in the middle of nowhere in the forest? Like a dog? That's the mythological version, the one that scares you. Or are you gonna give him a burial place like he deserves in the garden around the villa?"

Alvin thought it over.

"Depends on your goal. Whether you're trying to hide his death or pay tribute to him. I don't know, like imagine that one of his parents whacked him... Stuff like that happens, you've heard of those mothers who freeze their babies."

"Holy shit, you gotta be crazy to do something like that."

"Maybe the Lakes are... Especially Mason, the father, he always freaked me out."

"Why?"

"I dunno. His predator eyes, something like that. The way he stares at you. But anyway. Let's say they're not guilty of anything at all and that they just wanted to bury their son in their garden on the island, okay? So let's go back there and look around."

The two friends turned around to go back to the villa and started to look at the yard surrounding the house, using their phones whose batteries were falling drastically. Between the fringe of the forest and the lawn, they rummaged around for several long minutes, just like truffle hounds looking for the black or white pearls.

Then they took a rocky path leading to a creek

where the lake waters were gently chopping against the rocks, and both froze.

What they'd imagined was right there in front of them.

Up till now, it had been a mere fantasy. Something they believed, like they believed in the Tooth Fairy, or Santa.

Their macabre intuitions were confirmed.

They materialized themselves in a lopsided wooden cross.

Alvin Brown and Paul Tannent kneeled at the tomb.

CHAPTER 27
A big problem

ALVIN and I hopped into my Ranchero so we could continue this conversation sheltered from the freezing Boston weather. At this stage in the lawyer's story, I was startled, hands on the steering wheel of my car.

"It's not a legend then? There really is a grave in Sugar Island? A private and secret burial place for Brandon Lake? And you discovered it?"

Alvin scratched his head and made a face, troubled by what he was telling her.

"Yeah. There was a cross on the far end of the property, on the eastern side of the island facing the lake, with Lily Bay across from it. An old wooden cross all worm-eaten and full of moss because of the humidity."

"What did you do?"

"We looked at that burial plot. Well I said burial plot, but there's no guarantee because there wasn't a tombstone, or anything in marble or something like that. Plus the earth was flat there. No difference around the cross that would allow us to think that someone had dug here."

"If it goes back over twenty years, that's not illogical," I said. Nature had time to fight back. And was there anything engraved in the wood?"

"There was. But unfortunately, with time, the inscription was nearly illegible."

"Nearly? Meaning you could read a part of it?"

"We could make out some letters: an R, an O, and an N, in that order. For the rest, two dates that looked like 19-7 and then -000."

"1997 - 2000? Three years... Alvin, I can't believe I'm asking you a question like this in the parking lot of a baseball stadium in the middle of the night, but did you dig up the grave to be sure?"

The black man took his head between his hands and rocked towards the dashboard several times, as if he were hesitating to confess.

"Jesus! No, Karen, we didn't. Maybe we were drunk, but we wouldn't raid a grave. We couldn't do something like that. It was fun playing explorers, ghost hunters, but when all was said and done, we couldn't go any farther. If that was the place where Veronika's older brother was resting in peace, we couldn't desecrate his grave. However it had been dug. Plus, we didn't have a shovel or anything and we certainly weren't going to use our nails."

I understood their psychological reluctance of course but regretted they hadn't gone farther. This being said, I wondered what I would have done in their place.

"You went back to the villa after that? Did you tell the others? Or the authorities?"

The young man shook his head.

"That was our secret, Paul and me. The party was already a crazy one and we didn't want to add something like this. After all, it wasn't our business, was it? It was an old tale dating back to the beginning of the century, a private affair concerning the Lake family."

That made me lose my temper.

"A private affair? None of your business? And the tag on the Who poster? *Who killed Brandon?* You didn't think that was enough to trigger research, a procedure, an official investigation? You're a lawyer Alvin, and you must have thought there was something fishy going on there."

"We were just teens! We didn't want any problems. We forgot about it."

"Well I don't agree. I want to know, to understand. Alvin, do you remember where this cross was located?"

"Not really. It was dark, we walked all over, turned back. All I remember is that it overlooked one of the creeks leading to the lake, like I told you earlier. Why?"

"Because I want to go!" I declared emphatically. "And if I find it, I'll dig. And what if I asked you to come with me?"

"Karen, I'd say no," the young man replied, apologizing with his arms in the air. "First of all, I don't have the time. I've got a lot of work to do. Then because I don't want to go back to Sugar Island again. Never."

He looked at his watch.

"Karen, I really have to go now, sorry I couldn't help you more."

"No problem, Alvin, you already helped me a lot, you can be sure of that. Just by accepting to meet me. Thank you so much for your time and confidence."

He opened the door, ready to get out.

"I'll be available though, if you have any questions or doubts. You can call me."

"Thank you very much," I said as he closed the door.

I started up the car and left the now deserted Fenway Park parking lot.

My eyes looking up at the ceiling in my hotel, I couldn't sleep. Veronika's disappearance, the death of Brandon, the grave in Sugar Island, the forbidden room, the tagged poster of the Who: all these elements of the Lake puzzle were dancing in front of my eyes and tired me yet prevented me from sleeping.

CHAPTER 28
The common thread

NOISE FROM CARS, a jackhammer on a construction site that wasn't far from the hotel and the loud voice of the man in the adjacent room woke me much too early after I'd finally fallen asleep.

Motels in the suburbs of Boston certainly don't have – and far from it – the charm of the Greenville Inn, that I was already missing. I didn't have anything to do in Massachusetts anymore, so I decided to skip breakfast and go back to Maine. I wanted to return once again to Sugar Island, to investigate the property, using the information that Alvin Brown had given me.

Before starting off, I logged onto Facebook Messenger and sent off a short message to Paul Tannent to accompany my invitation, as Alvin had asked me to do. Step after step, testimonial after testimonial, I was hoping to find the truth – *and truths* – about the Lake family. But the more I advanced, the more clues I had that were sending me in a thousand different directions. I had to find the common thread.

My Ranchero was driving along the Atlantic roadway. Piled on the passenger seat was my lunch: potato chips, two salmon club sandwiches, and a bottle of mineral water. My thoughts were confused between all these threads holding them together. Threads that were entangled, without me being able to do anything about it, to other previously solved... or unsolved mysteries. Cans of worms like these were not unfamiliar to me and were the reason that I'd chosen to work in this field. As if untangling all these little threads would allow me to understand the breadcrumb trail of my own past, my own intimate wounds, this absence that haunted my life and my nights.

I mentally zoned out and my car began to cross the line. A sports car that was trying to pass me honked his horn loudly.

Three hours later I arrived in Greenville where fall seemed to be even more beautiful than when I'd left, though it was a mere twenty-four hours ago. I undoubtedly had not paid enough attention to the golds and yellows. Had I been a tourist, I would have stopped here for a couple of days in this little town, apparently so calm, next to the calm and clear waters of

Lake Moosehead. But I wasn't a tourist, and I knew that this postcard image was just an illusion. That behind this beautiful showcase there were terrible smothered secrets.

While going down Main Street, I saw lights from a car behind me, coming closer quickly. Flashing lights, easy to recognize.

Shoot, must be the local cops I presumed.

The vehicle overtook me. I had a look at it. *Town of Greenville Police*. The guy behind the wheel signaled me with his hand to pull over.

Which I immediately did, sure I hadn't broken any laws. I wasn't speeding with my old Ford, nor had I gone through a red light or failed to stop at a stop sign.

What the heck could this cop want with me?

I stopped my car and watched the cop in front of me get out of his patrol car, a white pickup, which was huge. The man in his dark blue uniform slowly got up from his seat, transporting his imposing stature above a gut that was beginning to strain his jacket. Younger, he must have been athletic, but now, at the age of forty-five or so, he seemed to have let himself go. Buzz cut formerly blond hair and a small beard; he was impressive.

I rolled down my window.

"Hello Officer," I said, in a relaxed tone. "Was I driving too fast?"

"Hello Ma'am. We'll see. Are you Karen Blackstone? The journalist?"

That was surprising.

"That I am. Why? Who wants to know?"

"Listen lady. I'm the one asking the questions here. I'm Chief Patterson, head of the Greenville police force. And I know quite well who you are and why you're sneaking around town."

"I'm not sneaking around, I'm staying here," I replied, defending myself.

The head of the local police force smiled ironically.

"Mrs. Blackstone, it doesn't matter how you describe your presence and acts. It's my duty to warn you that Greenville is a peaceful town, one without any problems, you understand? And as I guarantee the safety and peace of mind of its inhabitants, I must be vigilant."

"But Officer, how can my mere presence impact the peace of mind of the inhabitants of this town? I'm just doing my job. I meet people, talk to them, ask a few questions, nothing reprehensible. Unless the laws in Piscataquis County aren't the same as those in our large, free country."

"Don't try to get smart with me. People told me you were bothering them."

My eyes popped wide open.

"Me? Bothering people? Seriously..."

"Mrs. Blackstone, I can't prevent you from doing your job as a journalist, though I don't appreciate people in that line of work. On the other hand, I'll be there should there be any issues with law and order here. Understand?"

I nodded in agreement but without forgetting my

resources and my goals. Unfazed, I surprised the officer with a question he couldn't have been expecting.

"Chief Patterson, as I've now had the pleasure of meeting you, I've got a couple of questions to ask you about this affair which brought me to your beautiful little town. And I'm not asking the inhabitant, but the professional in law and order. As a citizen I'd like to exercise my right to information. Could I have an appointment? At the police station if possible?"

The Chief sighed loudly and shook his head.

"You don't back down, do you? I'm giving you a warning about your excessive curiosity and here you are trying to get information out of me. A true journalist, no filters, and shameless. Okay. Tomorrow morning at the police station, half an hour. Ten o'clock sharp. We'll clear the air once and for all and that'll be it. Okay with you?"

Considering how my relationship with Chief Patterson began, I feel like provoking him a bit.

"Perfect. Thank you. Can I go now? You're not arresting me?" I joked.

"Move along," he muttered in conclusion. "And don't make any waves."

"Yes, Sir," I said, starting the car up.

I nodded to him briefly and drove away as he saluted me with his index finger and middle finger against his forehead, fingers he then made a V with, pointing them at his eyes to tell me he'd be watching me. Strange guy, a modest head of a tiny police force who thought he was a sheriff in the Far West.

I drove away.

With the firm intention of going back to Sugar to look for Brandon Lake's grave.

CHAPTER 29
Ready to demolish

ONCE AGAIN, I drove to the Greenville Marina, hoping to find someone to take me to Sugar Island. And hoping to see my bearded fisherman. Luckily, Herman was docked to the wharf, cleaning up his boat after a day on the lake.

"Well, well," he said recognizing me. "Still here? How's things going? You look a little less white today."

"Hello, Herman. I'm fine thanks, and you?"

"Ahh! Like an old-timer. Each new day is one less day for me. How's your research going?"

"Not too bad," I replied vaguely. "I was actually wondering if…"

"If I could take you there again?" he said, cutting me of and pointing his chin toward the island.

"You're reading me like a book Herman. I'm so foreseeable, don't you think?"

"Foreseeable, I don't know. Curious and stubborn, that's for sure," he added, with a greasy and nicotine-filled laugh that unveiled a his yellowed and tobacco-stained teeth.

"Same price as last time, obviously."

The old, bearded man seemed to think things over for a couple of seconds.

"Can't say that it doesn't bother me to take your money, but I must admit that *it does put butter on my bread*... I'll do it. When do you want to go?"

"Now."

My answer took him by surprise.

"What? Did you check your watch? The sun will be setting in less than two hours, my little lady."

I told him that I did realize that but that didn't prevent me from persisting. To tell you the truth, I wanted to have the same atmosphere as the teens in the Clique in August 2017: spending a night on Sugar Island.

That's what I told Herman who raised an eyebrow.

"You're curious and stubborn but also nuts! With all due respect. You want me to take you now and pick you up tomorrow? Is that it?"

"Exactly. Just give me a half an hour to buy something to nibble on and get my sleeping bag, it's in my trunk, and we can set off, if it's alright with you."

Herman signaled me with his fingers, rubbing his thumb against his index. With a smile, I took out the sum we'd agreed on.

I came back to the marina after having ransacked the cookie aisle as well as other non-perishable goods for wannabe campers like me in the drugstore on Main Street.

Herman started up his boat just when the sun had begun to hide behind the hills on the western side of the lake.

From the stern of the boat I turned and looked back at Greenville, thinking that perhaps I'd seen a white pickup belonging to a certain policeman, who was standing and looking right at us.

We took the same route we'd taken the previous time, and I recognized Lily Bay before we reached the Sugar Island pontoon. I waved at Herman who said, "good luck tonight," before heading off as quickly as possible and disappearing behind the island.

Once again, I was alone on Sugar.

The sun was already setting little by little on the highest branches of the pine trees surrounding the Lake family's villa.

What had gotten into me? *A little too late to ask yourself questions like that, Miss Karen Blackstone*, I thought without however stopping my walk to Veronika's family's cabin. Had I really had that idiotic idea to sleep in one of the bedrooms of the abandoned cabin?

You did, murmured my subconscious, that little devil who sometimes whispered in my ear.

I went in through the summer kitchen, like I had the first time. This time the cabin was more familiar to me, but depending on what I was expecting to find, it already had an ominous aura that made me get goosebumps. Where would I sleep that night? Anyplace, except for the taboo room of the deceased child, of course. But that wasn't my priority.

Before night fell completely, I wanted to go to the place that Alvin Brown had described to me where the wooden cross was, and thus Brandon Lake's final resting place.

I dropped my stuff on the rug in the living room, between the two leather armchairs, and went back outside with only my phone to light the way. I saw a shed next to the patio by the kitchen. I went there hoping to find what I was looking for. I was right: it was a shed containing garden tools and I took a shovel that could be useful, though it was rusty.

There was no noise on the island outside of the sound of branches blowing slowly in the wind coming off the lake. But a heavy mist was coming in on Sugar. I followed the eastern coast of the island, looking for the creeks and hoping to find the one Alvin Brown had described. The only problem was that they all looked alike. I was walking slowly and awkwardly through the brush and bushes because I hadn't found any paths at all. At the same time though I shouldn't have been expecting a concrete boulevard on this uninhabited island. Sometimes I was so dumb. Night was falling, and I was losing hope, internally scolding myself for this stupid act and my illusions. What if Alvin had simply made this up and there wasn't a single cross here? But why would he have lied to me? Who knows. I continued my search, convinced that he had told me the truth.

On a little rocky crag, with a grassy mound, I finally saw what looked like a wooden cross.

I rushed over, stumbling against the roots and nearly fell flat on my face. When I reached the two pieces of wood nailed together at a right angle, I kneeled.

It really was a cross on a grave site, just like Brown had described, but now undoubtedly more worm-eaten and covered with moss. The inscriptions on it were now illegible.

Was little Brandon beneath my feet here?

I was torn between the desire to know and the fear of what would be required of me to find out.

Did I have the right to desecrate a burial place on private land?

Or anyplace incidentally.

I wanted to pick up that shovel I'd taken and dropped on the ground, next to the cross.

Driven by an instinct and determination that I didn't know I had, I stood up, grabbed the tool with both hands and raised it above my head.

Ready to demolish that tomb.

CHAPTER 30
More goosebumps

AND THEN LOWERED it with wrath to the ground.

The tip of the shovel went a couple of inches into the hard earth in the pine forest.

Then I froze. Like a wave had suddenly swept through me and I only felt guilt.

Nearly a rape.

I became aware that I was on the point of desecrating a tomb. On private property.

The shame linked to my gesture and the fear of police retaliation and legal consequences blocked my determination to find the truth.

But what truth ?

The one about Veronika Lake's disappearance or the one about the death of her brother, Brandon? Were both independent of each other?

I couldn't wait to answer those questions, but I didn't have the right to violate laws or his burial place.

I thought back to when I'd left Greenville, and when I saw Chief Patterson's pickup truck on the wharf of the marina, looking out at me on the boat. Just a few hours ago he had sufficiently warned me about my unhealthy curiosity of an investigative journalist, and I didn't want him to be right, nor give him a good reason to throw me out of town.

The best thing to do would be to bring up the subject of a burial place with him during our appointment together. This subject and a few others too.

My hands dropped from the shovel, which began to tilt and fell over, next to the cross.

I didn't realize it, but it was now dark outside, and it was getting cold. I took the flashlight out of my pocket and went back to the villa.

I was sheltered from the wind, but not from the cold, as the cabin wasn't heated, so I curled up in one of the armchairs in the living room and took out a blanket that I'd found in one of the bedrooms. I looked at the fireplace but was too tired to light it. *Hey, Karen, it'll be a night like when you camped out when you were little*, I said, trying to motivate myself.

I luckily had found the electric box and was able to turn the lights on.

I wasn't really cut off from the world, as I found that I could phone from the island, with 3G. I took a quick dinner break munching on what I'd purchased before leaving and found a Facebook notification.

Paul Tannent has accepted your invitation.

A few minutes later Paul sent me a direct message via Messenger.

Hi Karen. Alvin said you were going to contact me. So you're looking to find the truth about Veronika's disappearance too?

I was thrilled that Tannent wasn't beating around the bush. I preferred that to useless circumlocutions.

Thanks for accepting my invitation, Paul. I'm an investigative journalist specializing in cold cases, and I'm interested in the strange fate that the young lady you knew had. I hope you'll be able to tell me something, especially what could have happened during the night of August 26 to 27, 2017.

I'll try to use my memory. What exactly do you want to know?

Would it bother you if we talked by phone? That would be easier.

No problem, I'm all ears.

I gave him my phone number.

"Karen? This is Paul Tannent."

"Thanks for calling, Paul. I've got quite a few questions. Can we start?"

"Sure."

"To start, I want to tell you that I already talked to Tom Malone and Alvin Brown, Victor Martineau, the mayor of Greenville, and very briefly with Chief Patterson."

"You're in Greenville?" he asked, cutting me of.

"Almost. To be honest with you, right now I'm in the villa on Sugar Island."

"Holy shit!" Paul said, astonished. "You sure are a hands-on journalist! Nice house, isn't it?"

"Architecturally, yes. But the atmosphere is pretty cold when you think back on what went on here. By the way, did you know about the forbidden room? What do you think about the existence – and death – of Brandon Lake?"

"You want the truth, Karen? Even five years after, I still get goosebumps, just thinking of it. Alvin told you about our expedition to find that poor kid's tomb?"

I thought back on how I felt a bit early, between the pine forest and the lake.

"Of course. Paul, do you really think that Brandon could be buried there, in Sugar Island?"

I heard him sigh.

"Karen, I'd believe anything about the Lake family. They were so... so strange. I even wonder how I could have been close to them at that time."

"You were part of the Clique."

"That's true, that was our nickname back in the day. Our group of friends."

"And how did you get into the Clique, Paul?"

"Oh! No big deal, no entrance rites or stuff like that. It was just affinities between us, children from families who were well off or influent in Greenville. We all went to the same schools, were invited to the same parties, or even gala dinners or charity events in town. My parents had a thriving company of yacht and boat sales and maintenance, Alvin's dad was the county deputy, Cynthia's dad was a real estate promotor, Becky's dad, remember she went out with Alvin at that time, was the Greenville mayor..."

"What? Becky's the daughter of Victor Martineau, who's mayor?"

"The irremovable Martineau, you mean! Like he's the only person I ever knew as mayor of Greenville," Paul Tannent joked.

I had just picked up a new piece of information. Martineau was closer to the Lakes than he'd told me. Maybe nothing would come of that, but still, this wasn't something to be forgotten. I mentally drew up a list of Clique members.

"I also heard of another couple, Carlos and Dorothy. Who were they?"

"Carlos is the son of a famous author, who wrote several best sellers back in the day. They sold like hotcakes all over the country and she decided to spend her millions here in Maine, on a cabin overlooking the lakes. As for Dorothy, well you know, she was a Patterson."

I jumped.

"Patterson, like the chief of the local police force?"

"That's right, she's his daughter."

I was beginning to think that the circle was getting tighter around a handful of people. The younger generation and their influential parents. They hung out together.

Did they also influence each other?

CHAPTER 31
Chips in the armor

THE WIND WAS HOWLING SHARPLY above the Lake family's villa, and I was having problems making out what Tannent was saying.

"Paul, tell me what you think about Veronika's disappearance. What do you think happened to her? Your personal theory?"

There was a long silence, and I was afraid we had been cut off. But Paul was simply thinking things over.

"You know, Karen, I think we all said, thought, envisaged everything possible about this subject. The craziest theories and the most improbable fantasies. The only certitude we have is that Saturday Veronika was with us and on Sunday morning, none of us were able to affirm where she was. Those are the facts. Black or white. Yes or no. Present or absent. Living or... dead. Outside of the facts though, there's what we all felt. I'm not a psychologist – for that you'd have to ask Carlos Iglesias who was majoring in psychology at the university, I don't know if he graduated – but that doesn't stop me from thinking."

"So, what do you think?"

"I've always thought that one day or another, Veronika could harm herself," he finally said.

This sentence sparked a type of list of all the different ways she could do this.

Kidnapping.

Running away.

A murder.

An accident.

Suicide...

Up till now I'd never thought of the last one.

"Like she wanted to kill herself?"

"Possibly. Anyway she wanted to end the type of life she was living at that time."

"Why? Didn't she have everything a young lady of her age could dream of? Beauty, wealth, love, a bright future..."

"Appearances Karen, appearances. We're all the same you know; we only show people what we want them to see. All the rest is buried deep inside us. Sometimes there are deep crevasses and chips in the armor where our secrets slip out. Sometimes Veronika's shell shattered. She let people see her faults, her fears, her apprehensions."

"What was she afraid of? Or who?"

"Of herself, I imagine."

"That's strange. Can you be afraid of yourself?"

Paul thought that over and reformulated his sentence.

"Maybe not real fear, rather disgust with herself."

"How can you affirm that? Did she admit it or insinuate it? Did she tell you her secrets? Did she tell anyone her secrets? Guys or girls?"

"No, she didn't tell me anything. Cynthia was her listening ear. Those two were really close. Besties. No, I'm just thinking of something that happened that night in Sugar Island. I think it was after dinner when we were grilling marshmallows at the campfire. Yeah, that's it, we decided to play a game. An idiotic game that kids our age loved to play, well not really kids anymore, almost young adults."

I was intrigued by Tannent. He was dragging on his syllables as if he'd never end his sentence.

"What game?"

"You must know it. You must have played it too with your friends. That night, at the poolside in the Lake villa, we played *Truth or Dare*."

CHAPTER 32
In flames from Hell

SUMMER OF 2017, *Sugar Island.*

A SORT of torpidity was weighing down the group of young party makers. Suddenly someone spoke up.

"Hey guys, how about a little game of Truth or Dare?"

This proposal came from Carlos, who was always ready to light a party back up when its fires seemed to be going out.

Some grumbled, but most of the group welcomed that decision.

The eight guests quickly sat down in a circle around a coffee table next to the pool, full of empty beer cans and glasses of cocktails.

"Let's go over the rules," suggested Carlos, the self-proclaimed leader. "We'll flip a coin. Heads, it'll be

'Truth' and tails, it'll be 'Dare'. Everyone okay with that?"

They all unanimously nodded.

"And to decide who will be responding to the questions and who'll be asking them, we'll spin this empty beer bottle on the table clockwise. Wherever the bottleneck stops, that'll be the players. Go!"

Carlos grabbed the bottle which started to spin on the table in slower and slower circles, stopping in front of Becky with its imaginary finger.

"Becky, you're first. Let's see who you're going to challenge."

Once again, the bottle turned, stopping in front of Paul this time.

"Now the coin."

He flipped it and it landed on its heads side: Truth.

The young lady put her index in front of her lips, pretending to think deeply, while glancing maliciously at Paul. She cleared her throat.

"Paul, tell us the truth. Out of everyone here tonight, who would you like to go out with?"

The young man blushed, but no one saw this as it was getting dark.

"Too easy," said Alvin mockingly. "Everyone knows the answer to that question."

"Maybe I'll surprise you," Paul replied. "What if I said it was you, Becky?"

"Don't cheat Paulo, you gotta tell the truth and the whole truth. If not, you'll burn forever in the flames of Hell," said Becky. "Spit it out."

"Shit, gimme a break guys."

"That's the game, kiddo."

"Come on, who?"

Paul Tannent looked down at his nervous fingers.

"Okay, if I really had to choose, it'd be Cynthia. Happy now?"

He was awarded by whistles, "wows!" of encouragement and hearty laughs.

"So what if we continued with the next action then," Dorothy proposed. "Paul, you gotta go kiss your heart's desire…"

"No, no," Carlos jumped in. "That's against the rules. The bottle is the decider, and you only get one Truth or one Dare each turn. Next up then."

The bottle and coin pointed to a truth Alvin asked.

"Dorothy. Could you tell us a Truth you don't want to tell anyone or a Dare that you wouldn't do for anything in the world?"

The devious question was admired by all.

"Wow, what a sneaky question, Alvin. Let me tell you I'm glad I'm not in your head. It must be a fucking mess in there. But, okay, let me think it over. Got it. There's one thing I couldn't do is to strip butt naked in front of you all."

"That's too bad! But glad we know."

"Shut up, Alvin," said Carlos, Dorothy's boyfriend, who was hoping to have the monopoly of her many charms. "Next."

"Well, you're sure in a hurry."

"She answered your question, didn't she? That's the rule. So next."

"Come on, this is just a game," said Alvin, before spinning the bottle. A Dare for Alvin from Carlos.

"Oh. This is going to be fun. Alvin, you have to... use your tongue to kiss someone on their bellybutton... I'm being nice and giving you the choice. I don't hold a grudge."

"So I can lick your girl's bellybutton then?"

"You can. But you'll end up with my fist in your face as a prize."

"Your little fists? You make me laugh."

"Hey, you two roosters in the farm," interrupted Veronika. "This isn't a boxing ring."

Alvin turned to Becky, his *steady*.

"Honey, may I?"

"That's disgusting!" she protested but did uncover her stomach.

"Hey there!" Carlos said. "What the hell? Choosing your own girlfriend, that's not fair!"

Alvin wasn't listening to this remark and was busy with his tongue all around Becky's navel.

"That tickles!" the young lady complained, moving away.

Everyone burst out laughing and had a drink of their beer or cocktail before going back to the game.

Then Tom Malone asked Dorothy for a Truth.

"Dorothy, tell us about your most powerful orgasm."

Carlos couldn't wait to hear his girlfriend's answer, but she surprised them all.

"A what? An or...ga...sm? Never had one!"

His eyes popped wide open, taken aback by Dorothy's amusing answer. Of course everyone else was laughing.

"Good answer, Do," said Tom, congratulating her. "We're gonna hear less from Carlos now."

Carlos raised his middle finger towards Malone, who raised his beer like a true diplomat.

But Tom was the next on the list. Carlos gave him a Dare that he could not refuse.

"Tommy, watch out for the boomerang. As you can't keep your big mouth shut, let's see if you have enough balls for this. You have to dive in from the high diving board."

"Easy peasy," laughed Tommy, walking to the pool.

"But there's one more condition. You have to dive in... naked!"

"You don't give up, do you?" Malone complained. "You just want to see what a real man's sex looks like, right? Because we all understood that yours didn't satisfy Dorothy."

"Yeah, sure, you can say whatever you want but take your suit off."

"Take it off! Take it off! Take it off!" they all said, except Veronika, who was looking elsewhere.

Tom nodded his head, as if weighing the pros and cons, his thumbs in the belt of his swimming trunks. Then, to prove he was in, he took it off and butt naked, slowly walked up the ladder leading to the diving board. He walked slowly to the end of it, his male attributes easy to see, raised his arms and awkwardly dove into the pool, just missing a belly flop that his body would have regretted.

Admirative whistles followed his dive: he had the guts to meet the challenge.

When Tom came out and put his trunks back on, it was Veronika's turn to say the Truth that Paul Tannent asked her.

"Vero, what part of your body are you the proudest of?"

The young lady seemed to be daydreaming, no longer interested in the game.

"What?"

"I asked you what you preferred. On your body. The part of your body you like the best."

The group at the poolside was silent. An owl hooted grimly. Veronika finally answered.

"Nothing."

That was it. One word summed up the lack of consideration she had for herself.

"Sweetheart, stop," Tom said. "You're the most magnificent girl here."

"Oh!" Dorothy cut him off. "You're exaggerating."

"Tommy's right you know," said Cynthia. "You are the most beautiful of all of us. Stop belittling yourself."

"No," replied Veronika. "I'm disgusted by everything in me, inside and out. And you know it too well, Cynthia. You understand me, I'm sure."

Veronika's voice had been rising, she was now screaming.

"Fuck off all of you with this idiotic game! You all just fuck off, no one understands me."

She was sobbing, tears now streaming down her cheeks. Sad pearls that were sparkling in the full moon at Sugar Island.

Veronika got up and ran into the cabin, hiding her shame and anger.

CHAPTER 33
An ordinary person

I LISTENED ATTENTIVELY to Paul Tennent on the phone. He was telling me what had happened in this exact place, where I was right now, on Sugar Island. Though the events had taken place five years ago, I could almost hear the teens shouting behind me, around the pool.

"A game that didn't go well then."

"That's often the case," Paul agreed. "Daring to tell the truth, doing things you don't want to, that's complicated. Things that usually don't end well. That's what happened that night with Veronika. I knew she had to be having some problems, and the game finished her off. All it did was to strengthen her unhappiness that had been growing for months. And she let us all know it that night."

"For months... What made you say that, Paul?"

The gamer didn't answer right away.

"I'm sorry, I'm probably not the best person to talk

about Veronika. You'd be better off talking to Tom Malone or Cynthia Favor, her best friend. I'm sure she knew everything, they didn't have any secrets, you'd learn more from her. All I can say is that I remember Veronika as being someone who wasn't very stable."

"Meaning?"

"What can I say? Someone who quickly went from euphoria to stress, almost depression, even if that's a strong word. She could invite you one day and then cancel the invitation the next day without any reason. She would also disappear for days on end, without telling anyone."

"Disappear?" I said, caught in the middle of that word again. "Like she ran away?"

"I don't know if she ran away, but she often missed high school for a couple of days and then she'd come back. I have no idea what she told them to justify her absences. But once again, talk to Tom or Cynthia, they'll probably know more."

I looked at my phone and as it was getting late, I was ready to thank Paul Tennent when I had another idea.

"Oh. I almost forgot. I'm sorry to ask you this question Paul, but I have to understand. I learned that on that Saturday night, someone surprised Veronika in a delicate position, not alone, in one of the bedrooms of the villa. See what I mean?"

"Yeah… I see. Please continue."

"Well, the person who was with her wasn't, contrary to the person she should have been with, Tom

Malone, and your name came up. It's delicate Paul, but that night were you in bed with Veronika Lake?"

"What the hell? I hope you don't believe a single word of that lie. Okay, I was single at that time, and I must admit that Veronika was a good-looking gal. But she was going steady with a friend. I never would have done something like that. Plus I was attracted to Cynthia, who also didn't have a boyfriend at that time. My goal was clear! I even played Truth or Dare... I'm white as snow. Cross my heart!"

"Paul, I believe you. But I had to ask the question. Who do you think it was then? Any idea?"

"Nope. Sorry."

"Do you think there was anyone else that weekend in Sugar? Who might have snuck in, maybe invited by Veronika herself?"

"Frankly? No, I don't. There's just no way we couldn't have seen them."

I hung up after having asked him if he had any idea where Cynthia was, with new questions in my brain again.

WHY ALL THESE REPEATED DISAPPEARANCES? Were they like rehearsals before her final disappearance in August 2017?

And her unhappiness and euphoria-depression cycles made me think of someone who perhaps had a bipolar disorder? How come? And what did that mean?

Plus the disgust she had with herself, the way she depreciated herself.

I had to contact Cynthia Favor and noted that on top of my to do list. Plus talk to Tom about this.

I yawned and rubbed my eyes. I suddenly couldn't stay awake. A mental and physical fatigue. I had been thinking about the Lake family's enigmas for days now, without seeming to make any headway.

I unrolled my sleeping bag and went in, still with the feeling that I was violating the Lake's private property. But I needed a total immersion. I luckily slept like a baby.

EARLY IN THE MORNING, before meeting Herman at the pontoon, then going to the appointment Chief Patterson had given me, I decided to keep some proof of my stay on Sugar Island. I took my phone out and took pictures of what I thought were the most important elements.

The infant's room.

The tagged Who poster.

The burial place with the cross.

Could all those elements suffice to reopen the cold case?

At least that was what I was hoping would happen, and who knows - maybe solve a few underlying riddles.

I couldn't wait to talk to Patterson at Greenville police station.

The Chief didn't really welcome me with open arms. It was clear we hadn't gotten off to a good start. I still had my goals in mind, even if that meant upsetting the peace and order he aimed for in Greenville.

"So, Mrs. Blackstone, you're a boater then?" he said as I walked in.

Okay! So it was him then, on the dock of the marina when I was leaving with old Herman.

"Isn't boating one of the favorite activities of tourists in Greenville?"

"Don't try to be cute with me. Where were you heading? Sugar Island? And what were you doing there?"

After all I thought, if that was where he wanted to go, I was all for it.

"We can't hide anything from you Chief. You're a cop with formidable insight. Yes, I did go to that island, and I've actually got a couple of questions to ask if you have the answers. As a policeman, I'd imagine that you've got loads of information that I as an ordinary person, don't have access to."

Patterson sat back in his chair and cleared his throat.

"So, to start with, Mrs. Blackstone, please note that your status as a journalist - and do you actually have a press card - does not authorize you more than anyone, to penetrate into private property with the owner's agreement. And Sugar Island, as you know, belongs to the Lake family. Did they say you could go there and spend the night?"

I shook my head with a mischievous little kid's frown.

"Secondly, though I do have access to confidential information, nothing says I have to share it with you. So please don't abuse my indulgence and remain in a police-press framework. Till now, I've tolerated your presence here in town, but if you do anything that disturbs law and order here I'll expulse you. Understand?"

"Very clear, Chief. So, as a journalist I'd like to know the conclusions of your investigation when Veronika Lake disappeared, five years ago."

The policeman spread his hands apart showing this was evident.

"Like you said, the conclusion was a disappearance."

"Yes, but that's only the finality of the event, and doesn't explain it. Or even tell us what happened. What did you do to understand and explain her disappearance?"

"Mrs. Blackstone, are you insinuating that our services were incompetent or insufficient? That we screwed up? You don't seem to have a good opinion of the police. Of course, we did our utmost with all our resources to try to find Veronika, dead or alive. Our teams, firefighters, and numerous volunteers searched the entire island, we flew over the lake and coastline in helicopters, we searched the forest with our K9[*], Clever, dredged many parts of Lake Moosehead and all the ponds on Sugar Island. We put police roadblocks all over in the county rapidly as soon as we'd been notified of her disappearance. We put up missing person signs. So, we tried everything, albeit unsuccessfully. Plus we questioned all the teens at that party in August of 2017, as well as their friends and families. We talked to everyone who knew Veronika: her family, friends, classmates, neighbors, professors, and I'm sure I'm forgetting some. But we just ran up against walls of incomprehension. And we never localized the trace of the young lady or her body. So if you're smarter than the police, okay, tell me what you discovered and maybe we'll make progress together. But please, don't give me any lessons on what we didn't do right or didn't do enough of."

Patterson's speech nearly made me like him. Yet some of the details bothered me and made me believe that the investigation could have been more thorough. In my mind, the Veronika Lake mystery was inseparable from the death of her brother, Brandon, and the policeman didn't mention this. I opened my phone and showed the Chief the Who poster, the photo I'd taken a bit earlier.

"As you searched all over in Sugar Island, as well as inside the cabin, I'm sure you couldn't have missed this worrying detail, Mr. Patterson?"

---

[*] K9 = Canine, police dogs.

I showed him the tagged *Who killed Brandon?* poster.

I hit bullseye. I saw Patterson's eyes open wide and he began to frown. A sign of surprise or a feeling of being caught red-handed in a lie or an omission?

His response surprised me though.

"I know this poster, that was thumbtacked in the baby's room in the villa. However, I can assure you than in August of 2017, during our investigation, there was nothing at all written on it..."

CHAPTER 34
Shedding light

PATTERSON and I looked at each other without a word for a few long seconds, both thinking. He was thinking because he'd discovered something new, and I was thinking because the poster seemed to have been tagged *after* Veronika Lake's disappearance, giving me even more questions to answer. When did someone write this? Who? And why?

"Mr. Patterson, are you sure?"

"That I am. We took photos of course on the premises. It would be easy to find the ones of the bedroom and I'm sure that they'd substantiate what I just told you. The poster was on the wall, but there was no writing on it."

He stopped speaking.

"Mrs. Blackstone, maybe you had fun writing this on the poster to make some incriminating evidence to match your ridiculous hypotheses?"

I didn't believe my ears.

"You must be joking. What would I do that? Your image of journalism is poor..."

"Just like your image of our police force. Let's say we're at a tie then. Okay. You do realize that I could cause a few problems for you for the picture that you took inside the Lake family's private villa?"

"I do. But that's not going to prevent me from seeking the truth about this affair and the Brandon Lake affair too."

"What Brandon Lake affair? There's no Brandon Lake affair. It's in your mind, that's all."

"Because the death of a little kid and the absence of a tomb or an official civil registry act doesn't bother you, Chief Patterson?"

He put his head back and rolled his eyes.

"Jesus Christ! That dates back over twenty years. A kid died young, no one filed a complaint, no one contacted us. There wasn't any *affair*!"

"That may have been true before I discovered the tagged poster. But with this new element, you can't dismiss the idea that two people disappeared, the brother and then the Lake sister, and that these affairs are somehow linked to each other. Plus, there's another element in this collection of mysteries. This one."

I once again took out my phone.

"What is that shovel doing on the photo, Mrs. Blackstone?" asked Patterson roughly.

Shoot, I'd forgotten to move it before I took the picture.

"You must have seen this burial place when you searched Sugar Island," I said, reversing the roles.

"Don't tell me you defiled a gravesite... If you did, you're going to have problems, I can guarantee you that."

"No, I didn't. However, because of what we now know, I'd like your services to have a closer look at this burial place. I'm sure that Brandon Lake's remains are below it."

I tapped on the screen with my nail, showing him the grass-covered mound with the worm-eaten cross on top of it. Then I drove the nail in.

"A witness told me that back in the day, you could read the letters *R, O,* and *N,* as well as the dates *1997-2000*. You can't doubt this."

"Jesus," Patterson said, hitting his desk with the palm of his hand. "In 2000, I wasn't even here in Greenville, and I ignored all that."

"Would it be possible to order the search of this tomb, Mr. Patterson? Would that be enough to reopen the investigation?"

"What investigation? Brandon or Veronika? The first one never existed and dates back over twenty years and the other one has been closed."

"Both of them. I'm sure they're linked and inseparable. I don't yet know how nor why, but my intuition is rarely wrong."

"The investigation could eventually be reopened by the State of Maine or on a federal level," Patterson sighed.

"Could you have the tomb dug up?"

"We could."

"What are you waiting for? By the way, I've also got a couple of questions about the absence of the Lake parents since their daughter went missing. Someone told me they now live in Florida. I'd imagine that you could confirm that, as, if my sources are correct, you and the Lakes were pretty close friends. And your daughters too."

I chuckled internally at the way Patterson looked at me. He hadn't been expecting that one.

"We did see each other, from time to time."

"Not too long ago, I think. Plus, Dorothy, your daughter, was on Sugar Island that night of August 26 to 27, 2017 when her friend Veronika, went missing... Knowing that, I just can't understand why you didn't do more to shed light on this affair. Unless..."

"Unless what?" the policeman grumbled, approaching his face to mine over the desk. "Why would I not try to solve this affair just because my daughter was a part of the protagonists that night? You're transgressing the bounds, Mrs. Blackstone, be careful."

"I wasn't insinuating anything. I was just surprised. Being as close as you were, in your shoes I would have pulled out all the stops to find the truth. Who questioned your daughter? Not you, I'd imagine."

"No, it was Lieutenant Shana Davidoff, my assistant. I always stick to procedures."

"Great, I didn't want to accuse you of professional misconduct."

"Okay. Time's flying and that's all the time I have for you today, sorry."

I nodded, comprehensive. I felt like I had accomplished something. But there was one detail that I wanted to bring up before leaving.

"One last question, please. I was able to meet the person who purchased the Lake's house in West Cove, Mr. Kissinger. And he told me that when he was having some work done in one of the rooms, he stumbled upon a bizarre USB flash drive. You know what I'm talking about?"

"A USB flash drive?" mumbled Patterson, astonished.

"That's what he told me. He added that he handed it over to the police here as it was his duty to show it to you, seeing its content… well, let's just say… sensitive. You still don't remember? Once again, it's something concerning the Lake family."

Robert Patterson thought it over before answering evasively.

"Let me see… Ah! Could be possible. It's coming back to me."

"What was on the flash drive? I'm sure you opened it. Could I access it?"

"We inspected it, but nothing proved it had belonged to the Lakes. Now it's been archived, and the general public can't access it."

"Not even a journalist?"

"Correct," said Chief Patterson with a smirk. "Now, if it's alright with you..." he concluded, getting up, signaling that our meeting was over.

He walked me to the door and before I left, I asked him to give me his daughter's contact details so I could talk to her. Much to my surprise, he gave me her phone number.

When I was leaving, I saw Lieutenant Davidoff, a good-looking brunette whose uniform looked nice on her.

"Be careful," she whispered to me with a discreet movement of her chin towards Patterson.

...my fault...

I spent so many years running after your ghost, my angel.

How many? Fifteen, twenty, even more? I can't remember.

Finding you is like the stations of the Cross. Jesus himself, in his immense sacrifice, couldn't have found it more difficult than me.

Each day that goes by since your disappearance represents one more station, one painful stage that tests me.

But I'll make it, I won't waver, though I may lose my life if I look too hard.

My youthfulness died with you. It also disappeared. Ever since that cursed day the pain I've had of not being able to, not wanting to, not having chosen to keep you, has been eating away at me.

What did they do with you?
What did you do to deserve that?

You didn't ask anyone for anything.
Me neither, incidentally...
So are we equal?
Unless I'm entirely to blame for this human drama...
Yes, I am. It's all my fault, now that's the way I feel.
I hate myself; I can't stand myself anymore.

And I must atone for this mistake, punish myself for having abandoned you, you, a tiny being without any way of defending yourself.

CHAPTER 35
Against the tide

I PUT my cup of coffee and notebook down. The Dockside Tavern and its homely decor impregnated me with its torpidity this afternoon. The workers and employees had finished their meals, and the grannies hadn't yet come in for their cups of tea.

I was suddenly mentally exhausted. I'd been running around for several days now, without thinking of anything except the Lake affairs – yes, now I say it in the plural. I'd love to have a few minutes just for myself. But work was more important. I remembered that my boss had left me a message when I was with Chief Patterson.

"Oh. My little Moosehead prawn," said Mrs. Fairbanks when she picked up. "Not too much news lately. You swimming against the tide? Can't touch bottom? Drowning in mysteries?"

"Hello, Myrtille. When you've finished with your

freshwater sailing metaphors, maybe we can talk seriously?"

"Karen, you don't have a sense of humor. Okay, let's talk shop. I'm listening, Miss Blackstone," she said in a falsely pinched tone, "could you please update me on your latest progress in immersion?"

"In immersion… You're continuing."

"Come on, jump into the deep end! Go with the flow!"

"You should write an almanac; it would be a bestseller. Why not a section in *TCM* while you're at it? So, listen up. I just got out of a meeting with the Greenville Chief of Police. I think he's hiding something. His daughter was one of the kids on Sugar that night. Plus, I've sort of got the impression that he's dissimulating important information about the 2017 investigation, but also something on some incriminating evidence - a USB flash drive that had photos… porno ones actually - that belonged to the Lakes. That stinks of complicity. Plus I discovered a non-official burial place that could be where Veronika's older brother is. I'm trying to get the grave dug up and trigger a new investigation."

"I'm pleased to see that you're not just a windmill. Rather in crawl mode," she said laughing. "No trace of Veronika then?"

"Nope. But I'm beginning to understand her and the circumstances surrounding her disappearance. But I still can't affirm anything about the cause of her disappearance: assassination, accident, running away, a suicide? Everything's possible. Is it linked to her brother's death? I can't affirm anything there either. I'm working on it. But now that Chief Patterson's got his eye on me, I can't do everything I want."

"Karen, whatever works for you. You know, all I want are facts and results. Speaking of which, I'd like you to write a preliminary article on the subject for me. Email it to me by tomorrow evening."

"What do you want me to say? I'm drowning in incomprehension."

"See? You like metaphors too. Do we need certitudes to fascinate our readers and make them bubble over? Sensational and enigmatic, that's what they want. Hun, I trust you. You know what to do, you've proved it to me many times. It's up to you, Bye!"

Click. As usual.

"More coffee, Karen?" asked Charlene, my favorite bubblegum waitress.

"Thanks, I'll need it," I signed, opening my laptop to start writing on Myrtille's article. *The earlier it's written, the earlier I can leave*, I thought.

I opened a file up and as I usually do, let myself be guided by my inspiration.

Start with an eye-catching title, then I'd add some subtitles in the article. That was always useful for people who never read the whole thing. A few keywords, photos that made people uncomfortable, and that was it.

A began typing a couple of minutes later. It would be:

The Moosehead Lake Ghosts.

CHAPTER 36
Thirst for Truth

THE MOOSEHEAD LAKE GHOSTS.

Greenville, Maine, October 2022.

For over five years now, a deep shadow has darkened the peaceful village of Greenville, a town of just over a thousand souls, nestled in the middle of Lake Moosehead. A shadow that was born over the waters, in nearby Sugar Island, a now deserted bit of land that the inhabitants of this town only call the "Cursed Island."

Until the summer of 2017, Greenville had enjoyed its legendary calm. A fishing and yachting town, a vacation place for retired people and families who enjoy swimming and water sports, this little town in Piscataquis County radiated happiness.

An atmosphere that is now flawed by doubts, fear, questions, and suspicious looks.

EVERYTHING WAS OVERTURNED on the night of August 26 to 27, 2017, during a party that took place on Sugar Island, the island that belonged to the infamous Lake family, a prosperous and influential family from Greenville. Veronika, their youngest daughter, aged seventeen, had invited some of her close friends for the weekend, those who were a part of her "Clique."

But during the heat of this weekend, the Clique was shattered.

In this implosion, there was a victim. Veronika Lake disappeared that very night and has never been seen since…

WHY? How? No one has yet solved this mystery.

BUT THE STORY doesn't end here, or should I say, it doesn't begin here.

THE ROOTS of this tragedy are anchored even deeper in the past of the Lake family… And in the black waters of Lake Moosehead.

If you dare hire a boat to set foot on Sugar Island

and you think you'll be finding a haven of peace, heaven on earth, an idyllic villa with a pool, tennis court, pine forests, in a nutshell, beauty and luxury, you're wrong: hell is what you'll find on Sugar Island.

If you dare go into the villa and have enough guts to go upstairs, to open the door of the "forbidden room," a child's bedroom with a little crib where a teddy bear is peacefully sleeping, you'll discover a poster thumbtacked on the wall, — something that doesn't belong in an infant's room — from an album of the Who, the famous British group. When you look closer, you'll see that this poster was defiled with these ominous words: *Who killed Brandon?*

And then, if you're brave enough to explore the untamed island, you'll walk down to the rocky creeks, and you might find yourself face to face with a burial place... a tomb that was dug directly into the ground, topped with a worm-eaten wooden cross, battered by the weather and years gone by.

Yet should you dare to look at this cross that has fallen on the ground, and your eyesight is good, you might make out a couple of letters and two dates.

The dates? 1997-2000.

The letters ? *R/O/N*. No, it's not Ron, because there are letters in between. This must be *Brandon*.

Who was Brandon? The Lake family's first child!

The innocent little angel who wasn't even three when his life ended.

. . .

Why? How? No one has yet solved this mystery.

Readers, please stop a moment to think about the horrible fate of the Lake family.

A little angel, who died and who was buried secretly on a private and deserted island, in the middle of a huge lake, surrounded by dark pine forests.

Their daughter, who disappeared seventeen years later in undetermined circumstances, on this same cursed island where the mortal remains of her brother are located.

Will my readers link these two tragedies together?

Is the Lake family cursed?

Can money not protect you from the worst horrors?

Immersed in the theater of this double tragedy, your favorite journalist Karen Blackstone is constantly working to solve this double mystery and ascertain the Truth, the only one that, as my readers know, is found on the pages of your dear *True Crime Mysteries*...

PS: Please contact our editors if you would like to help us in this search for the truth.

. . .

I saved my document and after having proofread it and corrected a few things, I mailed it off to Myrtille. At least she wouldn't be able to accuse me of doing nothing!

I noticed that the diner had filled up while I was busy writing my article. Charlene was slowly taking care of her customers, jaded as always.

A few tables from mine I glanced at an elderly man who immediately looked away when he noticed I was looking at him. I didn't feel any hostility, just a type of curiosity. Like hadn't he ever seen a lady working on a laptop? Was something like this so unusual in a place where mostly blue-collar workers had lunch or people from the neighboring shops, or retired people shooting the breeze were the main clients? The man, who must have been a good sixty, was wearing a checkered shirt with a scarf around his neck. Not bad looking either for an old fart with buzz cut white hair showing off a square face.

I nodded briefly at him, trying to be polite, and he responded before paying and saying goodbye to Charlene. You could tell he was a regular customer.

I got up to leave too.

"Who was that old guy with the white hair who just left?" I asked Charlene.

"It's Mr. Fenton. Barry Fenton, the former Greenville Chief of Police. A regular customer, polite, a nice guy. Everyone appreciated him when he was heading the police force. Not like Patterson who plays cops and robbers in B series movies," she added, still chewing her gum.

"Has he been retired for a long time?"

"Um, I don't really know. I'd say a good ten years."

I thanked Charlene, paid my bill, and left the Dockside.

I was anxious to get back to my room in the Greenville Inn, take a hot shower because I couldn't yesterday when I was in the Lake family villa in Sugar. Plus I'd forgotten to bring along my daily treatment and was worried about the side effects of not having taken it. The doctor had warned me to always keep a couple of pills on me. I swallowed my three pills, and decided to go to bed, without having dinner tonight.

I wasn't hungry... just thirsty for truth.

CHAPTER 37
No rest for the wicked

IT WAS GETTING COLDER and colder in Greenville. The water in the lake, now cool, reflected fall colors, with a metallic blue or nearly gray hue. The last campgrounds had closed up for the season and the tourists and boaters had gone back home. Now it would be hunters coming here.

The town had a different atmosphere, an unsettling calm in the streets. Perhaps a storm was coming?

The storm in my mind was in full blast. The more progress I made, the more I felt like I hadn't moved. The simple fact that I'd resumed my on-going investigation for the magazine showed me how the Lake affair – *or affairs* — were inextricable. But I'd find something, like each time I begin to search for the truth. Up till now I'd never failed… except once… The worst and most cruel failure!

. . .

I OPENED Myrtille's response to my email.

You're a killer, sweetie. In less time than it takes for Mr. Rabbit to please Mrs. Rabbit, you wrote me a great article. Chilling on glossy paper. A concentration of suspense, mystery, and emotion. Our readers are going to love it. So, Miss Blackstone, there's no rest for the wicked, I want results (concrete ones, or you can invent some) by next week. Bye!

I was happy to read these words that boosted my confidence. This confidence that was so hard to keep up, so fragile, like I am myself inside, contrary to the image of a warrior that I show to others.

AFTER HAVING WOLFED down a copious breakfast at the Greenville Inn, as I was starving, I walked downtown where the public library was located. I hoped to be able to consult the archives of local papers, in particular those from 1997 to 2017, a double decade and an important one for the Lake family. Sometimes just reading an ordinary article can lead you to a clue that seems to be initially insignificant, but when you put it in with what you've learned, it can tell you much more than you'd bet on. I've always preferred local to national news. News from the horse's mouth.

Shaw Public Library was on Lily Bay Road. The small one-storied building at first looked more like a Baptist church than a library. It was charming though and I went in. A middle-aged lady, probably a volunteer, welcomed me, smiling over her glasses that kept slipping down over her nose while she was reading a fashion magazine.

I asked her if she had archives of the local papers, either as a paper or a digital version.

"Paper, no, sorry, it's much too small here. But you can consult the digitalized papers here on this computer," she said, pointing to the back of the room. "But I don't think you're a library member. I've never seen you and I know just about everyone."

"I'm not," I admitted. "I'm a journalist and I thought that with my press card I could consult the papers here. But if you want me to get a library card, no problem, Ma'am. I'd be happy to contribute to the finances of this beautiful place. How much is it for a year?"

"Only ten dollars. We even have a three-week formula for our tourists who love to read."

"I'll take a year's card," I said with a smile, taking my wallet out.

"Thanks, I'll give you a receipt."

When she finished, she walked with me to the computer and explained how to carry out research on it. I thanked her and immediately started looking up the local papers: *Moosehead Messenger, Piscataquis Observer,* and *Newsbreak*. Some were no longer published, but were at the time I was interested in.

I started with the year 2000, when Veronika was born, and perhaps, when little Brandon Lake, if what was on the cross was correct, died. I put in a few key words in the search engine. *Lake, Veronika, Brandon,*

Mason, Janet, Sugar Island, Greenville... but had no joy. I tried other suggestions, hoping for some hits. The words *crime, death, accident, deceased*, brought up tons of articles. I read through some of them quickly but there was no reference to the Lake family. There were several articles about the virtues of the local police force when Chief Fenton, that elegant, retired person I ran across at the Dockside, was there.

But nothing that interested me. Nothing serious happening in this calm little town. Of course, as in many towns on lakes where people could go swimming, there was an accident every once in a while, a young tourist who drowned when her parents weren't watching her for a second, despite how quickly the rescuers came. But in 2000, only an unfortunately little five-year-old had tragically died in Greenville.

I was getting ready to go to another year after having gone through the three local papers when an article caught my eye.

An ordinary one.

But my senses were instantly alerted:

Young child dies from attack by family dog

CHAPTER 38
Rage

WHAT MADE me read that whole article that was nothing but a tragedy of daily life? My journalistic instinct?

Flavie Cunningham, who had written it, related the facts poignantly.

GREENVILLE IS MOURNING after the death of one of its children. The names of the protagonists have been modified, as the family wishes to remain anonymous. We nonetheless can affirm that this event has affected a very well-known family in our little town. Concurring sources have informed us that the event took place when the father, Martin, was on a business trip to New York. His wife, Jacqueline, pregnant with their second child, was at home and the family dog, we'll call it Goldie, suddenly went completely crazy. The beautiful Golden Retriever – one of the most popular dogs for families –

suddenly turned into a ferocious animal and without any apparent reason, attacked little Brian, a peaceful two-year old boy. He was bitten savagely in the carotid and passed away just a few minutes later. The rescue squad was not able to save him.

The animal, now considered to be a potential murderer – don't you say that a dog who has bitten will bite again – was supposedly put to sleep.

A tragedy like this is not that rare in the United States, where over 4.7 million people are bitten by dogs per year – that's nearly 500 every single hour – amongst them of course our brave mailmen, who are on the front line. Luckily only about forty of these bites are fatal. But the most frightening thing is that these tragedies often take place right in the middle of peaceful American households. And those that attack the most are not necessarily breeds said to be "attackers," such as Bulldogs, Pitbulls, Rottweilers, Malinois, or American Staffordshire's, amongst other - but much more frequently simple pets, those no one would ever be afraid of. Such as the Golden Retriever, the incarnation of a dog who lives inside with its owners, an affectionate one, a teddy bear with soft hair that children like to run their hands through, that they love to play with, roll around with, and if they're small enough, even ride.

Children are the main victims of these affectionate - seemingly so,- dogs.

As anger, craziness, biting, rage, those things can happen all too quickly.

An ear that is pulled too strongly, a tail unfortu-

nately trod upon, a hand in a mouth to retrieve a rubber ball, getting a bit too close to a dinner bowl... and it becomes dramatic, just like what happened to this family from Greenville, to whom, on behalf of the editors of Moosehead Messager, *we address our deepest sympathy.*

The Devil Wears Prada said Lauren Weisberger in his novel. I thought that a demon could also hide in original and unusual costumes. A clown, a doll, a dog.

I don't even know why this accident that took place in 2000 made me think about the Lake family. The date of course, which matched Brandon's supposed death. *A very well-known family in our little town,* the journalist wrote. Why not the Lakes? The disguised first names of Martin, Jacqueline and Brian chosen by the journalist had the same first letters as their names: Mason, Janet, and Brandon. A lady who was pregnant with a child who would be seventeen in 2017, just like Veronika Lake when she disappeared.

Too many clues, too many coincidences. Any journalist worth their salt knows that information is nearly certain only when it has come from three different sources. Here was one source and now it was up to me to find the others.

I scrolled down the other pages of the local papers but didn't find anything. I decided to fast forward to 2017, the second key date concerning the Lake family.

I'd logically find at least ten different articles that would validate what I'd already learned from the various witnesses I questioned since I'd arrived in Greenville. The editors spoke of the excellent work done by the investigators, both the local police force and the sheriff from Piscataquis County. They also praised the inhabitants who were ceaselessly continuing to look. The conclusions though remained the same: Veronika Lake had never been found and had never reappeared in Greenville or on Sugar Island. Or anywhere else. Not a trace. Weeks went by and the papers found other things to write about.

The Earth kept orbiting around the Sun, the waters of Lake Moosehead splashed new tourists and supplied the fisherman with good catches, the boaters and yachtsmen made waves when they took their boats out. Life went on in Greenville.

The Lake family sold their house in West Cove and moved to Florida, though they kept Sugar Island. That raised a question in my mind. Why hadn't they also sold their island, like they sold their house to the Kissinger's? That place that must have represented so many painful souvenirs for them. Getting out of Maine forever and spending the rest of their - happy - lives in sunny Florida. Why keep a home base in this most northern part of the United States? Especially as they could have sold it for a pretty penny to real estate developers who would have transformed Sugar Island into a luxury getaway for tourists.

But I told myself that this mystery wasn't really one, taking into consideration all the other enigmas that punctuated the Lake family's affairs.

. . .

I thanked the library volunteer, and she handed me my provisional library card. Outside it was raining icy drops that froze my backbone. I hiked up my collar, lowered my head and rushed off to the Dockside to have a couple of cups of hot chocolate.

There, sheltered from the wind and rain, an improbable surprise was awaiting me.

Sometimes when you're looking for a needle in a haystack, someone brings you a magnet. And it sure makes that needle easier to find!

CHAPTER 39
The end justifies the means

I HAD JUST STARTED to warm up with my second cup of hot chocolate when I felt a presence behind me, someone looking over my shoulder, as if they were trying to read on my laptop.

Even before I had time to turn around, I heard a deep voice behind me.

"So, you're interested in Veronika Lake?"

I spun around and discovered the affable face of the former head of police.

"What makes you say that?"

"Charlene told me about your projects. No one's really interested in this anymore today. It's been consigned to Greenville's oblivion, at least that's what some people here hope, I imagine. Can I sit down?"

I gestured with my hand for the white-bearded man to sit down across from me.

"Charlene, could you bring me some coffee, please?" he asked politely.

He held out his hand.

"Barry Fenton, the former Greenville Chief of Police. Retired and loving it since 2010 and an amateur fisherman. You're Karen Blackstone, right? A journalist and investigator for *True Crime Mysteries*?"

"What else do you know about me?"

"That this is your unofficial head office, but you're staying at the Greenville Inn, that you have an old but magnificent Ford Ranchero dating back to 1967, if my knowledge in cars is still reliable."

"I hope you don't know the color of my underwear... You must have been a very efficient policeman, Mr. Fenton."

"Please call me Barry."

"Only if you call me Karen."

"We gotta deal, Karen. And please be reassured, I'm totally indifferent about your lingerie. Too old to be interested in futilities like that. But you might consider readjusting your belt because I can see pink lace behind..."

I squirmed on my chair, distraught with the idea that people could see half of my butt. Barry burst out laughing.

"I was messing with you!"

I looked at him.

"Thank you."

"For what?"

"For making me laugh. That did me a world of good. With all the work I do on criminal affairs, it ends up sapping your morale."

"You're preaching to the choir! I often led investigations concerning crimes and misdemeanors. But luckily that wasn't the majority of our work, here in peaceful little Greenville. But for you, that must be your bread and butter, day in and day out. What's driving you, Karen?"

A question I don't like. One only a cop would ask.

"I hate unsolved crimes. I detest the idea that victims can be forgotten and that perpetrators can live out their lives without being caught for their crimes. I try to find the truth, all the truth, that's what drives me, Barry. You too, I'd imagine?"

"When I was a cop, yes. Now the only thing driving me is where the fish are biting."

Charlene brought him some coffee and went back to the bar, still noisily chewing on her gum. Barry Fenton continued.

"What if you told me everything you found out about Veronika Lake's disappearance? After that, I'm sure I can complete your info."

"Why are you doing this? I mean, why are you helping me? You don't have to."

"I know I don't have to and that's why I'm doing it. I like to choose. Plus I'm happy to see that someone is finally interested in reopening this cold case. Because if you're counting on Patterson, you'll be waiting forever."

Hmm, I thought. Not what I was hoping to hear.

"Barry, you don't seem to appreciate your successor. Why?"

"I'll get there. But for now tell me what you know."

Barry listened to me tell him about what I'd done since I came to Greenville a couple of days ago. For nearly fifteen minutes, he followed the events, with squinted eyes and concentration. I could imagine him listening to people in the same way when he was working. I didn't try to hide anything from him, straightaway having decided to trust him and sure that he'd have something to say that would complete, invalidate, or clarify my suspicions. He whistled admiratively when I finished.

"Not bad. You did a good job there. Though you were sometimes sailing close to the wind for lawfulness. But *the end justifies the means*, as the saying goes. But there are still a lot of threads to untangle, true? And everyone isn't going to help you. On the contrary, I think that some people would really be happy to see you leave Greenville before shedding light on what could have taken place here, from 2000 to 2017."

"Who are you thinking of?"

"The same ones as you, Karen. The same ones as you."

"Victor Martineau and Bob Patterson... The mayor and Chief of Police... They didn't exactly welcome me with open arms. All I'm doing is trying to find the truth, so that Veronika won't be forgotten."

Barry Fenton smiled, with perfectly white teeth.

"I don't think that the truth that you might discover would favor those two..."

CHAPTER 40
Eavesdroppers

RAIN WAS SLOWLY DRIPPING off the windows of the Dockside Tavern, like sad grayish pearl tears.

"Are you insinuating that the Chief of Police and Mayor of Greenville are trying to hide the truth? You think they're involved somehow? Guilty of something in Veronika's disappearance?"

Barry Fenton made a face, seemed to be eating the words he'd pronounced, weighing them.

"Directly guilty, no, I don't think so. Guilty of dissimulation of proof, why not? Guilty of negligence in the investigation, probably so."

My eyes popped wide open, astonished at what the former cop was saying.

"Serious stuff there. You're talking about the two most influential and official persons in Greenville."

"That I am."

"Do you have any proof of that?"

"Proof? Nothing material but very strong personal suspicions. Those two guys are as thick as thieves, you have to remember that. Just like their offspring, Rebecca and Dorothy, their respective daughters, who were always going out with the Lakes. And Mason and Janet were also very close to Patterson and Martineau. They all hung out together and supported each other."

I could visualize the painting, a pool of movers and shakers who felt they were above the laws, all protecting each other. Covering each other in more or less illegal affairs too?

"Barry, what's your opinion of the Lake family? You knew them well; you were head of the police force when Brandon died back in 2000. You must have opened an investigation?"

"I see what you're referring to and you have good intuitions. You discovered a child that had died because the family dog had attacked him, and you concluded that it was the Lake family. I don't want to disappoint you Karen, but I didn't open an investigation on the death of Mason and Janet's oldest son."

"How come?"

"Firstly because there wasn't the shadow of a doubt that his death was linked to the attack by the dog and secondly because it didn't take place here in Greenville, or even in Piscataquis County."

"Where did it happen then?"

"At their place in Florida, I think."

I was mentally putting the different pieces of the Lake puzzle together.

"So that would explain why there's no death certificate here then? And why there isn't a tombstone in the Greenville Cemetery. Barry, have you ever heard of the burial place on Sugar Island?"

He stared at me.

"What burial place?"

I quickly ran him through my discoveries, including the poster of the Who with *Who killed Brandon?* written on it as well as the legend of the child's grave, in a creek on Sugar.

"So I guess that legend isn't one," I finished, showing him the pictures I'd taken earlier.

Barry Fenton shook his head, incredulous.

"What the hell? I don't believe it," he muttered. "That's the first time I ever saw this."

He shook his head, then nodded, silently. I asked myself the same question out loud.

"So the answer to *Who killed Brandon?* is just his dog? Don't you think that's a bit incredible? Why would someone insinuate that someone else had killed Brandon when the cause of his death had been proved?"

"I agree," Barry said. "Something's not right here. Something I wouldn't mind finding out."

"It'll be easier with us two working together: two brains, two skill sets. You think we could have this burial place in Sugar reopened and analyzed?"

"Impossible twenty-two years after, without any new tangible elements," Barry replied regretfully.

"Wouldn't the simple fact that Brandon doesn't

have a grave elsewhere, plus the fact that there's no death certificate, be a new tangible element?"

"Karen, listen. The fact that you didn't *find* this type of document doesn't mean that *it doesn't exist*. It's the same legal principle as people presumed to be innocent if they haven't been judged to be guilty. Let's see what we can find in Florida."

"You want to go to Florida?"

"Why not? Before, I can try to get in touch with some of my old colleagues from Miami. Some are still working and would be able to access data such as the Lake's last known domicile."

"By the way, Barry, are you still close to them?"

"We were never very close, contrary to Patterson. We saw each other at official events, that's all. We never shared a turkey on Thanksgiving! My kids weren't a part of their Clique. Plus I was always quite distant from the inhabitants of Greenville when I was a cop. It's better not to mix your job - law and order here in town - and personal or affective links."

"Good motto there."

"I always tried to do my best. If not, you know how it goes, it's hard not to slip..."

'Like?"

The Dockside was starting to fill up. Barry turned his head to the surrounding tables that were starting to fill and smiled strangely.

"Let's talk outside." It had stopped raining. "Some things are not for the ears of eavesdroppers..."

CHAPTER 41
A little yapper

WALKING along the southern coast of Lake Moosehead without any swimmers or fishermen, Barry and I were completely alone. The former head of the Greenville police force was thus completely at ease in speaking to me.

"So, I think I told you, I was head of the police in 2000 when the Lake's lost their first child and Janet had Veronika. At that time Mason and Janet Lake were still people you could associate with, if I can put it like that. Things went downhill later. The tragedy must have hit them harder than they showed. When you lose a child like that, it's understandable. After that, I was reelected twice: in 2004 and in 2008. And I wasn't a candidate at my succession for the 2012 mandate. I'd done enough, seen enough. It was time for me to turn the page. I'd worked long enough to have a good pension and wanted to spend more time with my family. But it wasn't just my age that decided me. There was something else."

"What?" I asked Barry who suddenly seemed to be lost in his thoughts, as if he was reliving something.

"The atmosphere in the Greenville police station had changed. As if clans were forming. A couple of years ago, Robert Patterson had been hired as a patrolman, but he was quickly promoted as the deputy to replace a colleague who had been transferred to Arkansas. That meant that Patterson was number two in the police, just behind me. But we never got on well together. To be frank, as soon as he arrived, I didn't like the guy."

"Why?"

"To make a long story short, he was a little yapper with big teeth, I was even afraid that he'd scratch the floors in our offices. He was a guy who'd worked all over, in many different states, who was often transferred. I think he'd worked in Nevada, California, Florida, Idaho, and Texas. He claimed he was well-traveled, but personally someone who is transferred from town to town, there's something fishy about that. And here in Greenville, when he was a mere patrolman, he quickly did things that exceeded his pay grade."

"Things he shouldn't have done you mean?"

"No, not to the population, or if he did, I never knew about it. I mean he acted as if he was a deputy or the chief of police. He discussed direct orders, tried to get out of some missions or be assigned to others that I was in charge of. He made a mess of things plus causing a rotten atmosphere here in the department, despite the fact I reprimanded him several times as did the mayor, who we all report to."

"Martineau."

"*Himself*. So I'm sure you understand he didn't give a damn and even openly supported him, praised him in official speeches."

"He was the teacher's pet then?"

"Yeah. Like I said, they were as thick as thieves. So in 2012, when I resigned, the door was wide open for him. Before leaving, I'd submitted the candidacy of Lieutenant Shana Davidoff, a very competent gal, one who deserved to wear the Sheriff's star. You understand how local chiefs of police are appointed?"

"I think it varies from state to state, or even from town to town, but I get the basics. The decision is taken by the town council?"

"That's right, and the mayor has the last say in this. Get it?"

"Victor Martineau appointed Bob Patterson as the Chief of Police instead of Lieutenant Davidoff, the lady you'd suggested."

Barry sighed deeply.

"That's just one of his shortcomings. Nepotism. Aggravated favoritism, you can call it what you want."

"That's not good, but I'd imagine that things like that happen all over."

"It's inevitable. But that Greenville, my town, where I've always lived, is controlled by a son of a bitch like Patterson, that makes me sick to my stomach. I even doubt his probity in carrying out then investigation on Veronika's disappearance."

I was chomping at the bit. Barry Fenton had stuff to reveal, it was evident, but it looked like he wanted to make me wait for it. I jumped in.

"Barry, what are you insinuating? That the investigation was botched, even sabotaged, by Patterson and that Martineau covered it up? But you told me they were both good friends of the Lakes. I would imagine that they would have tried twice as hard to find the truth and find Veronika, their friends' daughter."

"Unless they had a vested interest in Veronika not being found."

"Good Lord!" I said, horrified. "What interest can there be in not finding someone who's gone missing?"

"Someone missing - especially if they never are found - can no longer speak nor testify."

"Testify what?"

"Testify on something they could have seen or been a part of and that Patterson and - or - Martineau, had been a part of."

CHAPTER 42
Partners-in-crime

BARRY FENTON'S last words puzzled me. Was Veronika Lake an embarrassing witness in an affair that the mayor of Greenville and the local Chief of Police didn't want solved? Never would I have thought of this as a cause of her disappearance.

"Barry, are you trying to tell me that Patterson and Martineau were the cause of Veronika Lake's disappearance?"

"No, not really, just that they had the means and resources to sabotage the investigation. That doesn't make them guilty, though you could say they were partners-in-crime in this affair. Guilty of failure to assist a person in danger."

"Maybe of misappropriation of proof? Or subordination of witnesses? Or concealing the truth? Or sabotaging the investigation... The spectrum is wide. Do you think that the daughters of the mayor and chief, Becky Martineau and Dorothy Patterson, could know something about that? Or even worse, that they could also be accomplices or guilty of the disappearance of their friend?"

When I formulated this question, I realized I still hadn't spoken to either of these girls about the weekend in August of 2017, and everything else that Barry Fenton had just told me.

It was starting to get dark and the streetlights in Greenville were lighting up, street after street, while we were walking towards the center of the town. The darker it got, the colder it was.

I realized that I hadn't questioned Barry about one thing and wanted to know his opinion of it. I quickly told him about how I'd been to see Liam Kissinger, the new owner of the West Cove Point residence as well as about the USB flash drive that he'd found in the Lake family's house when he was doing some work there. Considering the unflattering portrait of Chief Patterson that Barry Fenton had just described, it seemed even stranger that he was so evasive, or even elusive when I talked to him about it.

"You said that he handed the flash drive over to Patterson in 2017?" Barry asked.

"That's right, after they'd moved to Florida."

"And you think there's some kind of link with Veronika's disappearance a couple of months earlier?"

"I don't think anything, this is a question. What if Patterson had tried once again to dissimilate some incriminating evidence linked to the preceding investigation? From what you've told me that wouldn't be impossible."

Running his hand through his straight hair, as if he were scratching his gray matter, Barry Fenton seemed to be thinking.

"Patterson is capable of anything. From bad... to the worst! That makes me think of an anecdote dating back to right before I left the squad. And it was about a stupid affair. But Patterson's methods here show what he's capable of when he's protecting his friends."

∽

Greenville, winter of 2010

The wind was gusting in Piscataquis County this January 2010. Winter in Greenville was going to be freezing. The Arctic wind licked the lake with its frozen tongue and the salt spray blew up against the windows of the local police station. In Chief Barry Fenton's office, the atmosphere was just as cold inside as out. Fenton had called his deputies, patrolmen and Lieutenant Shana Davidoff in for a meeting. At this time the department had eight members, without forgetting Malika, a female German Shepard K9 member who was both beautiful and efficient.

"What the hell are you doing you guys? What's the population going to think of us?" asked Barry Fenton angrily.

Some of the cops lowered their eyes while others looked annoyed. Only deputy Bob Patterson dared to look his boss in the eyes, ironically.

"Let me tell you," Chief Fenton continued, "we look like a bunch of hicks, Keystone Cops, police wannabes who don't even know how to carry out an investigation."

The dog, hearing Barry Fenton speak loudly like this, sat down at his feet, below his desk, his ears low, his muzzle touching the ground, whimpering.

"Sorry Barry," Lieutenant Davidoff said. "I understand, but you shouldn't be yelling at me as personally I didn't play a part in this story. I did my job, up until..."

The young lieutenant punctuated her unfinished sentence with a movement of her chin, towards Patterson.

"Someone experienced had to head the investigation," said Patterson.

"I didn't need a chaperon, Bob, and I told you so loud and clear. You might be a deputy and me a lieutenant, but that doesn't give you the right to short circuit my investigation. It was given to me and it's none of your business."

"Shana's right, Bob," Chief Fenton said. "When everyone does their own job, the squad is more efficient. At one moment or another did I ever give you the impression I was authorizing you to stick your nose into the Jansen affair? Who do you think you are? You wanna be the boss, right?"

Patterson didn't answer the question, contenting himself with a smile that presaged his short or mid-term intensions. But he did speak up.

"It seemed to me that my skills and relations could be used to progress."

"Because I'm incompetent, is that what you're saying?" shouted Shana Davidoff. "That what you're insinuating? Hell Barry! You're letting this asshole insinuate that I'm no good? Or that a female cop isn't capable of heading an investigation alone? Coming from someone like you," she said, pointing at Patterson, "nothing surprises me anymore."

Patterson raised his hands above his head, trying to act falsely innocent.

"What I was saying," he defended himself, "was that I was just giving her a helping hand. Trying to get the ball rolling in the right direction."

"You really think that was the right direction?" asked Barry Fenton. "The general public is making fun of us. And as I'm the chief here, making fun of me."

"Not for a long time," said Patterson softly.

"What do you mean by that Bob? You trying to get my job? Can't wait, can you?"

"I didn't say that Barry, relax. All I'm saying is that soon you'll be retired. And you'll need someone to take your place. That's all."

"We all understood Bob, don't worry. But for now, I'm the boss and you do what I tell you to. So, for the Jensen investigation, Shana is the one in charge, got it?"

"Whatever," Patterson grumbled. "But don't complain then later that you haven't solved it."

"Of course," said Shana. "And if our dear Sir wants to undermine the investigation because he and Jensen are good friends..."

"Oh, what a spiteful tongue!" Bob said. "Shana, is it that time of the month for you?"

"Can it Bob," Barry said. "For the moment anyway, I'm the boss here. And I'm repeating myself clearly here, Lieutenant Davidoff and no one else is heading the Jensen affair. Everyone is there to assist her, if required. But not to go in front of her, for any reason whatsoever. Especially if we can be suspected of not carrying out the investigation properly because of friendships."

"If we can't even have friends anymore," muttered Deputy Patterson, leaving the room without having asked permission to do so.

"So that's what the atmosphere was at that time, Karen," said Barry to conclude this internal episode at the Greenville Police Station. "It was like that. And that was just a glimpse of Patterson's methods and character. He already saw himself chief in my shoes, king of the hill."

"Like the Jensen affair was just a repetition before the Lake affair?"

"I'm sure that Patterson hasn't changed a bit. And

knowing how close he is to the Lakes, hand on heart I'd say that he's hiding this USB flash drive that they found at the West Cove Point residence someplace. But why? What was on it?"

"Disgusting photos with children, Kissinger told me."

"With whom else?"

"The Lakes? Patterson himself? I don't know."

"Who does he want to protect? I'd give anything to know."

"Maybe we can take a peek at this USB flash drive?"

"I'll ask Shana to have a look around. I'm sure you understood that he is not her best friend…"

CHAPTER 43
In horror novels

I LEFT Barry Fenton after we both promised to let each other know if we found anything else out and stopped in a takeaway to get something to eat. I was nibbling on it in my room at the Greenville Inn while writing a resume of what I now knew and what I still had to clarify.

I divided my file into two columns: on the left what I knew, or thought I knew, and on the right what I still didn't know. But when I looked at them, the right one was still much longer than the left one.

I found Dorothy Patterson's number in my notes and phoned her. It was about time I spoke to her, as she had played a dual role in this story: first as Veronika's friend and a member of their Clique, and secondly as Patterson's daughter, now the head of the Greenville Police Force, but with a controversial behavior.

She didn't pick up. I didn't leave a message, preferring to call back. Sometimes people don't follow up on their messages whereas when you call them, they cooperate more easily.

I turned on the TV in my room, something I rarely do, and let CNN give me some background noise. The images and the titles on the band at the bottom of the screen were enough for me. In the meanwhile, I finished my dinner while continuing my notes.

Finally the third time I called her, she picked up.

"If it's to sell me insurance or air conditioning, I've got what I need, thanks," Dorothy Patterson said abruptly instead of a mere hello, with a rough tone that I imagine she inherited to her sweet father.

"Not at all, Miss Patterson. My name is Karen Blackstone, I'm a journalist for a magazine and your father gave me your number. I'm investigating the disappearance of your friend, Veronika Lake."

Silence on the other side of the line. I even wondered if she'd hung up as soon as I said her friend's first name.

"*Pfff*, who'd still be interested in an old story like that?" Dorothy sighed. "There's nothing more to say about it, I mean it happened over five years ago now. What could I tell you that I hadn't already repeated a hundred times?"

"Excuse me, but who did you repeat all these things to?"

"Umm, first of all to that lady cop who works with my dad, Shauna, Fiona, something like that."

"Shana. Lieutenant Shana Davidoff. Anyone else?"

"Yeah. My father. Several times. I don't know

what he was trying to find out, but I don't think I have any key info about this affair. I just told him what I knew. So I don't see how I could help you. But if my dad gave you my number, I'll try. But I don't have a lot of time. What do you want to know exactly?"

Dorothy Patterson's attitude was puzzling me. I could understand that five years after this event that she was a part of, she wasn't exactly enchanted to have me bringing the subject back up again. I took time to apologize for having bothered her and carefully chose my questions and words so she wouldn't slip through my hands.

Rather than trying to pry things out of her, I told her what I already learned and asked her to confirm or invalidate the info and tell me anything else that might influence my hypotheses.

So it was mostly what the other members of the Clique had already told me. The party where alcohol was flowing freely, Tom who was able to access the forbidden room, how he grabbed the teddy bear and threw it into the pool and shouted "*Fly, Winnie, and swim!*" Then the fight that Tommy and Veronika had. And she also remembered the Truth or Dare game and some of the questions, after I'd read them off from my notes.

On the other hand, she never had heard about The Who poster with the question on it and knew nothing about Brandon's death, as it was before she was born.

"But it's true that Veronika always refused to talk

about her brother. It was taboo. I never wanted to insist."

But she was horrified when I asked her if the tomb on Sugar Island could have been Brandon Lake's last resting place.

"That would be horrible, atrocious. I can't believe that. Shit, you only see stuff like that in horror novels, like *Tales from the Crypt*! No, no, that can't be."

I heard some kids crying in the background, which Dorothy confirmed.

"I'm sorry, Mrs. Blackstone. I have to hang up, my son woke up and it's time for supper for him."

"Oh! I understand, I'm sorry to have called you so late, I didn't know you had a little baby. Congratulations. I envy you."

"Yeah, you don't have any kids, otherwise you wouldn't say that," she joked.

"I've still got other questions. Could you call me back later, even if it's real late?"

We hung up. I was overwhelmed by the little infant's crying in the background. Nothing unusual about hearing little kids cry or make little noises. Yet, when confronted with something emotional like this, I sometimes still break out in tears.

I would love to hold a baby in my arms and calm its tears...

CHAPTER 44
Silent as a grave

DOROTHY PATTERSON CALLED me back an hour later. I looked at the clock on the wall, and it was a bit after ten.

"Thanks for calling back? Is your baby sleeping? Is it a boy?"

"Yup, a little boy. Nolan. My little baby. His father took off as soon as he was born, so I have to take care of everything by myself. It's not always easy you know."

"I understand," I replied, thinking of "those bastards."

"What else do you want to know, Karen?"

"Just what you think about why Veronika disappeared. For me, anything is possible. She ran away, had an accident, killed herself, was murdered. Dorothy, what do you think? You were friends when you were little plus when you were teens, you were with her for her last hours. Any details that come back to you about the weekend in August of 2017 in Sugar Island?

Anything that could explain her disappearance? What kind of mood was she in? Did she tell you any secrets?"

"No, not really. Her best friend was Cynthia. Those two were inseparable. Actually, now that you mention it, I remember that the night she disappeared, no one could find either of them for a while. I think someone had talked about having a midnight swim. I can't remember what time it was, but it was really late. Maybe three in the morning! You gotta remember that we all had had a lot to drink, and we'd also smoked some grass, so we were pretty out of it. We were young, and crazy and alone on an island. So anyway, we couldn't find either of them. So we all stripped and went in, without them. The guys couldn't have cared less about showing their nuts to everyone. Us girls, well Becky and me, we were cracked up to see them diving from the diving board, their ridiculous little johns swinging around. After that, I think only Cynthia came back. Or actually Tommy found her on the beach on the southern part of the island. She was alone, looking out over the water, a bit absent, Tom told us."

"So, if I understand correctly Dorothy, you're telling me that the last person who saw Veronika was Cynthia?"

"I don't know if we can conclude that. All I'm saying is that no one could find Cynthia and Veronika, and then after that, only Cynthia came back. That doesn't mean that they left together, though I would think so, but they were best friends."

"Could Cynthia have harmed her best friend?"

Dorothy Patterson hesitated a few instants.

"Human nature can sometimes be surprising. Who can say they know everything about their friends or family? A husband who slaughters his wife, a mother who puts her infant in the freezer, a father who rapes his daughter, you think that's logical? A best friend who kills her BFF and makes her disappear forever, you know, in today's world anything can happen!"

I could only agree with that because in my job, I'd run across things that apparently were impossible yet were true. I still had a few questions.

"I was told that Veronika's behavior was a bit strange in the months preceding her disappearance. Mood swings, melancholy, absences, anger. Did you notice any of this?"

"Now that you say it, she was really sad at the end. Preoccupied. By what? Got me. And yes, she did miss school more and more. Sometimes for two or three days. When we asked, she changed the subject. She told us not to worry, or that she'd tell us later, or to leave her alone, or that it was none of our business. Then one day she cracked. She told me her absences were for medical appointments in Portland."

"She was sick?"

"I suppose so. You don't go see a doctor to talk about the last movie you saw or the results of the elections."

"True. I mean, did she complain about something? And did her health deteriorate visibly? Did she tell you what she had? Cancer? Some incurable or degenerative pathology?"

"No, she was as silent as a grave about that. She just had regular doctor's appointments. I think she went to Portland General Hospital, but who knows. Maybe Cynthia..."

I suddenly had an unsettling idea, a morbid thought. *Can you want to shorten the suffering of someone though you love them?*

Could Cynthia have dared, obeying her best friend's insistence, because she was suffering from an incurable disease, help her end it all?

I now had a new hypothesis on Veronika's disappearance.

Was Cynthia guilty of euthanasia?

...this crap eating away me...

Am I going to be able to continue for a long time with this sword of Damocles hanging over my head?

This crap that has been eating away at me for years, that I try to fight, will it ever go away?

The doctors are optimistic, at least that's what they tell me. Treatments are better and better and easier and easier, they add. The side effects are better controlled, they affirm.

What the hell do they know? Are they in my body?

Can they put themselves in my shoes, in my head, in my thoughts?

What do they know about my dark thoughts, my moments of weakness where I'm afraid to tip over into the dark side? Except for what I tell them.

Two types of doctors take care of me. Doctors for the body. The ones that only talk about cells, blood, organs, remission. Then doctors for the soul, the ones who listen to your words, who guide you towards a better you, who try to help you understand yourself. I prefer soul doctors. At least with them, I can talk, I can evacuate my pain and untie the knots in my brain. I can trust them as I don't have anyone else to confide in.

Despite that, there are days when I doubt like days where the wind is gusting. When it gusts inside my head, when it's hard for me to survive with this shit inside, I nourish the idea of abandoning everything, stopping my treatment, and letting myself slide to the bottom, until I disappear...

CHAPTER 45
What followed after

THE SUN ROSE on a new day in Maine with its fall colors. The bright red leaves on the trees next to the Greenville Inn welcomed me through my windows.

Last night I'd worked late after having talked to Dorothy Patterson on the phone. The latest revelations of that single mom had left me in an unprecedented quagmire of thoughts.

Was Veronika Lake thinking of committing suicide to escape the disease eating away at her?

What disease?

Could she have asked, or solicited the complicity in legal speak, Cynthia, her best friend, to help her in this terrible project? This hypothesis was beyond my comprehension, yet I couldn't ignore it.

Hadn't Arthur Conon Doyle written: "When you have eliminated the impossible, whatever remains, however improbable, must be the truth?"

Meaning I had to eliminate what was impossible, inaudible, unspeakable, and continue.

Reach Cynthia, undoubtedly one of the best people able to shed some light on her last instants and last wishes. Veronika… and her parents, whose trace I hadn't yet been able to find, despite my research and questions each time I'd spoken to people. No one was able to give me their address in Florida. Neither Liam Kissinger, who'd purchased their house in West Cove Point, nor Victor Martineau or Chief Patterson, both close friends.

But I wasn't giving up. Perhaps Barry Fenton or Shana Davidoff would be able to find it. I tried another search on social networks. Last time, I'd written their full names but without any results. The most plausible explanation was that they didn't use social networks. Many people of their generation don't have a Facebook, Twitter, or Instagram account. Another possibility is that they had hidden their identities by eliminating the vowels from their names, or things like that. I keyed in *Jnt Lk* and *Msn Lk*, unsuccessfully. Or they chose pseudonyms, unconventional names like *JanouLakou, MisterMason*, or who knows. No way I could have guessed those.

I gave up.

But I'd be back.

FOR NOW, all I want is a break. People don't realize the emotional load that carrying out an investigation with multiple ramifications, like the Veronika Lake affair, implies. And doing that for days on end. I felt that, behind the scenes, there would be heavy truths to be uncovered, like lifting granite stones, where you would risk hurting yourself. I needed a break before continuing.

Of course, I could have left Greenville for a few days and gone back home, it was only a couple of hours away. But why? No one was waiting for me, except Myrtille Fairbanks, my boss, but we didn't spend our weekends together. My parents had retired in Colorado. There was no one. I didn't have a good friend to spend a couple of days with. Not even a pet, a cat, a guinea pig, no one to feed.

And I'd never been able to get close to a man. Each time a relationship started to get serious, my past caught up with me, my past with a myriad of demons. So I fled happiness, perhaps afraid that happiness would flee me first. Always staying one step ahead.

But I was always one step behind.

I'm a single forty-year-old who only thinks of work and my personal and intimate quest, the one that never leaves me.

So now and then, it's vital for me to take a break, and this was the case at the present time.

I decided to stay in Grcenville. Enjoy the town like a tourist.

. . .

During the summer the little town was undoubtedly a tourist trap, with boaters and campers all staying in various cottages around Lake Moosehead. The advantage of the end of October is that they'd all left. And I was alone at the beginning of this cool morning, strolling down Main Street.

In the middle of summer I probably wouldn't have noticed the car that was just behind me, as if following me.

I probably wouldn't have paid any attention to the man who was driving it, one hand on the steering wheel and the other casually resting on the door with the window open, despite the cool weather. I would not have heard the engine of his vehicle, a sedan with a temporary license plate and would not have jotted it down. I would not have felt him going in front of me while I was walking quickly on the wet sidewalk.

I would not have turned my head in his direction, not have looked into the eyes of the man driving and not have been intrigued by his questioning air and his half-smile.

Had I decided to take my break elsewhere than in Greenville, even had it been in Lily Bay, or someplace isolated on Sugar Island, I would not have gone into the *Stress-Free Moose Pub* to warm up.

Where, half an hour later, I would not have noticed the same man, on the other side of the pub, staring at me.

The same man I'd seen a bit earlier in the road, the man driving the sedan.

Undoubtedly with *ifs* and *buts*, what followed would have been completely different...

CHAPTER 46
The darkest parts of human souls

I LOOKED AWAY from this individual who - but maybe I was wrong - kept on staring at me. What did he want? Why was he following me?

I internally reprimanded myself. *Come on Karen, time to go back to Earth. This guy has the right to be in the same place as you at the same time, it's not a crime. Like it's not a huge town here, we're not in New York or Los Angeles. It's just Greenville, Maine, and there's not much to do around here at this time of the year. If he wants to have a cold beer in the same pub where you're having your tea, it's neither shocking nor abnormal. Just relax, kid. You see evil everywhere when you focus on your work. Always investigating crimes and misdemeanors, often thinking about the darkest parts of human souls, it's hard for you to distinguish good from evil. As if your mental cursor was going crazy, not knowing where the north is.*

I was trying to chase my ridiculous ideas out of my head when the phone rang, helping me.

"Karen? Barry Fenton here. Do you have a few minutes?"

"Sure Barry. What can I do for you?"

"Nothing, but I can do something for you. I just had an interesting talk with Lieutenant Shana Davidoff. About the USB flash drive that Patterson was said to have received in the beginning of 2018 from Liam Kissinger, the guy who bought the Lake's home in West Cove Point."

"And?"

"And she remembers the day that Kissinger came in very clearly. She's the one he talked to first. And here's what she said..."

∽

Greenville Police Department, January 2018.

Shana Davidoff was warming her hands on the radiator behind the front desk when a man entered, flicking off the snow from his coat. It was winter in Greenville. The tops of the pine trees on the coast of the lake were immaculately white making the scenery very soothing.

"What weather!" the man mumbled as he walked in. "Hello, Ma'am, I'd like to make a statement or a deposit, I don't really know what the right term is in your police jargon.

"Hello, Sir. Tell me about it."

"So, I was doing some work in a room of the house we bought a couple of months ago, you know to modernize it and so that we'd feel at home, and when I moved a piece of furniture, I found this," he explained, showing her a yellow USB flash drive. "It must have fallen between the blades of the floor and the former owners didn't notice it. And excuse me, but I looked at what was on it."

"That's normal, Mr....?"

"Kissinger. Liam Kissinger. We moved to Greenville last November. My wife, two daughters and me."

"Perfect. Welcome to Greenville, Mr. Kissinger. I hope you'll like it here. So, you discovered this thumb drive and looked at it. What did you find?"

"Stuff that wasn't nice, that's for sure. I'm even ashamed to tell you about it, you, a lady and maybe a mother."

"What type of not nice stuff?" insisted Lieutenant Davidoff. "Even though I'm a lady, I'm still a police officer and thus apt to listen to what you have to tell me, even though it may be difficult."

"It would be easier to show it to you."

"Of course, but I'm sure this thumb drive

belonged to the former owners of your house. Who were they, please?"

"I bought the last house on West Cove Point, and it was owned by a family named Lake", said Kissinger, handing the drive to the lieutenant.

Chief Patterson, when he heard the name Lake pronounced, rushed out of his office.

"Wait a sec, Lieutenant. I'll take care of this gentleman. Come into my office."

His hand on Kissinger's shoulder - who was still holding the flash drive, - he showed him into his office and closed the door behind them.

When the new Greenville inhabitant walked out of the Chief's office a few minutes later, he no longer had the flash drive. He said goodbye to the lieutenant and went outside into the icy winter weather.

"JUST ANOTHER EXAMPLE of Patterson's stranglehold on everything concerning the Lake family," I said, when Barry had finished telling me about the conversation he'd had with Shana.

"Just another example of an authoritarian way of hiding proof of something fishy," Barry added.

"We have to find that flash drive."

"Shana promised to try as soon as possible, without letting Patterson know of course."

"He probably didn't keep it after these five years," I

said sadly. "If what was on it was embarrassing, he probably destroyed it or deleted the content."

"Not so sure," said Barry. "As Lieutenant Davidoff had seen him with the flash drive, Patterson can't hide it, as he'd risk being accused of dissimulation of proof. Plus he had to write a report after Kissinger came, and both had to sign it. So there is an official trace, one we can't deny. On the other hand, he probably put the flash drive somewhere safe and somewhere no one could find it."

"But you think you can, is that it? But how?"

"Shana is on the night shift tonight. She'll have a look around Patterson's office…"

CHAPTER 47
My own demons

BARRY AND I HUNG UP, with a bit of hope of finding the USB flash drive, probably hidden in the Chief of Police's office, as it was not with any of the evidence stored in the dedicated evidence room.

Upon leaving the Stress-Free, I glanced over at the table where the man with the well-maintained brown beard was sitting. I was sure he was staring at me as I left. But why?

I wasn't the type of girl men looked at.

The wind had picked up but that didn't discourage me, and I left, my head lowered and hands in my coat pockets. I saw the car I thought had been following me before in the parking lot. I glanced inside of it discreetly. Walked around to examine the inside. There was a pair of gloves in the back seat, and a bright yellow raincoat. On the floor of the passenger side, there were empty soda cans with plastic sandwich wrappings, and

I thought I spied an empty bottle of J&B too. A guy's car.

I quickly forgot the man, his car, and his raincoat while I walked towards the Greenville Inn, hoping to get warm and dry. The slow walk did me good, with drops from the drizzle running down my forehead.

I took my time. Time for myself. Time to forget Veronika Lake a while, everything orbiting around her, all these horrible things.

Time to think about my own demons. To gather, again, information that would be useful for my never-ending quest.

Rehashing the information I'd received, my feet mechanically brought me back to the inn. The Greenville Inn manager greeted me and asked me if I'd like a cup of hot tea to warm me up. I accepted gratefully and asked her to bring it up.

"Of course, Mrs. Blackstone."

I went into my room, took my wet clothing off and rushed into the shower. What an idiot I was to go walking in the rain! The hot water penetrated my pores, I basked in it, washed my hair, my head leaning back, eyes closed. I emptied my head out, cleaned my dark thoughts from it.

While I was putting a towel over my wet hair, someone knocked at the door.

"Your tea," said one of the employees.

I thanked her, put the tray on my bedside table and pulled the duvet over me, opening my laptop.

Here we go again. Karen Blackstone the hunter. I

logged into several official sites, scrolled downloads of web pages, closed and opened tabs, gathered information, file numbers, email addresses and URLs. I'd already visited these sites many a time trying to find the right information. But it was like looking for a needle in a haystack.

I wondered how I could be so efficient when tracking down individuals that were unknown to me for work and at the same time, so terribly incapable of untangling my own past.

You must say though that American administration is neither transparent nor centralized. Each state, each county, each city has its own databases, and you're quickly confronted with a mass of contradictory information or even worse, a total void.

Plus all of this dated back for a long time! Nearly twenty-five years. I was just eighteen, almost the same age as Veronika when she disappeared, when my life was destroyed, when my body and my heart were broken in two by fate. *In the wrong place at the wrong time*, was what I repeated to myself. Yes, just eighteen when my life tilted from innocent to cruel reality. I've never forgotten the date. February 19, 1998. I was a student in Philadelphia. I lived in a cheap studio that my parents paid for despite their modest resources. They would have done anything for their only daughter. They spent all they had so I could study, have a place to live, eat. To exist in a nutshell.

But I ceased to exist on that day of February 19, 1998. After that, all I did was survive.

People said that *you could blame it on bad luck*, while others said I'd deserved it. I didn't care what they said, that didn't bother me. I was past all that.

That night, I'd run across two guys who'd given me two... poisoned gifts. I'd like to get rid of one of them. As for the other, for years I've been wanting to see him again.

So I keep on looking.

My heart suddenly jumped. How could I have missed this site after all those nights of looking all over? I entered a day into their search engine, febrile as the hourglass showed the seconds while the online server was going through all its data before giving me the result.

Good Lord! I couldn't believe what I was reading.

Tears began to flow; my computer screen was misty behind a curtain of tears. I began to sob.

Sitting cross-legged on the bed, I began to tremble. I'd been going through forms on sites, emails, phone calls, from disappointments to deceptions.

Today I finally had a glint of hope.

I filled in the form and closed my laptop.

I felt emptied.

I fell asleep, ensconced in my towel, lying on the duvet.

CHAPTER 48
Disgusting images

I WOKE up the following morning from a deep sleep, with the light coming in through the window. I must have slept twelve hours straight. Last night I didn't even lower the shades. And I hadn't touched my tea. My stomach was empty, and it was growling. I rushed to the breakfast room and wolfed down some scrambled eggs and pickled vegetables with my morning coffee.

I felt like I could conquer the world this morning.

Especially when I got Barry Fenton's text.

"KAREN, we hit the jackpot! Let's meet Shana at my place. Easier to talk there."

AND HE GAVE me his address on Mayhem Manor Road.

I quickly finished my breakfast and got ready.

I left the Greenville Inn to hop into my car - I wasn't going to walk again today in the rain - and my heart skipped a beat.

I stopped. The vehicle with the temporary plate was parked next to mine. The boots and yellow raincoat were still in the back seat.

Was it just chance that the man had decided to stay in the Greenville Inn? There were no vacancies elsewhere? Was that where he usually stayed?

Why was I running into him so often?

I pushed those unsettling thoughts out of my mind and got into my Ranchero, driving to Mayhem Manor Road.

I LUCKILY TOOK my car to see Barry Fenton. When I parked, the gusts of wind pushed the door of my Ford wide open while I was getting out. Black clouds, full of electricity, could be seen over Greenville.

"Come on in Karen," said Barry on his porch. "Hurry up, the storm's almost here, we'll be better inside. Shana's already here. We'll sit in the patio; it's heated and light. In the other rooms, with this weather, you'd think you're at a funeral."

I took off my coat and shook it before hanging it up. There was a lady at the end of the hall.

"Madeline, my wife," Barry said. "Thanks for the coffee," he said to her, taking the tray she'd handed him before going back into the kitchen.

Barry escorted me through the house to the veranda in the back. Lieutenant Davidoff, wearing civil clothing, got up and greeted me.

He put the tray down next to the main table, that had a laptop that was open on it. Right next to it was the yellow USB flash drive.

"You found it."

"That I did. Like Barry told me, all I had to do was search Patterson's desk. I waited till that SOB left the building and my team member went to sleep in the spare room to start looking for it."

At night, in the Greenville Police Department

The police station was serene as Lieutenant Davidoff was the only person still up as patrolman Aaron Ziegler had gone to bed. She waited a few minutes before going into Chief Patterson's office. When she opened the door, she felt like she was violating a forbidden sanctuary. She went in though and walked right up to his desk. As Barry had imagined, one of the doors was locked. Both were convinced that he was hiding the flash drive in there. All she had to do was find it now.

Shana looked around, trying to guess where he could have hidden the key. She put her hand beneath the desk, looked under the leather blotter on it, rummaged his box of pens, examined the content of the other drawers. Nothing. There was a jacket on the back of Patterson's armchair where he sat his fat butt, she inspected all the pockets. Nothing here either.

There were shelves on the wall behind the armchair. She looked at them, pushed the files, opened the boxes of archives, looked beneath the books, ran her fingers behind the piles of magazines. No key there either. She accidentally tipped a pile of archives over, making a lot of noise.

"Sh...oot," she said, picking up the pieces of paper and putting the files back into the box, before putting it back in its place on the third shelf.

There was another jacket on the coat rack. Shana hoped this would be the place and went to it, but suddenly stopped. There were footsteps approaching.

"Shana?"

Shit, it was Aaron. What did that idiot want? He was supposed to be asleep. She quickly left the office and came face to face with him in the hall.

"Oh. You're there? I heard some noise. Everything okay?"

"Yeah, don't worry Aaron. You can go back to bed. I tripped over my purse and spilled a box of archives."

"Okay. I'm back then."

"Sleep well, everything's under control here!"

She was back in Patterson's office a few minutes later and went right up to the coat rack. She put her hands in the pockets of the jacket, but only found a package of cigarettes, a box of matches and some candy.

"So that's where he gets his fat ass from. When you eat candy on the sly."

But candy doesn't open locked drawers.

She was starting to despair, fearing that the Chief was devious enough to keep the key on him, around his neck for example. She was ready to give up when she saw the little painting that masked the safe where Patterson kept his service gun. Maybe...

Except Lieutenant Davidoff didn't know the combination. Only the heads of the department did.

"Shit."

She had an idea and sent off a quick text message, fearing that at this time of the night, she wouldn't get an answer. But she got one just a few minutes later.

If the code hasn't changed since I was there, it's: 0-7-0-4-1-7-7-6. July 4th, 1776. Good luck. Barry.

Shana smiled. Of course ! Independence Day. A symbol.

The lieutenant turned the rotary selector on the safe with the code. The door opened. Inside there was a box of munitions with his service arm as well as other objects including a porno magazine that Shana pushed aside with disgust, imagining what the Chief did during the nights he was on duty, and a box of matches that she shook. There was the characteristic noise of something metallic in the box. She opened it, finding a small key.

She put it into the locked drawer. And turned it to open it.

In the drawer, at the very back, behind a stack of sheets of paper, there was a yellow USB flash drive.

"Have you already looked at it?" I asked Barry and Shana.

"We were waiting for you Karen," said Barry, picking up the flash drive to put it in his computer.

A window immediately opened, showing a series of images, without a preview feature.

Barry selected all of them and launched a slide show.

I'll never be able to forget those sickening images.

CHAPTER 49
Invisible

IN MY CAREER of nearly twenty years, I've seen, read, heard atrocities. But what we saw, Lieutenant Shana Davidoff, Barry Fenton, and I, made us all sick to our stomachs. I could read brute wrath in Barry's eyes, and a visceral nausea behind Shana's hand that she was holding against her mouth. I was petrified.

"Jesus, how can you do that to kids?" asked Shana.

"They're not that young," replied Barry.

"The girls," I said. "Unless I'm mistaken, I only saw girls."

"Yeah, barely pubescent ones. Long hair, hips not yet developed, budding breasts."

On most of the pictures on this flash drive, the protagonists are all adolescents, but their faces were masked by their hair. They were alone or there were two or three of them in the same picture. But they were all just wearing tiny white cotton panties.

Someone must have asked them to pose that way, nearly nude, in suggestive poses that teens like that wouldn't naturally have. Girl of? Twelve of thirteen?

On other pictures you could see a hand running through their hair or holding on to a ponytail. A man's hand, with dark hair on his fingers.

On another even more abject one, an even more degrading act. The little girl was kneeling between two legs - hairy ones too - that were spread. And the man was holding her down with her hair between his two fat thighs. The girl's head was masking his dick...

"Jesus, Mary, and Joseph, that's disgusting," Shana said. "Who is that pig? Who?"

"I'd pay a lot to know," replied Barry. "And I can assure you that if I run across that son of a bitch, I'm gonna make him swallow his birth certificate, the bastard."

"The bastards," the lieutenant said. "Look at this photo, it's not the same legs or the same hand. There were several of them."

"Without considering the one who took the photos and of course he's not on them. Look at this one, it couldn't have been taken in POV."

"POV?"

"Point of view," I explained. "It's a way of taking pictures or movies as if the lens was in the photographer's eye. Like a photographic immersion. Like in the photo where you could only see the guy's thighs, as if you observed this with your own eyes. But here, on this last picture, there's another person taking the photo because you see the back of the little girl kneeling in front of that fat asshole."

We were all fuming upon seeing this offensive slideshow, one that was wrongful and criminal.

Punishable.

"Punishable if we can identity the authors and accomplices of this ignominy," seethed Shana. "But how to recognize one of these dirty bastards..."

And it was true that the few times that you could see the men, they'd hidden their faces behind a ski mask or a carnival mask.

"Like they're parading, those fuckers!" shouted Barry. "Hell, I've seen enough. How can they like such evil acts? What pleasure can they have fondling young girls like that? How can they force them to commit acts like that? Perverts! Repressed! Like they don't have a wife within reach of their dicks?"

"I just hope they're not priests," I said.

The rain was pounding down on Barry's veranda, now mixed with sleet and hail, making a deafening noise, but we were silent.

"We can't let something like that remain unpunished," complained Shana Davidoff. "We have to talk to Patterson. If he did all that to hide incriminating evidence like this, that means he knows something, that he's protecting someone. One of these guys?"

"I'm sure of it. When were these photos taken? Can we find out?"

"Yeah, wait a sec," said Barry.

He right-clicked on one of them and in the pop-up menu, clicked on *properties*.

There was the name of the file, its type and size, as well as two different dates, one above the other. The one they were interested in was the date when the picture was taken: February 28, 2013.

"Almost ten years ago," Shana calculated. "Provided that the date was correctly configured in the camera."

"But that seems to be the case, if you look at the date when it was transferred to the USB support, which says March 2, 2013, just a few days later."

I looked at the long list of properties of the file and stopped at the last date the file was opened. February 19, 2018.

"The day I saw Liam Kissinger who came to the station and when Patterson came out and took it with him in his office. It's not a surprise but of course Bob opened the files in presence of Kissinger."

"And then he wrote up the deposit report and stuffed the drive into his locked door," added Barry. "There you go, the end, the affair is hushed. *Invisible*. Whereas there was enough evidence to carry out an investigation for pedophilia. You can't deny it, those little girls pleasuring those pigs weren't sexually adults at that time."

I suddenly had an idea. I shared it with my teammates.

"If these little girls were like thirteen when this

took place, how old are they now? Twenty-two, twenty-three?"

"That's right."

"Exactly how old Veronika Lake would have been, had she lived..."

CHAPTER 50
A puzzle to put together

BARRY FENTON CLOSED HIS LAPTOP. He'd put the yellow USB flash drive that Lieutenant Davidoff had taken from Patterson's locked drawer, that powerfully unsettling one, on the table next to it.

The hail was now accompanied by thunder and lightning. A terrible storm was crashing down on the town and our scarred hearts because of those abject photos dating back to 2013.

Barry, Shana, and I remained silent, deafened by the storm outside and shell-shocked by what we'd just seen and what I'd just said.

Could Veronika Lake had been one of those half-naked teens kneeling in front of those perverted men?

Beginning with that hypothesis, as a good investigative journalist, I extrapolated and drew up several scenarios.

What if, forever impacted by this terrible experience, Veronika couldn't bear such a psychological weight and had killed herself?

Or even worse – adding a crime to the act – what if one of the men in the photos with the little girls had wanted to eliminate one of them to avoid her telling her parents or the authorities?

In 2017, when she disappeared, was Veronika going to speak out?

And threaten the men?

One of them maybe wanted to silence her?

I put it to the others like that: Barry Fenton, the former Chief of Police, and Shana Davidoff, a lieutenant working in the Greenville police station, under Bob Patterson's command. Two priceless allies in my quest for the truth about the Lake affair. An affair that motivated them as much as me. Now there were three of us who want to bring justice to the young lady who went missing.

We divvied up what needed doing.

"We should meet Patterson, give him the USB flash drive and see what he has to say," I proposed. "Get him to spill the beans once and for all."

"I think we should hit harder and aim higher," Shana said. "I'm ready to contact the State Attorney[*] so he'll order the opening of an investigation on what happened in 2013."

"And incur the wrath of Patterson?" asked Barry. "Your boss?"

---

[*] This is the State-level prosecutor.

"I'm not scared. When I look at those pictures, and I know I'll never be able to forget them, I can't shut up or do nothing. Tough luck for the consequences. You can't do stuff like that to kids!"

"Good for you Shana," I said while the storm was subsiding slowly. "I want to see Tom Malone again. I don't think he told me everything about his girlfriend. I'd like to know what he thinks. And what about Veronika's repeated absences? Her visits to the hospital, her eventual illness? He couldn't ignore stuff like that. Why didn't he say something? That intrigues me."

Barry Fenton's phone rang at that very moment.

"Excuse me, I think this is important," he said before picking up. "Hello... Yes, speaking... Fantastic news!... Just a sec till I get a pen and a piece of paper..."

With his phone between his ear and shoulder, he got up and opened a drawer of a little table in the corner of the veranda and took out a sheet of paper and a pen.

"Okay... 351 Paloma Drive... Coconut Grove... Miami... Thanks, that's great. You wouldn't happen to have a phone number, would you? No problem, I'll make do. Thanks so much Lester. I owe you one."

I understood, even without asking Barry, while he was writing the address down. He'd just found where the Lake family lived.

He proudly waved the sheet of paper in front of us. "Anyone need some sun?"

We all looked up at the black sky here in Greenville.

"I'll book a ticket right now for Florida," I said without hesitating, delighted to talk to Veronika's parents, key components in the puzzle to put together on the young lady who went missing five years ago and who now had been strangely absent - or elusive - from the picture since the beginning of my investigation.

CHAPTER 51
A surprise

I CERTAINLY WASN'T GOING to leave Greenville without making sure that the Lakes were at home, in Miami. On the other hand though, I was hoping to surprise them and wasn't going to tell them I was coming. I wanted to use the effect of surprise to avoid them saying no, and perhaps fleeing.

Using Shana and Barry's help, a patrol car swung by their house in Florida to make sure they were there before I left.

As they were, I reserved a seat on a Bangor-Miami flight with a stopover in Philadelphia. Barry offered to drive me to the airport, but I refused, not wanting him to do any extra work while my Ford Ranchero, like me, just wanted to see other scenery than Greenville, and hit the road.

In the beginning of the afternoon, after having stopped at the Greenville Inn, I put my bag and my treatment into the trunk of my car, protected by the hood of my raincoat. I sat down behind the wheel, ranting about the crappy weather and dreaming of the sun in the south. I turned on the windshield wipers and headlights, it was so dark out, turned my blinker on to turn left after the parking lot and didn't believe what I saw.

On the road going into town, there was a man who was walking slowly in the rain, protected by a raincoat with a big hood. When I went past him, I swerved so I wouldn't splash him, he saluted me military style, his hand horizontal on his temple, an ambiguous smile on his lips, lost in the middle of his black beard.

I recognized this strange person who seemed to be wherever I happened to be.

Though it bothered me, I calmed down thinking of the hours of flight that would distance me from Maine for a while.

HOW DIFFERENT ORANGES and pumpkins are.

That's what I thought when we were landing in Miami. How different Florida is from Maine.

That's the magic of the United States, this vast country where, in just a couple of hours you can go from fall to summer, from rain to sun.

When I landed in Miami, it was already dark, but as soon as I went outside, I could feel the warmth. I hailed a taxi and gave him the address of the hotel, not too far from where the Lakes now lived. Just like lots of retired people, they'd moved to a place where it's always nice. I guess it's good for rheumatism. Wonder if it's also good to forget past tragedies?

I had killed time in the plane by writing a long email to Myrtille to tell her about my latest discoveries – especially the USB flash drive – and inform her not to be astonished when she'd receive an American Airlines invoice as well as expense slips from Florida. When the Boeing landed and we could connect, the email was sent north. A few minutes later, before I picked up my bags, I got my boss's answer.

"Hi my little Chickie! That's not an article or even a series that you'll be writing about the Lake affair, but a complete special edition for True Crime Mysteries! Count me in! Have fun in the sun, you lucky girl. Watch out though if you think you'll be having a vacation all expenses paid. Have fun anyway, my little princess."

Yeah, sure, *princess*, I thought in the taxi. Palm trees lit up by modern and well-designed streetlights. Behind this curtain of orangish lights and exotic vegetation, I could imagine the islands or peninsulas, as they were linked by the road, of Virginia Key and Key Biscayne. After Sugar Island, another decor, but still islands, still water. I could even make them out from my hotel room.

Before going to bed, exhausted by yet another

emotion-filled day, I sent of a quick text message to Tom Malone, as if casting a net in the water and seeing if I'd catch anything.

Tom, why didn't you tell me about Veronika's health issues? You must have known. Please call as soon as possible. Karen Blackstone.

Then I put my phone in airplane mode. It was time to sleep, not to work.

When I woke up, I saw that he'd replied.

Yes, I knew about that. Veronika was feeling worse and worse both in her body and in her mind. But I'd gotten used to how crazy the Lake family was. I swear to you Karen, they were all nuts in that family. All of them... But I think the parents were the worst. Tom.

CHAPTER 52
Dogs chasing a fox

SO, if Tom was right, I'd be meeting a couple of crazy people here in Miami, this morning.

The Coconut Grove neighborhood was one of the most expensive ones in Florida. Why didn't it surprise me that the Lakes lived here, as they'd always liked luxury and seemed to have plenty of money?

I was able to walk from my hotel to Veronika's parents' house. It was on one of the many islets that were off the Miami coast. Isla Grande was the name of their neighborhood, and you took Coconut Road to get there. Walking down the road where the Lake family lived, I saw a host of totally beautiful houses, villas with lime-treated white walls, most of them two stories high, with turrets, columns, and balconies, surrounded by palm trees, banyan trees, yews, or coconut trees. The houses didn't have fences and their perfectly mown lawns going right up to the street and driveways made from beautifully set interlocking paving tiles. I felt like I was looking at a postcard... or in Playmobil Land. When I reached number 351, I was happy to see that the Lakes didn't have a fence or a huge hedge. I imagine it was less dangerous to live in Coconut Grove than in Liberty City, in the north of Miami.

I don't know why but I was nervous about meeting Mason and Janet Lake. They were like mythological characters that I'd heard of several times while doubting that they actually existed. But their name was written on the mailbox shaped like a birdhouse. The house seemed calm.

I walked down the driveway and rang their bell.

Seconds turned into hours in my head before the door opened and I saw a tall and tanned man, with perfectly combed white hair. He was wearing flannel slacks and a golf shirt. And his eyes, his eyes seemed to go right through me. Dark eyes stared at me head to foot.

"Yeah?" he asked.

"Mr. Lake? Mason Lake?"

"Himself. And you are?"

"Karen Blackstone, journalist."

I held my hand out, but he didn't shake it. On the other hand, the word "journalist" made him frown.

"What do you want with me?" he asked. "Something happen in the neighborhood?"

As he was defensive, I decided to play it straight.

"Mr. Lake, I'm not going to beat around the bush. I work for the magazine *True Crime Mysteries*, and I'm investigating the unexplained disappearance of your daughter, Veronika, in August 2017, in Greenville. I have to talk to you and your wife Janet. I've got too many unanswered questions about your daughter and your son, Brandon."

"Mrs. Blackstone, that's it? I don't need to talk to you so I'm inviting you to leave immediately, or I'll call the cops."

"No need to call them Mr. Lake, I already did."

"What?"

"You understood. The Miami police force already knows that I'm here at your house and they also told me that you would be at home before I left. Up till now, I couldn't reach you and I'm very sorry about it because I'm sure that you have a lot of things to tell me. So, I'm giving you the choice: either you let me in, and we'll have a nice little chat, or I'll ask the authorities to speak to you as a witness – *a minima* – in the affair of the disappearance of your daughter. Which would you prefer?"

Right then we heard a voice from inside the house.

"Who is it dear? Another salesman? They never give up, to they?"

Mason Lake thought my proposal over. I could almost hear him thinking by looking at the way he was twisting his mouth around, as if he was trying to get a piece of meat stuck between two teeth out. He finally answered his wife directly.

"Don't worry, it's nothing. I'll take care of it."

Then he spoke to me.

"We'll talk in the yard."

"No. I want to talk to both of you."

"You journalists are incredible. Worse than dogs chasing a fox."

"Speaking of which, I also have to talk to you about a dog. May I come in?"

He sighed noisily but moved away.

Ten minutes later we were all outside sitting around a table with three glasses of lemonade on it. The backyard overlooked the Biscayne Bay inlet, a type of canal that snaked between houses and forests.

"I can't understand that our tragedies interest you, Mrs. Blackstone," said Janet softly. "Do you like rehashing old and painful stories? Plus, you came here, disturbing us retired people to harass us with that. It's cruel!"

Veronika and Brandon's mother was tiny, the opposite of her husband. A shy and discrete wife, the traditional housewife over the age of fifty, discrete, gray hair, blue emotionless eyes, a tiny mouth, one you had to pay attention to when she was speaking.

"Mrs. Lake," I answered in a voice trying to be soothing, "I'm not intending to rub salt into your wound. All I'm trying to do is understand everything about your daughter's disappearance. Isn't that the same thing you want? If only to bring justice to her... Unless you already know the truth?"

"What truth?" Mason Lake said angrily. "You don't think that we never tried to find it? There was an investigation in 2017, but with no result, unfortunately. Today all we want to do is forget it, so we also don't lose hope."

"Mr. Lake, are you sure the investigation was carried out correctly?"

"What are you insinuating?"

"I've got a few doubts about Chief Patterson's total involvement in the affair concerning your daughter. You were very close to the Pattersons."

"So? How could that be incompatible with a serious investigation?"

"That's exactly what I'm trying to find out. You know, I was able to speak to quite a few people. Friends of your daughter, influent people in Greenville such as the mayor and the head of the police department. Also a guy named Liam Kissinger, remember him?"

"Should I?"

"That's the person who sold you house in West Cove Point to."

"I didn't know his name," said Mason. "The transaction was managed by a real estate agent. The house was sold, we were paid. No problem. Why are you talking to us about this man?"

I opened my purse.

"Could you believe that the new owner, when he was doing some work at your old house, discovered quite a curious object that must have fallen beneath a piece of furniture. Here it is. Do you know what it is?"

"I'm not a prehistoric idiot. I know that it's a USB flash drive and even know how to use it," replied Lake ironically.

"You know what it contains?"

"Why the hell should I know what's on that flash drive that I didn't even know existed, Mrs. Blackstone?"

Once again, I put my hand in my purse and took two photos out, that Barry had printed last night, chosen amongst the most explicit. I put them down on the table next to the glasses of lemonade.

"Good Lord!" said Janet. "Please put those atrocities away! That's shocking!"

Veronika's mother turned her head away.

"I had the same reaction. Yes, it is shocking. The drive comes from your house. You must recognize it..."

Mason Lake got up, outraged.

"Mrs. Blackstone, what you just said is revolting. We never saw this object at home, and we totally ignored its abject content. How can you insinuate things like that?"

"Excuse me, I wasn't insinuating anything. Just asking a question. You don't know anything about this?"

"Nothing at all!" Mason shouted. "Plus what could that have to do with our daughter's disappearance?"

"I'm not sure yet. Perhaps it was just an enormous

and unfortunate coincidence. This is simply the way I'm seeing things."

"Continue."

"This flash drive was found *at your house* after you left Greenville and given to the police. Then *Chief Patterson* took it and dissimilated it to close the claim. And *you and Patterson* are on pretty good terms. So I concluded, perhaps naively, that he did this because he wanted to *cover you*."

"You're not far from calumny. Watch out what you're saying. You could go to court for this."

"Don't get angry Mr. Lake. I'm just wondering, that's all. Let's just say then that you have no idea what this is and go one to another subject that also intrigues me."

"If you must," said Janet dryly. "As it looks like you've decided to torture is with all this old stories."

I didn't know how to introduce this without hurting them. I was quite aware that I'd be talking about painful events in their past, but I was sure that they had the keys that could unlock some of the mysteries that I'd been trying to solve for days.

"What I'm about to say isn't easy to hear. Please excuse me, in advance. So, I went to Sugar Island, an island that belongs to you in full ownership, is that right?"

Mason Lake nodded.

"Why didn't you also sell it off when you left Maine, like you sold your home in West Cove Point?

Why keep a deserted island in the middle of Lake Moosehead?"

"That is none of your business, Mrs. Blackstone," replied Mason dryly.

"Is it because this island is the home to a grave that you want to keep?"

The couples' eyes both opened wide, taken aback.

"You are completely crazy," said Janet. "How abject can you get?"

I didn't let her intimidate me.

"Or because the villa is in reality a sanctuary? Because there's a forbidden child's room there? Your son Brandon's room, who died when he was two?"

When she heard this Janet made an involuntary little noise that she smothered by putting her hand in front of her mouth. Her husband rubbed her arm to tell her he'd reply.

"Have you decided to torture us Mrs. Blackstone? Haven't we suffered enough for over twenty years? Losing our son so young, our first child, then our second one seventeen years later, leaving us faced with this impossible double bereavement…"

I had to say that I was moved. Yet I persisted in my relentless logic.

"Aren't this island, this villa, and this bedroom a huge tomb for your son? Isn't that why you wouldn't sell it for anything at all? Because the grave here" - I showed it to them on my phone –" is Brandon's grave?"

Tears were streaming down Janet Lake's face. I was contrite, especially when she was able to speak, between two muffled sobs.

"Our son is buried in the Miami Cemetery, 1800 Northeast, 2nd Avenue. Sector IV, row 23. We went there yesterday to put flowers on his grave."

CHAPTER 53
A hidden monster

JANET, Mason Lake, and I were silent. I felt like an intruder here, with my difficult questions, answers that were so hard to hear and the terrible confessions they were giving me. But did I have a choice? Could I leave without knowing their feelings on several elements that were not correctly coming together in my mind? I kept on, with genuine repentance.

"I'm so sorry to rekindle your pain, Mrs. Lake, but there are still a few gray areas that disturb me."

"What else do you want to know? What other poisoned arrows are you aiming at us?" asked Janet. "The damage is done. Let's get this over with!"

"You saw, as I did, these barely legible inscriptions on the old cross on the grave in Sugar Island. Are the dates, 1997 - 2000 the dates of the birth and death of Brandon?"

"They are."

"And the letters that we can make out, though

faded. An R, an O, and an N... of your son's name. Who is buried there, if not Brandon?"

Veronika's mother lowered her head and put her two hands against her closed eyes.

"When Brandon was born, in 1997, we also adopted a dog. A marvelous Golden Retriever puppy. We thought our baby would be happy to grow up with this cute little pet. Really a dog for families."

"But one with a hidden monster inside..." I added.

Janet Lake swallowed, as if she had a huge ball of something stuck in her throat.

"I was eight months pregnant when it happened."

∽

Miami, February 2000

The Lake family liked to spend their winters in Florida rather than in cold Maine. As they had the choice, they preferred warm Florida over snow filled Greenville with its twenty below weather. With a two-year-old in her arms and an eight-month fetus in her stomach, Janet also preferred their Miami residence. They were planning to stay until their second baby was born.

A daughter, the doctor had told them. The couple was delighted, they had the *king's choice*!

It looked like it was going to be a nice day, as it generally was in Florida in the winter. Janet had heard the door close softly behind Mason, who had an all-morning meeting in downtown Miami, in the business district. She had also heard him lock the door, which reassured her. Brandon couldn't leave the house. She was still in bed, a hand caressing her round stomach, smiling and happy. She had fallen back to sleep until she heard the pitter patter of little feet in the bedroom.

"Mommy, hungry," the little brunette angel had said.

Opening her eyes, still buried under the stratum of sleep caused by a difficult night where she couldn't find a comfortable position because of her huge bump, Janet had replied "Coming sweetie."

Then she invited him on the bed, in Mason's place. Brandon climbed up and fell asleep next to her for nearly an hour. Both were awakened when the dog jumped on the bed and began to lick Janet's and Brandon's faces.

"I think we have to get up," had said Janet stifling a yawn.

She had prepared breakfast for both of them and filled the dog's bowl with dog food, then slowed down by her huge stomach, had asked Brandon to play by himself for a couple of minutes in his playroom, next to their bedroom.

Janet sat down to read her novel but quickly fell back asleep. As she had to stay in bed as much as possible, she was able to read, something she loved doing, though this routine was sometimes difficult.

She had just dozed off when her son's

babbling was mixed with the Golden's discreet little barks. Sometimes she could hear Brandon laughing out loud. Janet didn't regret having adopted the dog for her son. As Brandon had gotten bigger, the dog had become his best friend, his best toy, just after Winnie the Pooh, his inseparable teddy bear who had first place in his heart and on his bed. At night, the dog couldn't go into the little boy's room, but he made up for this during the day.

Suddenly sharp screams woke her up.

Janet got up in a fraction of a second, alerted by this unusual hullabaloo. The child's cries, the dog's growling, fierce and loud barking.

"Brandon!" she'd shouted from her bed.

Suddenly she was doubled over by a sharp pain, her hands on her stomach. Janet was in pain, but the noise had increased in the adjacent room, and she forced herself to move, get out of bed, or rather slide out, as she was suffering so much.

She dragged herself along the hardwood floor, atrocious images in her mind, almost like a dried-out worm on the road during a heatwave.

"Brandon!" she kept on shouting, progressing too slowly, her voice broken.

But the dog kept on growling, while the child's

cries became more muffled, nearly inaudible, drowned out by the animal's furor.

She'd made it down the hall, out of breath, her stomach stretched and painful, to the playroom.

But no one was playing...

A horrible vision hit her brain which at first refused to believe the reality of the scene. And her vision was troubled by a curtain of tears.

The first thing she saw was all the blood on the Disney rug below Brandon's body.

The same blood soiling the dog's mouth, its chops raised and trembling, and sharp yellow teeth showing in the jaws of the furious animal.

"Nooooooo!"

Janet's shout ripped the silence apart that had fallen upon the room when the dog saw her come in. As if it realized what it had just done, the animal sat down, then put his front legs out in front and sat down with his head against Brandon's inert body.

Janet crawled to them.

The dog was now whimpering, making squeaking noises, his red muzzle glued to the child's empty face, licking the blood flowing from his throat.

"Get out of there! Go away!"

The mother crawled to them, her face red, eyes crazy, dragging herself, pushing the dog away with huge gestures of her arms.

The animal walked away, still whimpering, its tail between its legs as if it had finally understood what it had done.

A mistake? A crime!

Janet Lake bent over her child's body; her baby who was barely two years old. Her hands were rubbing on Brandon's bloody throat. She had a glint of hope when she felt a weak pulse.

"My baby, my sweetie, stay with me, don't leave!"

She collapsed a few seconds on her son, her body wracked with sobs and spasms, her stomach with contractions. The infant inside her was kicking as if it also wanted to be a part of this tragedy.

Then she came to her senses and was able to reach her phone, that was on the bedside table. She keyed in 9-1-1.

When the rescue squad arrived at 351 Paloma Drive, there was nothing they could do for the poor Brandon Lake, an angel who had flown away too early.

CHAPTER 54
The mud of the past

I DIDN'T KNOW what to say after hearing Janet. Her story had been told with so much emotion, a broken voice, red eyes, that it was as if I had been there too. But it had actually taken place here, under this very roof, just a few yards from where we were now sitting.

Mason Lake put a comforting hand on his wife's shoulder, who was bent over by this painful memory of the tragedy that had taken place over twenty years ago, though she had not forgotten one instant of it.

"We had to have Brownie put down," said Mason. "Once a dog has bitten, it'll bite again."

"Especially as it just didn't bite, but it killed!" added Janet. "Dogs don't go to jail. They get put down immediately. I still have no idea what happened. We trusted Brownie so much. Brandon and the dog were best friends. And then... We never found out what triggered this. Perhaps Brandon bothered the dog, or bit it, or walked on its tail, I have no idea. But up to this day I feel responsible for my son's death. Because I was in my last weeks of pregnancy, a difficult one, I had to stay in bed all day. I often slept, I found it hard to wake up, I was completely out of it for most of the day. Plus I felt like a cow who was about to explode, lugging my stomach like a burden. Those abdominal pains prevented me from arriving in time to save our son. Would I have been able to have prevented it had I arrived just a few seconds earlier in the playroom? I've been asking myself about that for twenty years. Those images never leave me, they turn in slow motion in my head each time I close my eyes to try to sleep. Ah! If I hadn't been pregnant, Brandon wouldn't have died."

"I'm so sorry, Mrs. Lake," I said with sincerity. "I read an article in the paper that explained how things like this can happen. And you've given me a true and poignant explanation. I can't imagine your pain. The pain a mother has. A mother who will soon be giving birth."

"A child who's born never replaces the death of your first one, Mrs. Blackstone, if you're insinuating that everything was hunky dory when Veronika was born."

"No, I'm so sorry, I didn't mean that. I meant the opposite. I'd imagine that your heartache must have been multiplied by ten, as pregnant women always feel exacerbated emotions! I'm a woman too. And this symbolic, Good Lord, a child who's not yet born when the other…"

I couldn't finish my sentence. Janet broke down once again.

"This is what happens when you disturb the mud of the past," said Mason. "Do you have a heart of stone, Mrs. Blackstone?"

My heart was broken too when I heard this. How could it humanly be supported? I personally had to hear it though, to clarify all the doubts and suspicions I had about the Lakes. Which is what I told them, asking them once again to please pardon me for this intrusive interrogation. I reminded them that I was just looking for the truth, nothing but the truth, and who knows, trying to find a trace of Veronika, dead or alive.

But a detail suddenly popped into my mind.

"Mr. Lake, you told me you had Brownie put to sleep."

"It was required by the law. Why?"

"Brownie. Your dog was named Brownie?"

"It's a common name you know. Not an unusual one for a dog. Plus for a Golden Retriever, a chocolate-colored one, this name fit perfectly."

"I'm sure it did. But that's not what disturbed me. You said you adopted it in 1997 and put it down when your son died, in 2000. So Brandon and the dog have the same dates for their birth and death. And they also share, I can't miss it now, three letters of their first names. Brandon and Brownie. An R, an O, and an N…

Like the three letters you can still make out on the cross on the grave in Sugar Island."

"Of course! Because that's where we buried Brownie."

CHAPTER 55
In the shadows

"MRS. Blackstone, you actually thought that we'd buried our son like a dog on a deserted island in the middle of a lake in Maine?" continued Mason Lake angrily. "You think we're heartless? Brandon has his own tombstone, which you can see if you go to Miami Cemetery. Brownie is buried on Sugar Island."

"I'm so sorry... I realize now that my associations of ideas weren't the right ones. But some of them still seem strange. Can I continue?"

"Go ahead if you must, keep on trying to destroy us. Janet, will you be able to stand other allegations from our visitor?"

Her response surprised me.

"If that can help us understand why our daughter disappeared."

I hopped on that bandwagon.

"Like I was saying, some things still intrigue me. For example, in Brandon's room in Sugar Island, I discovered a poster hanging on the wall above his bed. A poster from an album by *The Who*. See what I'm talking about?"

"Of course," replied Mason Lake immediately. "*Who's Next*, an album that I often listened to, and I bought that poster at one of their concerts in Portland. But it's surprising that you saw in it our son's room."

"Meaning?"

"The poster was in my office!"

"So someone must have moved it then. To give us a clear message. Especially as what was written on it is frightening."

"I don't understand."

"After the title *Who's Next*, someone added a red question mark and below, a question: *Who killed Brandon?*"

The couple seemed flabbergasted.

"How revolting," sighed Janet.

"I don't understand," added Mason. "When we moved out of Greenville after our daughter's disappearance, I can assure you that this poster was still hanging in my office above my desk and nothing that abject was written on it. Especially, there's no doubt about this: Brownie killed Brandon."

"How can people propagate lies like that?" complained Janet. "Who could think that was funny to spread horrors like that? Plus breaking into a private property to do something like that too."

I didn't add anything here, knowing that that was

exactly what I'd also done. But they didn't seem to resent it.

"Have you any ideas about who could have done that?" I tried.

"Not at all," Mason replied immediately. "Someone crazy. You can't be sane and do something like that. Or someone who totally hates us."

"Why would someone hate you? What could you have done for people to harass you like that?"

Neither Mason nor Janet answered, both shaking their heads. It was as if my visit and speaking of the past had knocked them out. I still had another zone in the shadows to speak about with them before leaving them in peace.

"I'm not going to bother you any longer," I began. "But before I leave, I'd like to know your feelings about the disappearance of your daughter. I imagine that everything was said about this subject. All the hypotheses: kidnapping, assassination, running away, suicide - please excuse these harsh words - everything seems possible, but nothing has been proven. This has turned into a cold case, and that's why I'm working on it. It's my specialization, I could say. But you, her parents, you're the ones who know her better than anyone. What's your intimate belief? Could you have anticipated a tragedy like this? Were there any early warning signs? People told me that a couple of months before she went missing, that Veronika had a lot of doctor's appointments at the hospital. Did she have an incurable disease?"

No answer. I noticed that none of us had touched our glasses of lemonade. Janet, after a minute or so, decided to speak.

"It's probably stupid of me to admit this, but I did think that it could have been possible. Several years ago, a bit after Brandon was killed and Veronika was born, - this is a subject I've always been interested in - I read a book about the emotions that future babies can have, *in utero* babies I mean. A fetus can feel everything that their mother feels and has emotions too. It's a nearly chemical process, anyway one that has been medically proved. So you can easily imagine what my daughter must have felt the day Brandon died. I was screaming, Brownie was growling, Brandon must have been frightened, and maybe even my own body's pheromones, when I knew that Brandon was dying."

I was troubled by what Janet Lake had told me. I personally don't believe in esoterism like this but could easily understand that she did. I let her continue.

"So I think that Veronika was born with this fear inside her. And she must have grown up with it too, like a second skin she couldn't get rid of. Our daughter was often melancholic, - that's not astonishing – and she was terrified of dogs. You can understand why. Anyway when she became a teenager, this melancholy increased. Maybe because of hormones. And a few months before she went missing, she told us she wanted to talk to a psychologist. She saw one in Portland. She went there alone after school."

"Veronika was uncomfortable, out of her element,"

added Mason. "At first, we thought that was normal for a teen, but it didn't get better as time went by. Quite the opposite. We didn't know what to do for her. So when she disappeared, the first thing we thought was that she ran way, because she was terribly unhappy and uneasy. We couldn't explain it."

"Unhappiness that would have led her to commit suicide?"

"I don't know. I think she would have left a message. Or that we would have found her. Mrs. Blackstone, if you really want to know what *incurable disease* Veronika was suffering from, I'd say it was that she was... *tired of living*."

This sentence seemed like a logical conclusion to our talk. I thanked Mr. and Mrs. Lake for their time and apologized once again for having come and having asked them all these questions.

"Mrs. Blackstone, we sincerely told you everything we know," Mason Lake, who now seemed to be apologizing himself said as we walked to the door.

He no longer seemed to be on the defensive, but rather relieved to think that someone was investigating what happened to Veronika.

He shook my hand at the front door. A limp handshake.

At that instant something tickled my brain, but I couldn't tell you what it was. A type of uneasiness linked to an elusive souvenir.

A feeling of *déjà-vu* triggering a disproportionate amount of disgust...

CHAPTER 56
Crying out

BEFORE LEAVING FLORIDA, where I no longer had anything to do, I wanted to see with my own eyes what the Lake couple had told me.

I took a cab to the north-east side of town and walked into the Miami Cemetery's main entrance. I saw a site map and looked for Sector IV, Row 23. The sun was still up at this time of day, and it was hot for the beginning of November. As I'd lived most of my life in the northern states, I was always surprised by this climate.

I walked slowly, reading the names on the tombstones or crosses. There were all kinds of tombs. Cemeteries have an artistic type of architecture and can subjugate you just as if you were visiting a museum or antique archeological ruins.

I began to doubt the veracity of what the Lakes had told me when I saw a sign at the end of Row 23, for the Angel's Area.

Of course.

Amongst fifty or so miniature graves, I found the one I'd been looking for.

Brandon Lake
1997-2000
R.I.P.

Now I couldn't doubt it.

Yet something else would be coming...

I found a flight back to Maine that evening. I landed in Bangor and drove to Greenville, arriving at nightfall at my hotel where I plopped down on the bed with relief.

People often say that *travel broadens the mind*, I think it distorts it!

I just had time for a quick shower and brushed my teeth, took my meds, and I fell straight asleep.

But I had lots of nightmares and dark thoughts. I should have been used to this as each time I carry out an investigation, my subconscious nocturnal visions are harrowing, nourished by what I'd seen that day. Not surprisingly, in this one I saw teeth dripping with blood and enraged chops.

In the morning I woke up as exhausted as when I'd gone to bed the night before but was even more motivated to continue my investigation, even if it jeopardized my energy and health.

I went down for breakfast. Last night I hadn't eaten, and I was famished.

When I went in, as it was late, there were only a few people still having breakfast: coffee or tea, Danish pastries, scrambled eggs and bacon, pancakes, or other delicious things.

I could see the back of a brown-haired man, a fork in his hand, a cup of coffee in the other, reading the local paper.

I went up to the buffet and sat down at a table on the other side of the room. I like to take my time for breakfast, and don't vouch for anything if I haven't had my first cup of coffee.

But my good mood was going to be unusually vexed when, as I looked up from my coffee, I saw the man looking right at me.

What the heck, I thought, frowning.

And it got worse when he gave me an ambiguous smile.

And I seethed when he raised his cup of coffee, as if he was toasting me.

I finally got up when he whispered, "Hello Karen," which I was able to lipread.

This time he would have to explain what he was doing.

I walked with determination up to him. He looked up.

"You're not getting tired of following me all over?" I said. "What do you want? Who are you? You think you know me?"

"Sort of," he responded with a soft voice that I couldn't have imagined in the throat of a bearded man like him.

Idiotic biased thought. Why must a man with a black beard have a deep voice?

"I don't think so," I replied. "I usually have a good memory of faces, and I don't recognize yours at all. Or perhaps we were students together and you've changed a lot?"

"As much as I would have liked to go to college with you Mrs. Blackstone, I don't really think we're from the same generation, no offense intended..."

True, the man must not have been over twenty-five. A baby next to me!

"How do you know my name?"

"You're not inconspicuous here in town. People talk, believe me. But please, sit down," he said, pointing at the chair across from him.

As I wanted to get to the bottom of this, I did sit down.

"I don't like being followed or observed, Mr..."

"Is that the impression I'm giving you?"

"Everywhere I go you seem to turn up. And look at me. You know I'm not someone that you can seduce just by looking at me. I could be your mother..."

But when I said that, I had a terrible pain in my chest, as if I'd been stabbed. What if?

No! It wasn't possible... and I ousted this thought from my mind.

"Calm down, I'm not trying to seduce you. I'm a faithful man."

"So what do you want then? You still haven't given me your name. The least of things, as you know who I am, would be to introduce yourself. Mr.?"

Right then his phone, next to the paper he was reading before I came, began to ring.

"Please excuse me," he said.

He picked up the phone and went out of the dining room so he wouldn't disturb those still having breakfast. He left, I was all alone, but I could hear him murmuring.

"Oh. Finally Cynthia! I was waiting for your call. I arrived safely, yes. When are you coming?"

Then he disappeared into the hall of the inn.

Did I hear this correctly? Cynthia?

Okay Karen. Don't start inventing stories just because you heard a simple first name, one that's common too. John Doe was a person too.

I waited for a few minutes at my breakfast table, hoping he'd be coming back, the least of things in my opinion. Like do you cut off a conversation between two people to pick up your phone and then not come back? But that was what happened. I left, furious. I didn't even finish my coffee and went right up to the front desk where the inn owner was. I smiled and asked her a question.

"Excuse me Mrs. Mayweather, I don't know if you saw a man with a brown beard talking on his phone here a couple of minutes ago. We were talking in the restaurant."

"I did, Mrs. Blackstone. He's a client here. Why?"

"Could you give me his name please?"

"Mrs. Blackstone, this is a bit delicate. We're not supposed to give out information like that. Our inn is known for its discretion."

"I'm sure it is, which is why I'm so at ease here. It's a real jewel in a beautiful showcase. But, as you know, I'm a journalist and I'm investigating the disappearance of Veronika Lake, and I'm not far from thinking that terrible things happened here in Greenville, that I still must clarify. I need these elements. Please know also that I'm working hand-in-hand with Lieutenant Shana Davidoff, from the police department, someone I'm sure you also know. If needed, I could ask her to phone you to get this information, something that's not even a secret. But I think we'd both gain time if you gave it to me directly."

Mrs. Mayweather seemed to be weighing the pros and the cons.

"Okay, but please, be discrete," she said, opening the reservations page on her computer. "This man is Mr. Lake."

I gasped, as if sucker punched in the plexus.

"Lake?" I repeated stupidly.

"Absolutely. It's Mr. Brandon Lake...."

CHAPTER 57
An inverted double Z

WAS I going to remain petrified in front of the Greenville Inn's front desk, my jaw hanging open, in front of Mrs. Mayweather? That was what I was wondering when I finally closed my mouth, speechless after this improbable revelation.

"Are you sure? Mr. Brandon Lake?"

Just yesterday I was kneeling at his grave in the Miami Cemetery.

"Are you sure?" I repeated.

"Yes, I am, Mrs. Blackstone. That's the name he gave me. Now, that's all I can tell you."

"Thank you very much."

I stood in the hall, hoping the man saying he was Brandon Lake would come back. I could understand that someone who wants to remain incognito would say they're John Doe or Jane Doe. But a guy vacationing in Greenville saying he's Brandon Lake, that was hard to comprehend. And something that would slash the probability of this being a fluke.

Or was that person lying about his identity with a predefined goal? So I'd pay attention to him?

A message to be conveyed to the Greenville community?

Or directly to me who is investigating Veronika Lake's disappearance, why Mason and Janet Lake left for Florida so quickly, as well as the death, twenty-two years earlier, of Brandon Lake?

I went upstairs to my room to get my phone and laptop, ready to spend the whole day in the lobby of the inn, so I couldn't miss this guy with his well-known name next time he came in.

Before going down, I phoned Barry Fenton to inform him of this incredible surprise and what happened when I was down in Florida. Then he told me that Lieutenant Davidoff had petitioned the public prosecutor of Main to open an investigation on the images in the USB flash drive that Liam Kissinger had found in the Lake family's former home in West Cove Point.

I quickly brushed my teeth and went back to the lobby, sat down in a comfortable armchair behind an oval table that had an embroidered tablecloth on it and opened my laptop. I'd be able to see everyone, whether they were coming or going. The *pseudo-Brandon Lake* couldn't escape.

I wrote an email to my dear boss. I love calling her *dear boss*. She calls me *hun*, or *sweetie*. I gave her all the juicy details of everything I'd just found out, my hypotheses, and who knows what else. I also attached my expenses: two plane tickets, the hotel bill, a couple of meals. When you think of it, I'm pretty cheap for my dear boss! Without forgetting that if I can finish my investigation with proof and certitudes, *True Crime Mysteries* will make a bundle, covering my expenses a hundredfold. Myrtille Fairbanks was a good financial manager, and I knew that she let me do what I wanted because she trusted me.

Just like a hound trailing a fox, I worked while keeping an eye out on clients coming and going, whether they were leaving and opening their umbrellas or coming back and shaking off the rain from their raincoats, soaked by this incessant rain. But I kept my eyes open sitting in this nice warm lobby.

But the so-called Mr. Lake didn't show. He'd been tailing me nearly ever since I came, and since we finally talked, no one.

While I was waiting, I decided to open the photos on the USB flash drive once again, as I'd copied them on my laptop.

It's always so unsettling to see half-naked teens being subjected to the forbidden pleasures of grown men. I don't know why I wanted to look at them one more time, perhaps an intuition. I often listened to my intuitions and gut feelings, and since I'd left Miami, this *déjà-vu* feeling had never left me. I was sure I'd seen some tiny detail, a little something or other, a nothing that was something.

Then suddenly a flash blinded my brain.

I was afraid to believe what I saw. I didn't dare believe that association of ideas that forced itself on me.

It was too horrible to be true... and yet!

That scar on the main holding the ponytail of one of the little girls.

That inverted double Z seemed too unique to be on two different people.

A scar I'd recently seen. That was what gave me that *déjà-vu* impression as I'd seen that detail for the first time when I saw the photos with Shana and Barry in his veranda.

And now I knew where I'd seen it for the second time!

Good Lord, no...

That inverted double Z, that unique scar, one I'd clearly seen yesterday on Mason Lake's hand when I was leaving...

CHAPTER 58
Simon says

THAT COULDN'T BE TRUE.

My brain was refusing to admit what my reason was telling it.

Mason Lake was a pervert? A bastard who was capable of abusing barely pubescent teens... and with total impunity?

No! This crime – because it was a crime – could not remain unpunished.

I seethed internally thinking about the multiple facets of the Lake family, a family that seemed to be perfect, with a clean and healthy facade, a very well-to-do family, but when you scratched the surface, a terribly abject one.

I would like to identify the other people on the photos that I kept on staring at on my laptop. I tried to seize the most minute details, find out who was hiding, who it was hiding behind the masks. Who were these men – yes, men because there were several of them – with Mason Lake in his private parties?

And who were these young teens, behind their hair masking their faces? Who were the preys of these men avid of fresh, pure, white, immaculate... virgin... flesh?

Once again, I was having trouble believing what my mind was thinking. I remember what I'd thought when we first opened the photo file: that these girls must have been Veronika's age when they were taken. Could Mason Lake have included his daughter in such disgusting acts?

I suddenly saw a detail that I'd missed up till now. A detail, not of the people, but of the decor. Yes, I couldn't no longer doubt it. I'd clearly recognized the pattern on the rug below the knees of the young girl kneeling between the thighs of one of the men.

The rug on the floor between the leather armchairs in the living room of the Sugar Island villa...

The same likeness between the armchair in the photo and the one where I spent the night in Sugar. Just to think that I'd sat on it made me sick.

I looked at the photos once again, this time scrutinizing the decor. Now a myriad of insignificant little details, at first sight, confirmed my thoughts. A large ashtray that I saw in a corner, the end of the coffee table, the fireplace in the background.

All of this was evidence: the private parties with the teenaged girls took place on Sugar Island.

What better place for such criminal activities?

A villa, on a private island, in the middle of a lake surrounded by forests.

They wouldn't have run any risk of being seen by too curious neighbors. A perfect hideout for the most evil and vicious acts.

Now I tried to imagine how these disgusting parties were organized. I could see the boat leaving from Greenville, the whole Clique arriving on the island. Would the girls have sensed what would happen to them? Had they dangled a dream weekend on the island in front of them, where they'd be able to swim in isolated creeks and bask on sandy beaches or in the huge swimming pool behind the villa? Thought they'd be able to have a blast together, with no parents, no curfews? Told they'd have fantastic barbecues, be able to dance, eat potato chips, drink as much soda as they wanted to, cook s'mores over the fire outside? A dream for teens!

Except, when the sun had set, the atmosphere changed. Playtime was over little girls…

Or perhaps: girls, we're going to start to play. But adult games, okay with you? We're even going to wear costumes, like a masked ball, if that's alright. We'll put on some music too.

Plus, as it's hot, we'll just wear our swimsuits, or if your suit isn't dry, you can change and just put on your panties. It's so hot out, you don't need anything else.

And girls, if you want, we'll even make you a little cocktail, you'll feel like fireworks are exploding in your heads. And if you're not afraid, you can even take a couple of puffs from our special cigarettes, get nice and relaxed. You'll fly above the clouds, see pink elephants.

Then we can start our games. We can play "Chicken," or "Truth or Dare," or even "Simon Says." They're all lots of fun.

"Simon says: kneel down."

"Simon says: close your eyes and hold out your hand."

"Simon says: guess what I put in your hand with your eyes closed. Don't open them, or else it's cheating."

"I didn't say: Simon says? Okay, sorry about that."

"So Simon says: touch my weenie."

"Simon says: open your mouth, keep your eyes closed and lower your head. Yes, like that…"

Disgusting!

Had things really happened like that or was it merely the fruit of my too vivid imagination fueled by those sordid pictures? I unfortunately didn't think I was far from reality.

But the question I still had was how could these teens have agreed to be a part of shameful games like that unless they were either drunk or drugged?

Or unless the adults, headed by Mason Lake, had threatened them? Forcing girls aged twelve or thirteen when you're a grown man, a seemingly respectable father doesn't seem to be impossible. Things like that unfortunately happen all the time. The power of authority!

Even more so when the authority is your own father?

I was probably extrapolating.

Where were their wives? Janet Lake and the wives of the other half-naked men? Were they unaware of what was going on? Did they approve of their husbands going off to a private island with thirteen-year-old girls?

I was going crazy thinking of things like that.

Without forgetting to remain on the lookout for clients coming and going, I called Barry Fenton again to tell him about what I suspected. The former Greenville Chief of Police was just as disgusted as I was. Even more so when he thought about everything that could have taken place in Sugar Island in 2012.

"I can't believe that's possible," he confessed, " but knowing the complicity there was between Patterson - like what happened when Liam Kissinger deposited the flash drive - and the Lake family, I'm starting to wonder if Bob wasn't covering his friend."

"Which would explain the feeling of impunity Mason Lake had, knowing that the Chief of Police was protecting him."

"Exactly. The whole group of them: the Lakes, Pattersons, and Martineau… all of them were in this up to their necks," said Barry angrily.

"You think Patterson and Martineau knew?"

"Partially, at least. They knew and they turned a blind eye."

"They turned a blind eye?" I asked. "Or they were a part of this...?"

...this disease eating away at you...

I feel dirty and dishonored.

My body was no longer mine, it belonged to everyone.

I'll never forget this episode of my life, so horrible, so unacceptable.

I know I'll be scarred for life. As if a red-hot iron had branded my skin, in the most intimate parts of myself. That from that instant, because of those acts, I'll never be the same again, I'll never allow myself to be touched again in that way.

I'll never see men in the same way. Now they all disgust me.

I'm aware that I'll never be able to be at ease with a man. I'll constantly be ashamed of my body, of my nudeness.

Making love will never be possible because now I understand that love doesn't exist.

That night there were three of them.
    My three torturers.
    Three guilty men.

They forced me, intimidated me, threatened me. I couldn't do anything.
    They hurt me so much that night.
    The worst evil, the disease eating away at you night and day, the one that causes that bitter feeling, that will never leave you: hating your own life.

There were three of them.
    Three guilty men.
    Sooner or later, they're going to have to pay.

CHAPTER 59
Judged and punished

THE DAY WENT BY, but the so-called Brandon didn't show. I glanced at the clock on my laptop, thinking I hadn't even had lunch at noon. I walked up to the front desk to talk to Mrs. Mayweather.

"Excuse me. I'm sorry to bother you again, but did you see Mr. Lake again today?"

"Of course. He checked out this morning, a bit after we spoke. He's gone now."

Shoot, he must have snuck away while I was getting my laptop from my room. Quite an elusive guy! He started out by following me, then fleeing from me, and as soon as we got acquainted, he slipped away again. What could he be up to now?

"Did he tell you where he was going?"

"Sorry, Mrs. Blackstone, but I didn't ask. That would have been impolite."

"True," I said, with a strained smile.

Smile or not, I was darn annoyed. How could I

have been so dumb? I should have tailed that Brandon. Stuck like glue on him and found out what he wanted and what he was doing in Greenville.

Unless he left because of me?

Just a couple minutes after that, Lieutenant Shana Davidoff called.

"Karen? Would you be willing to testify about that inverted double Z scar that made you think that Mason Lake was one of the men in the photos on the USB flash drive?"

"In a heartbeat. Why?"

"I'm planning on contacting the Miami police department and based on what you saw and the incriminating evidence we have in our possession, ask for the Lakes to be called in by my counterparts there. We have to step on it."

"Shana, I'm ready to go. What should I do?"

"You have to come down to the police station so I can officially hear your testimonial and report it."

Fifteen minutes later I was in Lieutenant Davidoff's office. I'd come to Greenville a week ago as a journalist investigating a cold case dating back to 2017, and I was now a witness in another affair that took place in 2012. But both concerned the Lake family.

Were these two affairs linked? Did Veronika disappear because of what took place in 2012?

A five-year gap, but in the same place: in the villa on Sugar Island.

And I hadn't even mentioned what happened in 2000.

This followed the examples of antique drama: unity of place, unity of time. And in this case: unity of place, unity of characters.

If I solved the 2012 case, would I find out what happened in 2017? At least that was what Lieutenant Davidoff and I certainly hoped. While I was leaving her office, we stumbled upon Chief Patterson. He looked us up and down.

"So Miss Blackstone, you're still hanging around here? Now what?"

I glanced at Shana, not knowing what to answer. She nodded, suggesting that I let her answer for me.

"I just registered Karen Blackstone's testimony about a suspicion she had about a USB flash drive that you've illegally kept in the safe in your office, Chief."

The sentence the lieutenant pronounced was as if Mike Tyson had socked Patterson right in his gut. It took him a while to answer.

"I don't know what you're talking about, Lieutenant. Just allegations."

Shana took the object in question out of her pocket.

"With all due respect, Chief, this is not an allegation, but rather a tangible and real piece of evidence. You probably should have gotten rid of it ten years ago."

The Chief got closer to his lieutenant, who didn't budge an inch.

"As for you, Lieutenant Davidoff, you'd better give me that flash drive right now," he ordered.

"No way. It's in the file I just opened."

"You obtained it illegally, Lieutenant. It's inadmissible."

"And you dissimulated it just as illegally ten years ago. Call it a tie!" said Shana, who I thought was very brave to stand up to her boss like that.

"Lieutenant Davidoff, you have to obey my orders," continued Patterson. "Give me that flash drive and that file immediately. As head of the department, I must validate it... or invalidate it."

"Too late for that Chief. I already petitioned the public prosecutor, and he ordered the investigation to be reopened. The train is on the tracks, you can't stop it now. What's in this file is too repugnant not to be judged and punished. And too bad for those you've been protecting. It was my duty to..."

"I'm the one who decides what your duty is or isn't," Patterson shouted. "I'm the boss here."

"Probably not for long though," said a voice at the door.

We all turned around.

At the doorstep of the police station stood the former head of police, Barry Fenton.

CHAPTER 60
Ninety-eight point six degrees of hemoglobin

"WHAT THE FUCK are you doing here, Fenton?" Bob Patterson said. "You don't understand who's the boss here now?"

Barry walked up to the man who'd taken his job ten years ago. The former policeman was still powerfully confident. The two men, nearly nose to nose, glared at each other. Barry warned him.

"Yeah, but it's not going to last long, Bob. I think an early retirement is knocking at your door. And it's time to tell the truth. Plus a little birdie told me that this truth is going to splatter on you. You and your little friends."

Patterson leaned over his predecessor with wrath he was trying to contain in his eyes. I could see him making a fist, ready to jump on Barry. I could also see that Shana was ready for this eventuality.

"Barry, I'd like to advise you to zip it now and get the hell out of my police station. If not, I'll throw you in jail for insulting a public official. You know what that's worth, right?" he added, putting his hand on Fenton's chest, and pushing him away firmly.

"Barry, it's okay," said Shana Davidoff, trying to calm them down. "We'll deal with this legally."

All four of us looked at each other. Barry and I finally took the wise decision to leave so the situation wouldn't degenerate any further, though we were afraid to leave Shana alone with Patterson in the police station. Luckily at that moment, two patrolmen walked in.

Patterson went into his office, slamming the door so hard we could hear it echoing in the road.

Things were calm in Greenville, at least in the police station.

Only for a short while though. We didn't know it then, but dramatic events would be taking place in the upcoming hours.

Night had fallen over Greenville.

Shana Davidoff called Barry and me that evening.

I was already in bed when Barry called me. One of his former colleagues, who had front row seats in the theater where the drama had unfolded, had informed him.

An hour earlier, an inhabitant who lived not too far from the town office had called the cops, saying that he had heard gunshots not too far from where he lived.

Though there were a lot of hunters in Greenville, gunshots were generally heard in the surrounding forests, not in the calm streets of the town.

Night had fallen a couple of hours ago when the noise disturbed this person who was dining on a four-cheese pizza he'd thawed while watching his favorite series on Netflix. As he was watching a detective series, at first, he thought that the noise had come from the TV, but quickly realized that something abnormal had taken place in town.

He'd walked up to the window and pushed the curtain away to look at the street, which was calm, lit only by streetlights with their orangish lights. The road was silent, as if Mike Balducci - his name - had simply imagined these gunshots. The wind whistled through the last leaves of the trees along the road, and it was drizzling in the deserted street. No one on the sidewalks : at this time of the night the inhabitants of Greenville preferred the warmth of their living rooms rather than the cold outside.

Dead calm in Greenville, Balducci had thought.

Up until he saw a dark shape on the sidewalk in front of the town hall.

An inert shape that he couldn't really make out in the nocturnal drizzle. *A garbage can that blew over?* he'd thought. Though he'd wanted to plop back into the couch, something had made him get up to see what it was. Balducci grabbed his raincoat, buttoning it up quickly on his front porch. Then he crossed the road, going towards that dark shape.

The closer he got, the more he was sure of what he was looking at.

When he leaned down, he saw a man in an ocean of blood spreading below him, like a smoking magma in the freezing rain.

Ninety-eight point six degrees of hemoglobin compared to thirty-five degrees outside...

When he saw the face — of the dead man? — Balducci recognized him immediately.

Greenville would be confronted with a new tragedy, five years after Veronika Lake's disappearance.

CHAPTER 61
Like wildfire

THE NEWS HAD SPREAD like wildfire in Greenville. In less than two hours, the entire town seemed to know what had happened.

When Barry Fenton informed me that Victor Martineau had been killed by three bullets in his chest upon leaving the town hall, I thought he must be joking. But then when he gave me the details, it was clear: the Mayor of Greenville had just been murdered.

Mike Balducci, the neighbor across the street, was the first person to call it in. When Lieutenant Davidoff and Chief Patterson arrived, Scott Stevens, the head of the fire department and his team had already done everything possible to try to save him, but in vain.

Three bullets in his chest, one that hit his heart and another in his lungs, there was nothing they could have done.

I joined Barry and Lieutenant Davidoff in the street where we sheltered ourselves under an awning of a fishing equipment shop, across from the town hall. The firemen were removing Victor Martineau's corpse, and his wife was sobbing. Shana told us what she'd learned from the first people she'd spoken to.

"Jocelyne Chastain, the administrative assistant, told me that Martineau had said he'd be leaving a bit later, when she looked into his office. She added that he often stayed late to work on his files, because he liked working in peace and quiet during the evening."

"She didn't notice anything special or unusual when she left?" Barry asked, with the reflexes of a former cop.

"She did. She said she'd heard Martineau shouting on the phone just a few minutes before she left. She said she thought he was talking to Chief Patterson and that the mayor had mentioned the name *Bob* a couple of times and that the two people seemed to know each other well. And when I asked her if the two men had talked about a flash drive, she said yes."

"Why am I not astonished?" said Barry, rubbing his chin. "Do we know when he left?"

"Balducci heard the gunshots – Shana opened her notebook using the light from the streetlight – at nine twelve. So I imagine that was when he left. We called Jocelyne, who unlocked the doors for us. We saw that Martineau had had dinner alone in his office: microwaved Chinese noodles. The box was still on his desk, next to the phone and a can of Budweiser."

"Find any shell casings?"

"Nope."

"So the murderer took his precautions then. Looking at the impacts Martineau received, the shots must have come from this side," Barry said, turning around to point at the buildings right behind us.

We turned around too, looking at the buildings and windows above them. The fishing equipment shop we were standing in front of was next to an insurance building on one side and a real estate agency on the other. A bit farther down there was a taco takeaway joint and a house. On the first floors of the stores and buildings it must have been either apartments rented out or the offices of the shops. Everything was closed at this time of night. Shana told us that auditions would be held the next morning. Barry had another question.

"Shana, were you able to talk to anyone else? What came of it?"

The lieutenant raised her hand and gestured out to the road with a circular motion of her arm.

"With this weather and at this time of night, no one was out in the street, as you can well imagine."

"No one saw anything, huh?"

"Nothing unusual."

"As if the murderer had planned this... the right place and the right time."

"We've been thinking of the murderer as a man, but we don't know," I added. "And he or she must have known that Martineau was working late tonight."

"Who could have known that?" wondered Barry.

"With what we now know, plus what we think, I'd say that a small handful of people knew that Victor

Martineau would be working after hours tonight. Jocelyne, obviously. Probably his wife, he must have told her to eat without him. And why not the person on the phone when Jocelyne was leaving..."

"Bob Patterson," rasped Barry. "Who was he talking to about a USB flash drive? Some incriminating evidence on an investigation that had just been reopened today. Could that have been a motive for killing Martineau?"

Both Shana and I thought that Barry's question was merely a hidden affirmation.

"Wait a sec, Barry. You really think that the Chief of Police shot the mayor down to prevent him from speaking?"

"Knowing Patterson like I do, nothing can surprise me anymore. Shana, we're going to have to pay close attention to Martineau's autopsy. See if the bullets came from one of the guns the Greenville police use."

We both shook our heads.

Then I had a question. I looked at Shana.

"Who's leading this investigation?"

"Chief Patterson," the lieutenant sighed, gritting her teeth.

CHAPTER 62
By way of a signature

TRUE CRIME MYSTERIES,
 November 4, 2022.

The tip of the iceberg.

YESTERDAY, in the peaceful little town of Greenville, Maine, tragedy once again struck its population. Victor Martineau, the town's mayor, was assassinated with three gunshot wounds in the chest upon leaving the town hall. He died before the rescue squad could do anything.

This tragedy is part of an on-going investigation, and as of date, no suspect has yet been formally identified by the local authorities.

But for those of you who read this magazine, I'm going to give what I believe is a plausible explanation.

In my opinion, this new tragedy is merely the tip of the iceberg, as the old saying goes.

The Lake family iceberg.

And as you know, the tip or visible part of an iceberg represents only 10%, the other 90% of its mass is under water, and cannot be seen.

Let's go back in time.

2022: Victor Martineau, the Mayor of Greenville and close friend of the Lake family, is assassinated.

2018: Disgusting photos of young girls in the company of mature men, including Mason Lake, the father, are discovered.

2017: The mysterious disappearance of Veronika, the Lake family's daughter, who would never been seen again.

2000: Accidental death in Miami of Brandon, Mason and Janet Lake's son.

As you can easily see, these four

tragic events converge towards the same point: the Lake family.

It's easy to jump to hasty conclusions... the Lakes are guilty. Or were the Lakes victims?

But that would be omitting other commonalities of this sordid spider's web.

For example, the omnipresent shadow of Robert Patterson, the Greenville Chief of Police and good friend of both the Lakes and Martineau.

Let's look at that closely:

2022: Right before he was assassinated, Martineau seemed to be having a heated phone conversation with Patterson about some compromising photos taken in 2012. Yet, the same Patterson is heading the investigation.

2018: Patterson steals the photos and buries the investigation.

2017: In Greenville, Patterson heads the investigation about Veronika's disappearance.

2000: We just learned, by studying Chief Patterson's career, that he was working in Coconut Grove, Miami, as a patrolman. Which is where the Lakes now live and where Brandon died.

I INVITE my readers to draw their own conclusions from this info, which is not a supposition, but rather facts!

THERE'S STILL MORE THOUGH. I'm a journalist and I like to get to the very bottom of things.

The most incredible mystery is the one I personally was confronted with in the past few days.

LET me tell you about it.

Readers, please imagine how worried I was to know I was being spied on and followed by an unknown person who came to Greenville three days ago.

Readers, please imagine how scared I was when I learned that this man was staying in the same hotel I was.

Readers, please try to imagine how amazed I was when, just a couple of hours ago, I learned that this unknown person checked in to the hotel giving the name of Brandon Lake.

Readers, please be as astonished as I am when I learned that this person can no longer be found in Greenville.

What do you think of that, my dear readers?

An unknown person appears on the premises of a series of tragedies that impacted the Lake family and has the same name as their son who died in 2000!

I don't write about anything that's supernatural or fantastic, but believe me, in this case, what logic and rational thinking could apply to these facts?

That's what your dear investigator will try to find as quickly as possible!

I CLOSED my laptop after having sent this article to Myrtille Fairbanks.

I'd written it without thinking, rapidly, driven by the necessity of summarizing the recent events, from a different point of view. Sometimes, when you write things down, and explain them from a simple point of view, it allows you to take a more measured journalistic look at the events.

That's what I decided to do at that precise moment, inspired by its title.

Because I honestly had to admit that it was not a title I'd invented, but one that was totally in line with the Lake affairs. Yes, in the plural.

And to be totally transparent, the title was given to me on a plate, as if it had fallen from heaven.

I was coming back from town after the tragic episode of the mayor's assassination and when I went into the inn, the night duty officer called me.

"Mrs. Blackstone, there's an envelope for you."

Quite astonished, I took the envelope and rushed upstairs to open it.

All that was written was my name, Karen Blackstone, in capital letters. It was closed by a band, the kind that you had to lick.

I opened it.

Inside, just a sheet from a notebook folded in half, where someone had written:

Martineau is just the tip of the iceberg. Dive in Karen, you'll find what's lurking underground...

Then, two simple initials by way of a signature: *B.L.*

CHAPTER 63
A thorn in their hearts

SO, the self-proclaimed Brandon Lake couldn't be that far, as he was able to drop off a letter for me at the Greenville Inn, while I was in town, where the mayor had just been assassinated.

He was still stalking me, but why? Was he playing getting even or was he being a whistle-blower? Or someone giving you a lesson?

Whatever, he seemed to know a lot of things, behind his improbable Brandon Lake identity.

If he really was the guy he was saying he was, I was missing something here. And as I didn't believe in what's irrational, there had to be a more cartesian explanation.

As he couldn't be the Brandon Lake who died in 2000 in Miami, who was he?

These unanswered yet key questions kept running through my brain.

Anyway, in the letter he sent me, he invited me to

dive in so I could discover the hidden part of the Lake iceberg. And he paradoxically suggested that I swim in the troubled waters to see things clearer.

Got it. I was going to listen to the advice this unknown person gave me, and dive into and swim in the Lake backwaters. Firstly, I'd follow this intuition that I had during my dream and nightmare-filled night. The faces of the members of the Lake family were dancing in a sinister parade. Mason, looking creepy, showing his inverted double Z scar on his hand; Janet with her head down, eyes saying she was *the wife of*; Brandon with his bloody and mauled throat; Veronika with her troubled face floating below the surface of the green waters of Lake Moosehead. Mixed in with them were the ruddy face of Martineau and the bossy and cunning face of Chief Patterson. Dancing in the background were three adolescent girls just wearing their panties, their faces hidden by their long hair. That was when I had that intuition, and I woke up as day was breaking.

Driven by a vague idea, I sent off a message to Tom Malone, Veronika's ex-boyfriend, hoping he'd be able to satisfy my curiosity.

Tom, sorry to bother you again. I've got another request. You were Veronika's steady for over two years, I'm sure you must have some photos of her, either paper ones or digital ones. Could you send me a few where she's wearing a swimsuit? Photos taken of her back, if you have any. That would be perfect. Thanks in advance. Karen Blackstone.

I JUST HAD time to take a shower and have breakfast downstairs where I'd seen *B.L.* yesterday, and my phone began to vibrate, informing me I'd received a series of MMSs from Tom Malone. I opened the jpeg files and read the lumberjack's note.

THIS IS what I found in my Google Photos file. You're right Karen, she was so cute when she was wearing a bikini that I couldn't help but take pictures of her, from the back. I've got other photos where she's wearing even less, but I didn't dare send them to you, I didn't want to shock you. Anyway this is all I've got, hope they'll be useful to you, and you'll find what you're looking for. You hear about Martineau? Tom.

I CALLED Tom Malone before opening the files.

"Thanks for the photos, Tom. I'm sure they'll be useful. I sort of had a front row seat, if I can put it like that, for the mayor. Speaking of which, do you have any idea who could have shot him in the chest three times?"

"Lots of people, here in Greenville and out of town too," scoffed Tom. "Just like Patterson and the whole group of beautiful people who were members of the

Rotary and stuff like that, those movers and shakers in town, those people have the gift of attracting trouble."

"Enough trouble to justify something like that?"

"Probably," Malone replied. "You know Karen, even though I went out with Veronika, and we hung around Becky and Dorothy, Martineau and Patterson's daughters, who I did like, I can't say the same thing about their genitors. I couldn't stand them. I couldn't tell you why though. Perhaps because they always seemed so superior or their predator type eyes. Eyes where you could see there was manipulation, contempt, mysteries. Eyes that told you: 'You open it kid, I'm gonna take care of you, and make you shut up.'"

"And Tom, did you have any reasons to open it and attract trouble? Do you have things to say about them?"

Silence.

"Me, no. Veronika, undoubtedly. But she's not here to testify. Her disappearance was, I think I understand now, relief for those guys."

"You mean that Veronika disturbed them? That she would have unveiled unholy things had she not disappeared?"

"One night, it was just the two of us, we were hanging out on Lily Bay beach, looking at the waves, and for the very first time she told me some secrets. Well, let me imagine things. And now with hindsight, I understand better what she wanted to say without putting it in words."

I remained silent so I wouldn't interrupt Tom Malone's confession.

"We talked about our parents. Mine were simple workers and employees, I loved them for their simplicity. Hers, you know them. She didn't love them, quite the opposite. She told me they could keep all their money; she didn't want a dime. That she would have preferred 'more love and less money.' Those are the very words she used. Little by little she began to cry. Then she told me some more confusing things, between two sobs. She told me that as long as she could remember, she'd never seen any love in their eyes. More like reproaches, as if they regretted she'd been born. That they never said, 'I love you.' That they lived with a ghost, like ghosts."

"The ghost of Brandon, their eldest son?" I asked.

"I think so. I think it was a permanent pain for them, like a thorn in their hearts, that they couldn't pull out. Mason and Janet Lake lived with the souvenir of Brandon. Veronika told me that night that it was as if he'd never died. Remember his room in Sugar Island, Karen?"

"Of course. And Winnie, the teddy bear you threw into the pool..."

"Well, she told me they had a similar room in Miami, as if he'd be coming back any day now."

I couldn't help thinking of this *B.L.*, who came back from the dead in Greenville.

"Tom? What if I told you that recently a guy spoke

to me, and he told me he was Brandon Lake? Would you think I was crazy?"

"What the fuck? I'd say that nothing would astonish me about the Lake family now. And what if I told you that Veronika said that night where she was telling me about when she was little, that her parents often dropped her off at a baby-sitter in Miami. That night on the lakefront, she told me she thought they didn't love her and that they were going to visit another child, an orphan that they loved more than her, and that they wanted to adopt him."

"A *substitute Brandon Lake...*" I said to myself, not daring to believe what my mouth just expressed.

CHAPTER 64
A mortal vortex

THE DEGREE of insanity the Lake family had appeared to me in a split second. The confirmation of their insanity, but also of their infamy.

All it took was a couple of pictures to confirm the suspicions I'd had for the past couple of days.

I perhaps had the key here, right below my eyes, the one that would allow me to understand the reason why Veronika Lake disappeared, what happened: suicide, assassination, running away, or kidnapping.

Right after I'd hung up with Tom Malone, I began to examine the photos he'd sent me, those where Veronika was wearing a bikini.

The young lady, because she was a young lady at the age of sixteen or seventeen on digital photos, was truly beautiful, without though looking like a fashion model. Her tiny breasts didn't even fill the top of her bikini, her buttocks didn't bulge from the bottom of her bikini like they did on most girls of her age, but a moving femininity emanated from her. I was sure she had a body that pleased the boys.

Or at least pleased Tom Malone, which was sufficient for them. On some of the pictures she seemed happy, at least on the photo. But what does a smile in a photo mean? A forced tic? The need to seem happy, happy at that moment? Once the photo was taken, the smile would fade away, the souvenirs would resurface, melancholy would return...

I tried not to get distracted when looking at these images of a young and fragile lady, who, and I was sure of this, had found herself trapped in an intelligently spun spiderweb, one that her parents and their friends had created. Those surrounding her drew her into an infernal whirlpool, like a hole in the waters in the middle of the lake - a mortal vortex - that could sink a fisherman's boat.

I studied the photos.

Then the evidence jumped out at me.

Terrifying, incredible, yet so true, so terribly true.

As I was afraid of being mistaken, that my brain would be playing tricks on me, I refused to draw too hasty conclusions. Time and time again I flicked through the handful of photos where the detail of Veronika's body couldn't be due to a simple defect in the picture, some dust on the lens, digital noise generated by the years gone by. But I couldn't doubt it anymore, as it was repeated on several photos.

The same defect on her skin. It wasn't a tattoo, like I first believed. It wasn't clean, that wasn't that right color, ink would have been artificially straight. Plus, you generally have to be of age to get tats.

The only thing it could have been was a birthmark, in the small of the young lady's back, right above the elastic of her bikini bottom.

By definition, you have a birthmark when you are born, and it is inevitably in the same place all your life.

This mark follows you, year after year, it's permanent – everyone remembers Gorbachev –, just as personal and identifiable as your DNA.

Following the same logic, it's something that couldn't have disappeared when you were twelve or thirteen.

So if you happen upon a photo of that person at that age and you see the same birthmark in the same place, on the right side in the small of the back, just above the elastic of the white cotton panties, you could be one hundred percent sure that this little girl was no one else than Veronika Lake.

The teen who had just reached maturity, wearing panties on the same series of photos where half-naked men are in suggestive poses... Amongst them, a certain Mason Lake, with an inverted double Z scar identified with no possible errors...

Her own father!

CHAPTER 65
The worst of all sins

FROM A DISCOVERY TO A MYSTERY SOLVED, I felt like I had jumped from the frying pan into the fire.

Where would my investigation lead me? Towards which abysses in Lake Moosehead?

I thought I'd hit the bottom of horror, but aghast, I knew it wasn't true. How could I admit these photos?

A father who gives his daughter to the lust of other men... friends just for that evening or old friends? Isn't this father – let's not be afraid of words – a pimp?

Whether he received money for this or not, that still made him a sex offender.

Organizing private parties between men and barely mature girls, isn't that one of the worst sins?

I was revolted just thinking about acts like that, a terrible nausea while closing my laptop and turning off my phone. I no longer wanted to see. I no longer wanted to believe.

Yet the facts were there, undeniable, vivid with their filthy truth.

My brain refused to admit the unacceptable yet couldn't help but imagining the worst. Even worse than letting other men take advantage of his daughter, how could I even think that this father would abuse her himself, during these private parties he must have organized.

Incest would thus be added to pimping, the worst of all sins.

The poor kid! I pity you, Veronika. I can understand your unease, your unhappiness, your desire to end it all after having been exposed to hell on earth at such an early age!

Literally nauseous, I rushed to the bathroom, leaned over the toilet, and vomited my hatred of these men.

Though I rinsed my mouth several times, there was still an acrid taste on my tongue. I washed my face with cold water, then phoned Lieutenant Davidoff to inform her of what I'd found out. Just like me, Shana was terribly shocked. And just like me she wanted to get to the root of this.

"I'll give my colleagues in Miami this info right now," she immediately said. "Mr. and Mrs. Lake will no longer be witnesses, they'll be suspects now, believe me. Karen, send me those photos right away. Those motherfuckers!"

Shana hung up, in a hurry to speed things up, to make the Lakes pay for their crimes.

I called Tom Malone.

"Tom, I have to see you now. I'd like to talk to you in person. Could you come to the Stress-Free in half an hour?"

The lumberjack was sitting across from me, a glass of pale ale in front of him that he hadn't even sipped, except to remove the foam. I'd just told him what the photos proved to me, and he was as despondent as I was. Like he couldn't believe what I'd just said.

"Tommy, you didn't know?"

He shook his head, several times, just like a kid who'd been scolded. But poor guy, it wasn't his fault. I pitied him.

"There wasn't anything that set off any alarm bells? I don't know, a sentence, a couple of words Veronika said, an unfortunate Freudian slip...?"

Tom Malone kept on shaking his head incredulously. He drank a third of his glass of beer then suddenly began to speak.

"Now that I know this, I can begin to understand some of Veronika's attitudes and behavior. I'm not a psychologist, like I don't know if this can explain that, if there's a link between the cause and the effect, but there probably is. I don't know really how to tell you this, Karen, but at the same time, when I do, maybe you'll see the logic in it."

"Tommy, you can tell me anything."

"So here we go. I always felt that Veronika wasn't at ease with her body when we were intimate. See what I mean? We met each other, I mean we started going out when she'd just turned fifteen and I was sixteen. At the beginning, we just flirted like good teenagers, everything was great. But then, well, it's human nature, I started to want a bit more. You know how men are below the belt. After a couple of months together, just kissing wasn't enough. I begged her to let me pet her a little and I wanted her to do the same with me. I asked her to do things, you know what I mean. But each time, she refused, pushed me away, as if she was afraid of me, afraid that I'd hurt her. At first, I thought it was normal because she'd never done that with a boy. I imagine that for girls it's a really big deal, the first time. I'd already done it once, so I could wait, not rush her. But I was getting impatient. I gave her an ultimatum. We nearly broke up there, because a Platonic relationship didn't interest me, all that bullshit! Playing doctors and nurses is for kids. So she finally agreed, but it was very complicated. She never wanted me to see her nude. When I told you earlier that I had photos that would make you blush, that was to show off. The few times where she agreed to make love, I always had to turn all the lights off. Plus, I'm ashamed to say that, but I don't think she really liked that and when I turned the lights back on, after she'd got dressed, she always cried. I never knew why. But now I understand."

Tom put his head between his hands and looked down at his beer. I could feel he was ready to break down.

"Tom, it's not your fault," I tried to relieve him. "Veronika went through hell and back and was psychologically destroyed. It's extremely difficult to live your sexuality and love life normally after acts like this, believe me!"

I let Tom contemplate this for a moment. Then I thought of another detail that Alvin Brown, I think, told me.

"I'm really sorry to insist here and rub salt into your wound, but I have to tell you something else that I learned in my investigation. Can I?"

"No one can go to jail now..."

"So, I don't know if you found out at that time, but I was told that during your last night in Sugar Island, in the August of 2017, Veronika was seen... um... with someone other than you... I'm sorry Tom..."

Tom clenched his jaw, just like his fists, as if getting ready to break the table. But he controlled himself.

"It couldn't have been her... It can't be her!"

"By elimination, I think so. Would you have any idea who...?"

"Hell no. Not with one of the guys from the Clique, that's for sure. I can't believe it. Anyway, only Paul wasn't dating, and he had his eyes on Cynthia, not Veronika. Plus I can't see how she could have done that with someone else than me, knowing that with me it was already difficult. And if she did, damn it, it's even worse for me..."

Then I had a bizarre idea.

"Tom let's think outside the box. As making love to a man seemed to disgust Veronika - and that's easily understandable - could she, on that night, have been in bed with... a girl?"

CHAPTER 66
Not a big loss

"YOU GOTTA BE KIDDING!" said Tom Malone when he heard my latest supposition. "Veronika, a lesbian? Karen, you are completely crazy, sorry to have to tell you this. Already imagining my girlfriend cheating on me with another guy, I don't think that's possible at all, but thinking she could do that with another girl, no! No, no and no, she wouldn't have been capable of doing that."

"So who was in her bed that night in Sugar Island?"

"No one! You know what? I'm sure those are just stories. Bullshit that one of the guys from the Clique fed to you. Just to piss me off, to dirty Veronika and me. Just stuff someone invented!" said Malone angrily, this time pounding his fist on the table and finishing off his beer in one gulp.

Heads turned around, curious, looking at us. The pub owner, behind the bar, looked at Tom and with a hand movement, told him to calm down. No fights or loud language here was what he seemed to be saying.

"Why would someone have done that? Tarnish your reputation of what, and why?"

"I have no fucking idea, and all of this is seriously starting to bust my balls. You gotta stop stirring the muck. Let those who are gone rest in peace, that's it."

"Someone who dies only rests in peace when the truth is out in the open and justice has been rendered," I said philosophically. "Revealing this truth is what's been driving me ever since I arrived in Greenville, Tom. I just need a little help. I think we're almost there and that the events will tell the truth. Let's look at Martineau's assassination."

"Not a big loss."

I nodded, not too far from sharing Tom Malone's opinion about the mayor of Greenville.

"I would imagine a part of the population shares that feeling. The thing is though that this murder is linked to the Lake affairs, whether they go back to 2000 or 2017. I'm trying to understand how they all fit together. Tom, would you be able to recognize some of the people on the photos of the USB flash drive I talked to you about? Outside of Veronika and her father, who have already been identified."

I went and sat next to the lumberjack, opening my laptop so we could both look at the photos. Tom tensed up when he saw his girlfriend in degrading poses. I could feel he was about to cry, and I saw him squeeze his fists even harder when I pointed out Mason Lake on the photos.

"What about the two other girls?"

"Maybe," he murmured. "But we can never clearly make out their faces, because of their hair. I couldn't say for sure who they are."

"So, let's consider this problem from another angle," I proposed. "Let's start with a line of thought that doesn't seem so extravagant now. Let's admit that the three men in question are close friends. I think you'd have to be to participate in parties like this, don't you agree?"

"I think they'd all have to be perverts, filthy pigs!"

"We know one of them is Mason Lake, so who are the others?"

"Martineau? That would justify his assassination and the message you got about the iceberg..."

"And the third one?"

"Patterson? Who would have smothered lots of things about the Lake family... and maybe also about Martineau, as he was maybe going to squeal."

"So from there, can we extrapolate and suppose that their private parties took place with them, and their own daughters, that they proposed to the sexual appetites of the two other men? We're sure that one of them is Veronika, Mason's daughter."

"And the two others would be Becky... Martineau and Dorothy... Patterson..."

CHAPTER 67
Vomited the truth

THREE REVOLTING FATHERS; a trio of furious daughters.

"That could be them, Becky and Dorothy," confirmed Tom Malone, shaking his head unbelievingly and looking at the photos sadly before I closed the file.

We'd seen enough.

"So why was Veronika the only one to disappear?" he asked. "Why isn't *she* the only one missing?"

"She probably was more fragile, psychologically speaking. The others were more resilient, I'd imagine."

Dumbfounded by our logic, Tom and I remained silent for a few minutes while the waitress at the Stress-Free Moosehead Pub brought us a second round of drinks and a plate of tapas. I was exceptionally accompanying Tom by drinking a glass of beer too. Perhaps hoping to get a buzz to ease the weight in my brain and heart, held down by all those horrors we'd discovered in just a few days?

I'd just had a long sip of my cold beer when my phone rang. I could see it was Shana Davidoff calling.

"Karen? It's Lieutenant Davidoff. Are you sitting down?"

"I got so much lead in my britches that I can't even move," I replied ironically. "Go ahead."

"Hold on, 'cos I got news from Miami…"

"You found Veronika?"

"No, not really. But during Mason and Janet Lake's audition, my colleagues received a confession from them."

"What kind?"

"Mason couldn't deny that he'd organized private parties with young girls, including Veronika. But when we told him that Martineau had been assassinated, his scruples disappeared, and he squealed on the mayor."

"And the third one? Patterson?"

"He's still holding out. On the other hand, here's something really crazy that my colleagues found out when they spoke of the man pretending to be Brandon Lake, who's been dead and buried for twenty-two years. They wanted to know their version of this. They questioned them separately, that's something that always works. And that's when Janet literally broke down. She spit, or even vomited, the truth."

"Gimme a break Shana, tell me what she said! Come on!"

"That Brandon Lake didn't die in 2000 after

Brownie attacked him," said Lieutenant Davidoff, pausing to milk this info.

It sure worked though: I was speechless.

"Brandon Lake is alive? That's impossible, I saw his grave in Miami."

"An empty one. Or should I say an empty coffin. With money and influence, you get whatever you want here, including the worst ignominies. Mr. and Mrs. Lake were experts at that game."

"So, that unknown person spying on me in Greenville... it was really him?"

"It still has to be proved, and we could imagine that yes, but the rest of the story makes me doubt this. Let me explain. Janet Lake told us, and as opposed to what she said when you were at her place, that their son had survived the attack, and that the rescue squad got there in time to save him. But it was too late to avoid neurological and physical complications. Because of all the blood he'd lost, and the lack of oxygen, the two-year-old became paralyzed for life and severely mentally disabled. Like a vegetable. *Alive outside but dead inside*

are the terms Janet used. And they were ashamed to have a son in a state like this. Isn't that horrible to hear from a mother? So they decided to secretly place him in a specialized institution. They visited him occasionally, but never with Veronika."

"They always left her with a babysitter, and the little girl was sure that they were off adopting another baby in an orphanage," I completed.

"How did you know that?"

"Tom Malone told me that Veronika told her. It all comes together. But who can that guy be who says he's Brandon Lake?"

"I'd pay a lot to know," said Shana Davidoff.

Right then fate seemed to knock at my door, or rather at my phone. I had a message that someone else was calling.

"Someone else is calling. I'll call you back Shana."

It wasn't a call, but it was an MMS coming from a number I didn't have in my contact list.

When I opened it, my heart jumped.

The photo that the unknown sender addressed to me was like a thunderclap. I recognized the location immediately, without a shadow of a doubt, and couldn't wait to read the message…

CHAPTER 68
In rigor mortis

RIGHT IN THE middle of the photo, as if it were personalized, I immediately recognized it. Just a couple of days earlier I'd seen that rectangular hole filled with thick, nearly black, foul water, with dead leaves and algae on the bottom. Though it was a digital image, I could nearly smell that odor of putrefaction, of abandon, as if there was a decomposing body beneath the surface.

I was sure of it. The abandoned pool behind the Sugar Island villa was filling the largest part of the picture. When this first moment of surprise had passed, a second wave of questions washed over me when I saw what was in the foreground.

There were two sunbeds, seen from their backs, facing the blackish water.

Lying on these sunbeds there were two languid people, their faces turned towards the swimming pool, as if they were admiring the antique wavy glints in the pool. Languid? Lying down? Laid out?

You couldn't tell if these two people had dozed off, were sleeping or - my brain forced me to think of this - or were dead...

Did their neck's strange angle leaning on a shoulder reveal an absence of tonus or post-mortem rigor mortis?

I zoomed in on the photo to try to identify the two individuals, while wondering who could have taken this picture. A third person or did they simply use the photo retarder feature?

I kept on enlarging the photo until I had a closeup of the back of the heads of the two people in front of the pool. I thought I recognized a haircut on one of them.

Now, I was sure. That man, on the sunbed on the left of the photo, could be the unknown person who'd said he was Brandon Lake.

But who was the other person?

It must have been a girl as she had long hair and a narrow nape.

A man and a woman... A couple?

Brandon Lake and?

I was in such a hurry to open the multimedia content in my MMS that I hadn't even read the message accompanying it.

Its unexpectedness rendered me breathless.

. . .

"We're having a blast.
   Come and join us!
   The water's nice and warm.
   Come and dive in.
   The more the merrier."
   B.L & C.F.

I TURNED to Tom Malone who was still sitting next to me in the Stress-Free Pub.

"C.F. You thinking about the same person as I am?"

"I have no idea, and I don't know what game she's playing in this picture, but it could be Cynthia Favor," the lumberjack confirmed, joining my initial idea.

CHAPTER 69
Ghosts of the past

THE FIRST QUESTION I had when I put my phone down was to find out how the so-called Brandon Lake had obtained my personal phone number. But for the moment that wasn't a priority. All that mattered to me was to progress in my investigation and to solve all these mysteries that had punctuated these past weeks.

"COME AND JOIN US! The more the merrier."

WHO WAS THIS *US*? Brandon Lake seemed to be wanting to gather a maximum number of people impacted by the Lake affairs in a symbolic and same place: Sugar Island, in the villa where those terrible events had taken place. The sordid parties Mason Lake had organized with his mates and the little girls.

Veronika's disappearance. Without forgetting the other things, such as steles and souvenirs like Brandon's sanctuary, Brownie's grave, and so on.

Just like a Hercule Poirot who gathered Agatha Christie's characters together in a Victorian living room, the pseudo-Brandon Lake had chosen the Sugar Island villa to – at least that was what I imagined – to untangle the yarn from the mysterious ball of the family in the presence of witnesses.

Unless it was a trap...

That was what I was thinking about as the boat was heading off on Lake Moosehead's black waters after we'd left the Greenville Marina. This *us* thus included myself, who had had the privilege of receiving the message, Tom Malone, who had wanted to come, Lieutenant Shana Davidoff, whom I'd immediately informed as soon as I'd received the MMS, and Barry Fenton who had insisted on coming. And of course, Chief Patterson had obviously imposed himself as the group's leader, and two patrolmen from the police department and Clever, their dog, accompanied them. The skipper was one of Patterson's cops on the police boat, whose ultra powerful light on the bow split through the darkness, skimming the waves towards Sugar.

But I had to really insist on trying to convince Patterson to allow us come, as he was playing the Lone Ranger though I'd handed him the message on a silver platter. He was used to taking all the credit and keeping his secrets.

I was sitting in the back of the boat, trying to protect myself from the frigid wind caused by the speed of the outboard motor and the spray. My coat collar was right up to my nose and my hood was down to my eyebrows, with only my eyes looking out over the shadows surrounding us. I looked at Robert Patterson, on the bow, wondering what role he'd played in the past, and what role he was now playing and would continue to do so in the upcoming hours. Would the Chief of Police be both the judge and the jury?

We soon could make out the rugged coastline of Sugar Island, and its main pontoon. In a few minutes we'd be landing, impromptu guests of a macabre party organized by a mysterious phantom...

"You, the civilians, you stay back," Patterson ordered. "The lieutenant and I will go first. No one takes any risks, understand?"

Barry Fenton looked at me.

"What an asshole!"

"Let him have his moment," I whispered, "because I'm not so sure it's going to last."

The flashlights of the policemen shone down on the path leading to the villa, about three hundred feet back from the rugged coast. The wind was blowing through the branches of the trees, forming dancing shadows on the ground and an uneven and unsettling hedge.

The villa seemed to be sleeping; there was no light coming from the inside. There was merely a foggy halo coming from the back of the house, probably from the classy stakes around the pool, which was where we were to meet. Our hosts sure knew how to put on a good show, I thought to myself.

The police squad advanced carefully, their arms in front of them, convinced that the author of the message was the one who had assassinated Martineau the day before. The bullets though had not yet been analyzed.

Our group was silent, and we could all hear the grim wind blowing and the sound of our footsteps on the carpet of fallen leaves. My heart was pounding, tensed by the imminence of an outcome, whatever it would be. What was waiting for us in this house that had brutally become the center of the stage?

I suddenly gasped.

Music violently broke through the silence coming from the speakers behind the house, those that the protagonists in 2017 had described for me during that fateful night in August. The decor was now the same: the pool, loud music, darkness. Except the frigid weather had replaced the heatwave in August, that we couldn't see any stars in the sky as it was now covered with clouds and the water in the pool was no longer blue, but slimy and black.

The water and lake were in the lyrics of the song welcoming us.

*"We need water
And maybe somebody's daughter*

*Gimme good water, ooh, baby
What I need
Indian Lake is burnin'"*

I IMMEDIATELY RECOGNIZED the voice of Roger Daltrey from *The Who*, with his unique way of singing. On the other hand, I'd never heard the song before, probably a B side of a record that I'd never listened to, not really being a huge fan of the group. The lyrics were spot on though. Water, a lake on fire, someone's daughter... Congratulations to the producers, what a first act!

We carefully went around the villa and arrived onto the back patio, with the pool behind it, its diving board covered with brown moss and two sunbeds next to the pool. The two sunbeds that were in the photo they'd sent me.

But there was no one in them.

Empty.

The cops looked high and low, their guns in front of them, around the pool, the house, the surrounding woods, trying to cover as much ground as possible.

"What's this thing floating in the water?" asked one of the policemen to Patterson.

And now I could also make out an object floating on the surface of the pool amid the fallen leaves and blackish algae. But I immediately recognized it.

"*Fly, Winnie! And swim!*" Tommy had shouted,

throwing little Brandon Lake's teddy bear into the pool that evening.

I looked at Tom Malone, now an adult, and saw that he also had understood the message.

"Shit," was all he said.

That was all that needed to be said to understand that tonight, the ghosts of the past would be hosting us here in Sugar Island.

CHAPTER 70
Stress

OUR HANDS ON OUR EARS, we walked by the speakers blasting out the song by The Who.

"Jesus, can't they shut the fuck up!" shouted Patterson.

But as his greatest quality didn't seem to be patience, he aimed his gun at the speakers and shot a bullet into each of them, killing the stereo and plunging us once again into the silence of the night.

I'd never heard a gun being fired at close range and was surprised by the detonation. Two huge deafening *blams* echoed through my head.

"He's trigger happy," I said to Shana who was in front of me.

"That idiot is capable of screwing things up pretty quickly," she confirmed, moving closer to her boss to show him she also had her word to say in this operation.

Light was coming from the back kitchen door,

which was ajar, the same one where I'd broken in a couple of days ago.

"This way," said the cop holding Clever. The dog began to bark and pull at his leash, eager to do his job and follow the trail out hosts had left.

Patterson walked in first.

"Anyone home? If you're in there, come out now, hands up. It's better for everyone. You're on private property here and in Maine this is a criminal offence."

No one answered his tirade. But I thought to myself if it was Brandon Lake, he certainly had the right to be here.

Clever sniffed the ground frenetically, still pulling on his leash, dragging the patrolman into the villa, into the huge living room where I had illegally spent the night.

It was completely silent inside. We walked slowly, in single file, as if we were following a hearse. We were all tense and nervous, like the calm before a storm.

Patterson and Davidoff's teammates went off right and left, their guns loaded and in front of them. Clever was still whining, sniffing all over in the living room and the other rooms on the first floor: a bedroom and a bathroom. They were all empty.

Quite naturally everyone looked at the big wooden staircase going upstairs, where Mason Lake's office was and where all the bedrooms were, including Brandon's room, the one that had never changed since he was a baby. For me Brandon as a grown man logically would be there.

Patterson, gesturing with his hand, told the group to follow him up the stairs. Agent Maxwell, holding an excited Clever firmly, was behind him. His master told him to calm down, which the well-trained police dog actually did. Now you could have heard a pin drop. Or those green flies that surround bodies when they're decomposing…

This new silence wasn't troubled by any insects, rather by quiet and muffled footsteps in the hall.

Patterson, a finger on his lips, eyes wide open, was urging us not to make the tiniest noise. Then he was the one who did.

"Whoever you are, come out calmly, hands in the air, we won't hurt you!"

These words though didn't seem to suit the person who was upstairs.

"You're the one who's going to calm down, Patterson," declared a feminine voice.

At the same moment, in an angle of the hall, we saw the barrel of a rifle pointing at us.

CHAPTER 71
In front of witnesses

A WOMAN WAS HOLDING the arm, her left hand on the wooden forearm and the index finger of her right hand on the trigger. Her face above the arm on her shoulder was closed and determined.

A face that Tom Malone instantly recognized.

"Cynthia?"

"Hey, Tommy. Nice to see you again. So you're part of this too? The more the merrier."

The policemen who were present now reacted, a cacophony of noises mixed by wrinkled clothing, the clink of weapons, the dog barking, footsteps on the wooden stairs, and Patterson's words, cutting Cynthia off.

"Drop that fucking gun, Favor! I'm not going to say it again!"

"Or else what?" replied Cynthia. "What are you going to do if I don't? Shoot me like a wild animal? In front of witnesses? In your shoes Patterson, I'd avoid making things worse."

"Quit trying to be a smart ass, put that gun down, hands in the air, and walk slowly downstairs. We won't hurt you."

Cynthia just shook her head.

"*Tsk, tsk, tsk*. Maybe I will, but after, not now."

"After what?" asked Patterson impatiently, his gun still pointing to her.

"After our little conversation. I think we've got lots to say to each other. In front of witnesses..."

I saw Patterson's jaw tense up, his arm too. He had his left hand on his right elbow, as if he was getting ready to fire a gun in a shooting range.

"Enough bullshit, Favor," he said.

"I know everything, Patterson. All the filth, all the dirty tricks that you and your little friends in Greenville and Miami have been playing for over twenty years."

Everyone, including me, was holding their breath. The Cynthia Favor - Patterson face-to-face was like a boxing match when the bell had just rung and the first blows were given by the young brunette, with her dark eyes... and her double-barreled shotgun.

"You don't know anything. You're bluffing. Don't forget I could charge you for insulting a public official."

"That's nothing compared with what you risk Patterson, with all due respect. Acts of pedophilia and pimping, insider trading, corruption, and homicide, just to mention the main ones. The list would be too long to complete here, in our little meeting amongst old friends, but I'm sure a federal judge will take time to detail it to you, when you'll be arrested. Which means, and I'm so very glad, that you won't be a public official much longer."

Patterson was getting impatient; his eyes were red with wrath. As if wanting to end this all, he started to run up the stairs.

"Don't take another step!" shouted Cynthia from the landing, her arm aiming at the policeman's chest. "Let me tell our guests the incredible story of Robert Patterson. It's a fun one, you'll see."

"I forbid you..."

"Let her continue," Lieutenant Davidoff suddenly said.

Patterson looked at his deputy, outraged.

"You..."

"You can continue, Cynthia," said Shana, now aiming at Patterson with her service weapon.

That reminded me of the expression "*Mexican showdown*," I think it was. The only difference here was that now two people were aiming at Patterson. The young lady began her story while Clever continued to growl.

"This story began in the last century. Or should I say in the last millennium as the Pattersons and Lakes knew each other and had been close friends since the 1990s. Mason and Robert, who both attended the same university - and here, are you all sitting down? -

also hung out with a guy named Victor Martineau. So these three young men all attended the University of Maine. They majored in different subjects, but they were all members of the Epsilon Fraternity. When they graduated, they all went their separate ways, but quickly saw each other again. Firstly in 2000, in the sunny state of Florida. So what happened then under the Miami sun? A cruel domestic accident, euthanasia of a Golden Retriever and the death of a poor kid... The death? Officially. Off the record though the burial of that poor child was a farce mounted by his parents, with the complicity of the funeral home employees who had been slipped a couple of bucks to accept to close an empty casket, one that a representative of the public administration had officially sealed. Someone named Robert Patterson, who at that time was working in Coconut Grove..."

"A bunch of bull," seethed Patterson from the bottom of the steps. "That's an awful fairy tale you're telling us Miss Favor. Such imagination! Congratulations! Did you ever think of writing novels or scenarios for TV series? And if what you say is true, what happened to Brandon Lake then? As you know it all..."

"I'll get there. Just let me continue the story. There's going to be a new chapter, many years later, but this time in a new place. Here we are in Maine where, - can you believe it? - our three mates are back together. One of them has become the mayor of the town, the other one was transferred to the local police department, and the other is one of the richest people in Greenville, if not *the* richest. I bet you all know the three little pigs I'm talking about. I did say *the three little pigs*, because you'll see, they're swine! Swine and accomplices in the same ignominy. Grown men and fathers whose favorite leisure activity consists in organizing little parties with their own daughters, all three just barely teens, but who already are forced to accommodate the deviance of these three sexual predators..."

A couple of us listening could understand what the young lady was alluding to, whereas others – Patterson's teammates – were rolling their incredulous eyes, not knowing how to react: shut the young lady up or let her vent? In the absence of a direct order, they let her continue.

"These three little piggies have been friends for a long time, we know that, and they support each other, they've got each other's backs, if I can use this expression. Each one *knows* that the two others *know* things that the public *must not know*. Each one also knows what he *owes* the two others. So between them, mum's the word. No one would say a thing about this scandalous new scene taking place right here in Sugar Island, Ladies and Gentlemen, right where you're standing! Isolated from the rest of the world on Mason Lake's private property! An island that he purchased for next to nothing thanks to the discreet support of Mayor Martineau, who officially signed the deed - I was talking about insider trading before, remember? - to allow his frat friend to become the only owner. Generous, wasn't he? Not really. Let's just say tit for tat.

Because a couple of years ago, this same Martineau owed his election to Mason Lake's political and financial support, as he threw greenbacks into the hands of the electors, strongly urging them to vote in favor of his friend. *I hold you, you hold me, By the chinny chin chin, The first one to giggle, Will lose and ... get shot in the head!"* Cynthia suddenly sang, smiling. "Or rather, if the local news is correct, three gunshot wounds in the chest," she added, alluding to yesterday's murder.

"Disgusting," said the policeman.

"Yet unfortunately true. Wait, who's the third little piggie? You are Patterson! Yeah, this swine owes his job as Chief of Police in Greenville to Victor Martineau himself - a job that Lieutenant Shana Davidoff should have had when Barry Fenton retired. They're both here today, like I said, he got this job thanks to Victor Martineau's support. The circle has been closed. Everyone's holding everyone else... by the balls!"

Now no one was protesting. We were all hanging on to Cynthia Favor's every word, listening to her fascinating tale and looking at the menace of her double-barreled shotgun.

"Now, the last chapter is more recent: the summer of 2017. Maybe you see where I'm going here. One of the young teens who had been sexually abused five years ago disappears in mysterious conditions, but we'll talk about that later, if that's alright with you. And even if it's not, I'm the one telling the story, so I'll do what I want. With this new tragedy, Mason and Janet Lake moved – or maybe they fled – to Florida and sold their house in West Cove Point. And then photos of the private parties in 2012 were discovered... and hidden away by the current Chief of Police. Yeah, you Patterson. How could you not want to hide compromising proof like that? And how could you not want to sabotage the investigation you were doing on Veronika as it resulted in one of your victims disappearing? Veronika couldn't be found, for you it was a bonus, she'd never talk."

"Unfounded lies," Patterson denied once again, his index finger on the trigger of his pistol.

"We'll see," Cynthia insisted. "My story is nearly finished, and we'll see what's left for you to defend yourself Patterson. And the last act of this story of friendship between three students from the University of Maine just began a week or two ago. A journalist specialized in cold cases, Karen Blackstone, who's also present tonight, came to Greenville, and started to stir up the muck of the past. She questioned everyone, some people wanted to talk, others no, she discovered things, she deduced other things and all of that disturbed quite a few people. Like dominoes, when you push the first one, all the others fall too. And then Mason and Janet Lake were arrested, and they confessed! And you Patterson, your legs began to quake. Same for Martineau. The mayor, probably the weakest link, tried to come clean, tried to confess, and tried to tell the whole truth. You two had a stormy conversation on the phone – we've got witnesses – and subsequently Martineau was assassinated a few hours later upon leaving the town hall. Just bad luck? Wrong place at the wrong time? *Tsk, tsk, tsk,*" the young lady started again. "One friend locked up, another one six feet under, all that's left is you, Robert Patterson, you who I declare for guilty for aiding and abetting of all these aforementioned acts!"

Our mouths were all hanging wide open here, but the silence was suddenly interrupted by bursts of laughter, like a hyena, I should say, from Chief Patterson, who nearly lost his breath.

"You haven't got an ounce of proof for all those lies that you just told, Favor. Not one!"

"I don't need any proof, Patterson. Just a confession and someone to testify."

"So who's gonna testify? Who told you this moving story?"

A voice replied from the hall upstairs.

"I did, Patterson."

A man came in from behind Cynthia, also holding a shotgun. And this man was no other than my surprise guest in Greenville, the self-proclaimed Brandon Lake.

"Who are you?" asked Patterson.

"An enemy who wants you behind bars, you scumbag!"

When he said these words, he put his shotgun to his shoulder, lowered his head to the sight and his fingers tensed up on the trigger.

In a nearly simultaneous movement, Patterson

extended his arm with the gun in it out and his index finger squeezed the trigger.

Everyone shouted "No!" "Stop!" "Down!" at the same time.

And we heard two gunshots.

A scream ripped through our eardrums.

CHAPTER 72
Scents of fear

THE SCENE WAS FROZEN for a fleeting moment, like in a Kodak picture. The odor of gunpowder was mixed with scents of fear and tension. Not a word was spoken and even Clever, his mouth hanging open, was incapable of barking. We all looked at one another, our eyes haggard.

Bob Patterson suddenly fell onto the first steps, dropping his gun. His left hand was supporting his bloody and trembling right hand.

Shana Davidoff was on my left, still aiming, her gun facing her boss.

"Maxwell, Carrington," she ordered the two patrolmen, "call ER right now. Get a helicopter to evacuate Bob."

"Roger, Lieutenant!"

Bob Patterson was squirming around on the floor, whimpering, suffering, gritting his teeth.

"You fucking assholes…"

Then he passed out.

Shana Davidoff picked up her boss's gun and put it into a holster in her uniform.

Upstairs, Cynthia Favor and Brandon Lake both lowered their guns but were not ready to turn themselves in. Why should they anyway? Neither of them had fired. The first detonation came from Patterson's gun and its impact was clearly visible on the wall right above Brandon's shoulder. The second one came from the lieutenant, who, using her reflexes, wanted to prevent a murder by disarming her boss, full of hatred.

"Now, we have to explain ourselves calmly," she said to the young couple. "First of all though, I'd like everyone to put their guns down, okay? We're going to have a little talk between responsible and peaceful adults."

Cynthia and Brandon looked at one another, weighing this proposal made by the new head of operations.

"Everyone, including you," said the young man softly.

"Totally," agreed Shana Davidoff, raising her arms, and then slowly putting her gun down on the coffee table behind her. She did the same thing with Patterson's gun. "Your turn," she calmly said to them.

After a few seconds they did the same thing, understanding that no one would win in a situation by playing cowboys. Their goal, meaning the neutralization of Patterson, the last of the three sexual predators, was achieved.

We all started up the stairs to meet Cynthia and Brandon, but Brandon put his arms out, palms up, in our direction.

"One minute," the bearded man said. "Everyone's not invited up."

"Your conditions are starting to bother me here," Shana said.

"No. With all due respect, Lieutenant Davidoff, we know you're on our side and thank you for everything you've done for us and for justice, but we have to tell our story first... let's say... in private. What we have to say can't be shouted out. We promise though that you'll know everything, and officially. But for now we just want to talk to Tommy... 'cos he's Tommy... and Karen, because we owe it to her."

Shana paused on the fourth step, made a face, hesitated, and looked at Malone, Fenton and I. Barry nodded his head and backed down, inviting her to follow him.

"Please," said the young man, from the top of the stairs.

"Okay," Lieutenant Davidoff abdicated.

Tommy and I went up the last steps to join Favor and Lake on the landing. They turned around and invited us to follow them. I immediately knew where they were going. Into Brandon Lake's sanctuary.

Cynthia went in and turned on the light. We went in, our heads down, one after the other, like for a funeral. Everything was exactly as it was a week ago: the crib, the wallpaper, the curtains, the toys, and rug with its Disney characters where Cynthia and Brandon sat down. We did the same thing, like kids playing in a circle. I felt like one of them was going to get up quickly and walk around us singing a nursery rhyme.

"Here we go round the mulberry bush,
 the mulberry bush, the mulberry bush.
 Here we go round the mulberry bush, on a cold and frosty morning."

And one of them was going to mime washing their hands or something.

Of course, nothing like that happened, but sometimes your imagination associated with a place sparks curious thoughts.

Tommy spoke up.

"How come you invited us here? What's going on? Jesus, Cynthia, this is freaking me out. Last time we saw each other, you and me, it was here in Sugar, five years ago, on the beach, next to the pontoon. Remember?"

"I do, Tommy. We even got in a little fight, right?"

"I know, that wasn't cool."

I observed the bearded man, listening to this discussion, and found him ambiguous, worried, and tense. I butted in.

"Can I know why and how you came precisely here right now?"

"It's because of you Karen, or thanks to you," Brandon informed me. "Let's say that your arrival in Greenville accelerated ours. We had been thinking of this for a while but hadn't dared to do it. And when we learned that someone wanted to reopen the file on Veronika's disappearance to understand the reasons and circumstances, it was like fate had knocked on our door."

When he said that he took Cynthia's hand. Their fingers touched tenderly. Not something that Tommy, next to me, really appreciated. Cynthia looked at me.

"Actually the grapevine worked here. You contacted Tommy, then Alvin, Paul, Carlos, and Dorothy. One of them contacted us then. After that, we read the articles that your magazine published, got your contact details, the name of the hotel where you were staying, and all that. And here we are."

"You're together?" Tom Malone asked.

Both nodded at the same time, something that was touching.

"We are," Tommy replied softly. "We're together."

Tommy squinted as if he was trying to imagine who the bearded man was. I felt like he was going to jump him and try to rip his beard off, thinking it was fake. He lowered his voice though.

"Who the hell are you? Did I miss something here? Okay, Brandon Lake didn't die, which explains why Karen couldn't find his death certificate. That's understandable. But, as I understand it, ever since the dog attacked him, he's like a vegetable, in a home for the disabled, with nurses who have to change his diapers several times per day. So, gimme a break man, no one's gonna believe that you're him. I'm not and no one else will either. Or we got told other lies. I'm fucking tired of all these lies and all these secrets! And I'd like to know what the hell you've all been hiding for over five years now!"

Tommy got up and I had to hold him back.

"Tommy, sit down. We're going to tell you the truth. And to start, I'm not Brandon Lake."

"Who are you then?"

"You'll find out pretty soon."

CHAPTER 73
With certitude

SITTING IN A CIRCLE, or should I have said, a square, each of us in a corner, Cynthia Favor, the one-who-is-not-Brandon-Lake, Tom Malone, and I all looked at each other, waiting for what would finally be said.

"Are you close to the Lake family?" I said in a pleasant voice, after Tommy had finished shouting.

"I suppose you could say that. But I don't have anything in common with their group of perverts, believe me."

"I'm sure of that. Could you tell us your name?"

"Of course I can. But not yet. Aren't there any more important gray areas you'd like to shed light on? For example, knowing what really happened to Veronika Lake?"

"Because you know?" This time I was the one shouting out.

"Without a shadow of doubt. Or to be even clearer: with certitude."

"Because you saw what happened?"

The young man looked at Cynthia next to him.

"Even better. Because Cynthia and I personally organized her disappearance..."

My mouth was hanging open so wide my jaw nearly fell off. My brain was working overtime.

"Veronika Lake is alive?"

Cynthia nodded, a smile on her lips for the first time.

"Where is she?" asked Tommy.

"Not too far," replied the young man. "For the time being, she's waiting for the right moment to enter, to reappear..."

Cynthia continued, without leaving us any time to digest this bombshell.

"So, here's what really happened that night in August of 2017..."

∽

Summer of 2017, *Sugar Island.*

The moon was shining over the forest in Sugar Island, easing the darkness with its soft and peaceful light. The speakers behind the two girls, set up around the pool in the villa were spitting out violent and irregular sounds, something useless at this time of the night.

Cynthia and Veronika, who were slowly walking to the creek facing Lily Bay, couldn't stand the blaring sounds anymore. They needed to be alone. Hand in hand, the two young ladies walked to the tiny sand beach.

"You ready?" asked Cynthia. "You're sure of this?"

"More than ever. I can't stand it anymore. It's time we take charge. I want to change and change now. Cynthia, are you still with me on this?"

"Whatever you want, Veronika."

"You'll join me? You won't dump me?"

"Stop inventing stories like that, Vero. Both of us agreed. We decided and it's now or never. The more we think about it, the less we'll be willing to actually do it. And of course we'll get together again, dummy! We organized everything, planned for everything. See this grain of sand?"

The young lady picked one up from the beach.

"This little grain of sand isn't going to stop us, okay? Neither it nor anyone else."

"You're right. Excuse me for freaking out like that. This is a big deal though. You don't think it would have been better to let the others know?"

"Are you crazy or what? So they'd try to stop us? So that they'd tell everyone else, and you wouldn't be able to disappear anymore? Okay, time to shake a leg now."

The two young ladies walked down to the shoreline, where the lake licked their toes with a slow and calm tiny noise. No waves that night on the peaceful Lake Moosehead, the water was still warm, and conditions were ideal. Veronika walked in up to her knees and turned to face Cynthia, who took her hands and hugged her. Tight. Skin against skin in their swimsuits, they both had goosebumps. But what kind? Fright? Cold? Desire? All three?

Their faces came together, and their lips joined in a kiss mixing passion, lust, fear, expectations and the hope of a more peaceful future.

Then Veronika pulled away from Cynthia, slowly, turned to face the lake, and step by step walked into the lake up to her chest and started to swim.

Sitting on the beach, looking towards Lily Bay, Cynthia saw her friend swim away, breaststroke after breaststroke. Veronika was an excellent swimmer, that wouldn't be a problem. Soon the light from the waxing moon no longer allowed her to see her, but Cynthia remained there, perhaps for even an hour, she no longer had any notion of time. She hoped that Veronika would soon make it to the mainland across, not even a third a mile. It wasn't too much to ask.

She suddenly heard footsteps coming from the villa, behind her. She turned around and immediately recognized him. She sighed.

Cynthia? Ah! There you are. You know where the hell Veronika is?

Tom Malone, holding a bottle of beer in his left hand, nervously pushed away the greasy strand of hair on his forehead, while running up, panicked to her.

Haven't seen her for a good half an hour, she replied

to the visibly drunk young man. Why ? I thought she was with you.

She was. But she took off.

Cynthia shook her head.

Tom Malone didn't believe his ears and let them know it.

"You two really made fun of me, didn't you!" he said. "Two fucking bitches, two fucking pussy eaters, huh? So you're the two that Alvin surprised having a good time in that bedroom that night?"

"Please, Tommy," Cynthia begged. "I can understand that you're angry. But we didn't have a choice."

"You still don't know everything about Veronika," the bearded man added. "There's a whole part of her personality that she never told you about."

"What the hell do you know?" Tom asked angrily. "Who the fuck are you to say that you know her better than I do? You finally gonna tell us?"

And he furiously stood up, pushing the unknown man with the brown beard on the chest.

"Tom don't do anything you might regret," I said, trying to calm him. "Let them explain."

Tension had ratcheted up a notch when the man also got up, defying Malone, nearly nose to nose now.

But what would happen next was something that no one had seen coming.

The unknown man turned around, his back facing

us, lifted his sweater and t-shirt with one hand and lowered his belt with the other.

I didn't think I had ever been so surprised in my whole life:

The nude skin we could now see had a birthmark on it, one that was impossible not to recognize.

"Veronika..." whispered Tommy, who'd also identified her.

CHAPTER 74
Costume

AFTER TOM MALONE'S exclamation when he saw Veronika's birthmark - a clearly identifiable one, the same one I'd also seen on her in the pictures taken when she was wearing a bikini, or those horrible ones from the pedophilia evenings - we were all in the same stupor. Though we were aware of something, the evident proof of her identity had left us speechless for several interminable seconds.

The bearded Veronika let her sweater fall back down over her brownish birthmark, and turned around, tears falling from her eyes.

"Tom, I'm sorry, I'm so terribly sorry, if you only knew how much."

She took Tom's hands and squeezed them strongly. She hugged Tom, put her forehead against him, and they remained like that, their heads touching for a few minutes without a word, their eyes damp and hearts pounding, I was sure. Cynthia and I were silent witnesses of this moving and slightly bizarre scene between two men who, five years ago, had been a heterosexual couple. Tommy finally backed away.

"Okay Veronika, why don't you take off your costume now."

"Tommy, what costume?"

"Well, the fake beard - very realistic, congrats - your men's clothing, all that."

"Tommy, I understand that it's hard for you to assimilate the whole story," Veronika murmured. "You don't understand... For you, maybe I'll always be Veronika, but Veronika has disappeared Tom! Veronika is dead. Now, I'm a man."

"Bullshit," Tom Malone persisted. "What? How could you have done that?"

"You mean change sexes?"

"Yeah, that's what I don't understand. Why? And how?"

"Let me try to explain it to you. Let's sit down."

Right then we heard the easily recognizable noise of helicopter blades above the villa, immediately followed by a powerful searchlight coming in through the shutters of the room. Undoubtedly for Patterson's evacuation.

Veronika took a deep breath and started to explain.

"To make things clear," she began, "you must understand that deep down inside of me and probably unconsciously at first, I've always felt that I wasn't born in the right body, in the right skin and most importantly, that I never had the right identity. More than a sex change or gender reassignment, whatever you want to call it, it was first and foremost an identity change. Some people would say I'm transgender. I'd define myself as transidentitary. So, as of now, please call me by my new first name... Virgil... I'm '*he*' and no longer '*she*.'"

"Virgil," Malone repeated mechanically. "It makes me think of virginity."

"You're right Tommy. That's why I chose that first name. I feel like a virgin. I'm a new man."

"Virgil what?"

"Virgil Favor," said the new man looking at Cynthia.

Tommy nodded, completely discouraged.

"We got married last year," said Cynthia, showing a golden wedding ring on her finger.

I noticed an identical wedding ring on Virgil's finger, a detail that had escaped me.

To put an end to that embarrassing moment, *Veronika-Virgil* continued.

"Before 2017, I understood that I wouldn't *become* a man, because deep down inside I *already* was one. I think that it's something you're born with and in your genes. Today I'm persuaded that even before I was born, this was my fate. After that, it was experience, what I'd done, things that happened in my life that triggered the necessity of shedding my feminine skin. Like a snake does. And you both know, for things that happened in my life, well, let's just say there were a lot of them... What happened to my brother Brandon, when my mother was pregnant with me, bedridden and incapable of moving fast enough because of her huge stomach. That's something that condemned me as of that very day, and I wasn't even born! Judged, sentenced, and jailed with no defense. I know that my parents, especially my mother, put the blame on me for my brother's near death, that son who was the world for them. I grew up as a non-desired daughter, unloved, rejected by two bitter parents. That was the first stone in the building of my desire to no longer be the person that my genes had decided for me."

Cynthia, Tommy and I didn't say a word, aware that Virgil needed to speak, as much as to explain everything to us as to understand himself. As for me, I realized that little by little I was seeing *her* shift to *him* in my mind.

"After that, even when I was little, as you can see on the few photos of me as a kid, my parents always 'disguised' me into the son they'd lost. Short hair, unisex clothing, trucks and cars, not a single doll. I'm not going to talk about stereotypes here, but it was really evident. They raised me as a substitute Brandon, a *Brandon-bis*. You have to understand that in conditions like those, it wasn't easy for me to have... my own feminine identity."

Everyone simultaneously nodded.

"But that was nothing compared to what was waiting for me. Rather than letting me *build* normally, they ended up *destroying* me, tearing me down. When I was about twelve and my hormones kicked in, contradicting my parents' revolting plans, giving me wider hips, boobs that began to grow, more feminine features, the substitute son of their dreams began to evaporate, escape them. But that was without counting on the fierce imagination of my father and ... and his friends, Patterson, and Martineau. What followed - well you already saw pictures of it, right? So I don't have to add anything except that symbolically, I segued from the status of *substitute son* to a *daughter-object*. Object of the sexual depravity of my father and his friends, who were just as disgusting as him. And the cowardice, ignorance, or complicity of their wives. So you can well imagine how revolted I was by my budding body of a woman, one that other pedophiles exploited. Yes, really revolted by this body, and by extension, by me. I saw myself as an atrocity, and felt I was the fruit of temptation. A few years later, when I was nude with a boy – and my poor Tommy, you know what I'm talking about here, – I was so ashamed and disgusted with myself and my new body that I couldn't bear to be touched intimately..."

Tommy nodded, understanding.

"That's when I knew that I had to change," Virgil continued. "I knew I had to eliminate this identity that was not mine, not me, this carnal envelope in which I no longer wanted to live. I was about sixteen when I began the slow process of changing sexes. I was gone more and more, missing school quite often, because I had doctor's appointments in Portland. It started with appointments with Dr. Verril, a psychologist, because you don't change your identity, your body, your sex, just by snapping your fingers. You must be mentally prepared before the medical and legal steps."

"Why didn't you ever tell me this?" Tommy asked regretfully, his voice broken by emotion.

"It was my secret. And on the other hand, I was still curiously attracted by you, Tommy. I loved you, in my own way. Little by little though, I accelerated the process. I began a masculinizing hormone replacement treatment. I kept going to Portland Hospital to meet with specialists, endocrinologists, anesthesiologists, surgeons, urologists and so on. Just like a butterfly, it was time for me to transform myself from a larva to a chrysalid. I needed a couple of years to mature and grow in my little cocoon and reappear later, completely transformed into a magnificent butterfly who would be able to fly away. That stage began in August of 2017, right here in Sugar Island."

CHAPTER 75
Getaway plan

WE COULD HEAR the helicopter's blades throbbing again as it flew away from Sugar Island, with the former Chief Patterson and his teammates, except for Lieutenant Shana Davidoff who remained at the villa.

In Brandon's mausoleum, Cynthia, Tommy and I were all hanging on to Virgil's every word as he related his transformation to us.

"It takes a long time to go from a woman's body to a man's body. I had to disappear far away and for quite a while to come back, if I was ever going to come back, only when no one would recognize me. And you didn't recognize me. Not even you Tommy, and you knew me so well. I wanted to totally delete Veronika Lake's existence. But it's hard to erase an identity and a body. A long-term undertaking. So I'm not going to bore you with all the medical and surgical details, but you can well understand that it took them a long time to shape the man's body in which I now live. My deeper voice, this brown beard that's real, the hair on my arms, my larger shoulders, my flattened chest, all of this can take up to five years of long hormonal testosterone treatments. And I'm not going to mention... what you can't see, if you get where I'm going," said Virgil trying to joke, though no one laughed, "but I can assure you that I am now a man, with all the equipment that goes with my masculinity. Veronika had to die so Virgil could be born. And that's why, with Cynthia, we drew up a getaway plan, that would take place on the weekend of August 26 to 27, 2017, during the party."

"You planned it all then," Tommy said softly. "In secret. Why the hell did you never tell me? Why did you hide all your problems from me? We were a couple, we loved each other..."

Virgil extended a soothing hand to Tommy, who now that he understood that his ex-girlfriend was a man, jumped back at this friendly gesture.

"Hey!" said Virgil. "I haven't changed."

"Well, a little bit..."

"Inside I'm still the same person. And yes, I did love you, a special kind of love undoubtedly... But I didn't want to burden you with all that. I just wanted to disappear to better reappear. So that's what Cynthia and I did that night. On Saturday morning, before we left for Sugar, we took two cars. We dropped one off near Lily Bay, on the edge of the forest. I hid the keys in the gas tank door, and I'd filled up. In the night of

Saturday to Sunday, I swam from Sugar to Lily Bay. You know Tommy, I've always been a good swimmer, and it wasn't that far. The water was warm, and no one could see me that night. And I'd also hidden a backpack with dry clothes and a towel on Lily Bay Beach. So when I got there, I dried myself off, got changed and walked to the car. I got the keys out from my hiding place and started the engine. I have to tell you though that at that moment, my emotions were mixed. Fear, regrets, desires, and joy too, but most of all, hope. And I stepped on it and drove off. I'd mapped out the fastest road to Canada and the first town there. And in a little over two hours, there I was safe in Saint-Theophile, in the Quebec province, just a few miles from the border. It must have been about five; the sun was beginning to rise. Cynthia knew that she couldn't alert you before that time, because I needed enough time to flee before the cops began to search for me and put roadblocks up around the lake and at the border. Everything went perfectly. I moved there and waited for Cynthia to join me. I continued and even accelerated my transformation, from a medical and legal point of view, including a new identity. I'm now a Canadian citizen named Virgil Favor," the young man concluded. "Veronika Lake is dead; Virgil Favor is a new man."

We were all totally awed after having heard Virgil's tale. What a destiny!

"Why did you decide to come back now?" I asked. "Why didn't you just stay in Quebec?"

"Because, like I said earlier, I needed to wipe the slate clean, and Karen, you gave me the opportunity. Without your investigation on my disappearance, I wouldn't have been strong enough to come back."

"There's a question I must ask you, about a logical coincidence. Virgil Favor, did you shoot Victor Martineau when he came out of the Town Hall? Because he'd abused you a couple of years ago?"

Virgil didn't answer immediately.

"If you ask me if I'm glad he's dead, the answer is yes. If you want to know if this is something I'd already thought of, the answer is yes. If you want to know if I killed him, the answer is no."

"Cynthia?"

"The answer is also no."

"So who killed that bastard?" wondered Tom Malone.

We got the answer to this question when someone knocked three times on the door.

It was Lieutenant Davidoff.

CHAPTER 76
Undeniable results

"EVERYTHING OKAY HERE? Excuse me for opening the door," said Shana, walking into Brandon Lake's room, "but I just got a message from the services who did Victor Martineau's autopsy. Ballistics seem to confirm your theory. The bullets they extracted from the mayor's body correspond without the shadow of a doubt to Sig-Sauer P226 bullets. The ones we use here in Greenville."

"Meaning the arm Chief Patterson used," I continued.

"Exactly. And that'll make things even worse for him, knowing that we've got materiel proof, photos, a motive, which was the necessity of making sure Martineau wouldn't talk, as well as testimonies from the mayor's secretary, and you. Plus now we've also got undeniable results from our scientific analyses. All that's left to do is to compare the bullets in Martineau's body with those here, that I took out from the wall upstairs. Methinks they're the same ones, and that they were fired from the same pistol. Patterson is done for, just like Mason and Janet Lake who are behind bars in Miami."

"Those three bastards are paying for their crimes," said Virgil Favor.

"You still have to explain it all to me," said the lieutenant with a skeptical frown to Cynthia and Virgil.

"We will," said the young man.

Shana Davidoff left nodding, and we could hear her steps on the stairs. We were also getting ready to leave Brandon Lake's room, when I glanced up at the wall and then had a question that hadn't yet been answered.

"This *The Who* poster," I asked them, "do you have any idea who wrote '*Who killed Brandon?*' on it?"

'I did," Cynthia said. "A few days after the cops had been there, I came back and took the poster down from the wall in the office and thumbtacked it to the wall here, adding the question."

"Which explains why I didn't see anything when I went into Brandon's room and took Winnie to throw it into the pool. You hadn't yet moved the poster," Tommy said.

"But how come?" I asked.

"I asked her to do it," Virgil said. "I could feel that one day or another we'd have to shake the coconut tree to have the truth fall from it. I thought that an enigmatic message like that would maybe do the trick. That one day or another someone would finally come back here, discover the sentence and trigger research about it plus all the other affairs in our family's life. And that's what happened, didn't it?"

"It did. And I dove right in, that's true. To try to find the truth."

This time we all left the bedroom. Virgil, the last person, turned the lights off and closed the door behind him. We joined Lieutenant Davidoff downstairs.

"I think we're done here," she said.

A few minutes later, we were all in the police boat, heading for Greenville. Virgil and Cynthia were sharing a blanket at the end, Tommy was next to them. I was with Shana in front. We also brought Barry back, as he'd been waiting for us downstairs too. The night was pitch black and Sugar Island quickly disappeared from our view. On the other side of the lake we could see the streetlights of the little town along the coast of Lake Moosehead.

It was late when I got back to Greenville Inn. I was exhausted, emptied out, as I was each time I finished an investigation where I didn't count my hours nor my efforts to try to solve it. Virgil Lake's sudden eruption had precipitated events, and I was glad. I would be able to go home, even though no one would be waiting for me, and take a few days off before writing my definitive articles for Myrtille, who would, and I could already imagine this, be dancing with joy when I'd tell her all the whys and wherefores of the Veronika Lake affair.

I pulled the warm covers over me in my bed and fell asleep in just a few minutes, my face against the pillow.

But I was awoken at about four in the morning by a nightmare, sweating, with a heavy head. Often during investigations, my brain gets all mixed up and the data that I'd gathered right and left joins together to form a mind of its own. That was what happened here.

IN THIS POWERFUL DREAM, I was on Sugar Island again, in a place that I'd never forget. I was walking slowly through the dense forest on the island, heading towards the creek where Brownie's grave, the Lake family's dog, was located. In my nocturnal thoughts, while nearing the grave, I saw the back of a man, leaning over the grave, with a shovel in his hand. I suddenly walked on a branch which cracked loudly, and the bearded man turned around. It was Virgil Favor, and I'd surprised him when he was refilling the grave. We didn't speak, but we understood each other just with looks. I walked up to the hole. At the bottom, half covered with shovelfuls of earth, there was the dead body of a young lady. Her legs were hidden beneath the earth, rocks, and brownish moss, but I could see her chest and face. Veronika Lake was at the bottom of the tomb. Virgil continued his work, throwing shovelful after shovelful into the grave, burying Veronika's body. The symbolic meaning was easy to understand. We didn't even talk about it. Time, in my dream, went by in an imprecise way, and a few seconds later, Virgil planted a wooden cross on the earth, after having trampled it down with his feet. These words were written on the cross:

Veronika Lake
2000-2017

CHAPTER 77
With ifs and buts

THE NEXT MORNING, I decided to stay in Greenville a few more days. It actually was quite a nice place for a vacation break.

Virgil and Cynthia had decided to go back to Quebec. For them, this town had too many painful memories. Before that though, they were going to go to Florida. I'd stayed in touch with Virgil, and a few days later he told me why.

The day before, before going our own way on the Greenville Marina, I told them - and they were astonished by this - that the real Brandon Lake had survived and gave him the address of the home where he'd been staying for years. Just in case...

~

COCONUT GROVE, Miami, November 2022.

. . .

The Coconut Grove Center for Disabled Adults was a functional, clean, and recent facility, though lacking any charm.

Virgil and Cynthia Favor went down the hall on the third floor, the one for long-term residents, to Room 312, which is the one the nurse at the information desk gave them.

There was a paper label inserted into a plastic case next to the door with the resident's name on it: Brandon Lake.

Virgil, with a pang of sadness upon seeing the name he'd illegally borrowed, knocked on the door, though it was ajar. No one answered. He slowly pushed the door open.

There was a small hall masking the view of the room, with a bathroom on the right side. Near the foot of the bed, he only saw a pair of slippers and two ankles and the bottom of a green pair of pajamas.

He walked a few feet further in and saw his knees, thighs, with hands on them, and finally a bust and an empty face, one that didn't have any expression, as if it had just been laid on a pair of shoulders.

The young Canadian man swallowed when he saw what had happened to his older brother, the one he'd never met before. Would Brandon have been like his parents? A despicable person? Or, had he lived a normal life, would he, like Veronika, have been subjected to physical and psychological violence from their parents? Could the two Lake children have grown up like two ordinary brothers and sisters? Fighting like cats and dogs? And, if so, would Veronika's fate have been different? Would her parents have accepted her? With *ifs* and *buts*...

Cynthia, seeing how troubled Virgil was, put her hand on his shoulder and encouraged him to walk up to the wheelchair.

"Brandon?" asked Virgil.

No reaction. Not the least movement of an eyebrow, a tiny smile, nor a twinkle in one of his eyes. Nothing. Brain dead. An empty shell.

"I'm..." Virgil hesitated. "Um, I'm your sister, Veronika."

"He was too young to remember you," said Cynthia.

"I know," sighed Virgil. "But, Jesus Christ, how many lives were destroyed, ruined?"

The young man talked to himself like that for a couple of minutes, going from the past to the present, but Brandon's eyes remained empty.

He just groaned suddenly. A throaty noise, coming from his chest, almost like a wild animal roaring. Then Brandon leaned his head to the side and a filet of saliva dripped from the corner of his mouth. He closed his eyes. Virgil put his hand on his older brother's hand, who didn't react to this contact any more than he had to visual or auditory solicitations. Karen had said he was a vegetable. Virgil wondered, before being ashamed by this thought, if a cucumber didn't have more reactions to stimuli.

"He must be having a bad day," said Cynthia. "Let's go now."

"A day like all the others for over twenty years for him," said Virgil.

They left the Center for Disabled Adults and took a cab to the airport when they jumped on the first available plane for Quebec.

I'D LOADED my bag in the trunk of my dear old Ford Ranchero. It was sleeting in Greenville and the sidewalks were slippery. In just a few days the landscape had changed completely. I felt like I'd been here for ages, in this tiny town in the middle of nowhere in Maine. So many events in so few days, a concentration of emotions that, as I was about to learn, that wasn't yet over.

My phone vibrated in my pocket. It was Lieutenant Davidoff.

"Karen? Shana here. Am I bothering you? Are you still in Greenville?"

"I was just about to leave. And no, you never bother me!"

"I've got some info to share with you. Are you up for a cup of joe at your regular hangout?"

Ten minutes later the lieutenant and I were sitting in a corner of the Dockside Tavern. I was happy to see Charlene again, the waitress who had been one of the first people to drop me a few breadcrumbs in my quest for the truth. It was nice to see her smile mixed with her jaws moving up and down chewing her gum one more time.

Shana blew on her cup of coffee.

"I just spoke to an expert in ballistics from Portland about the bullets we found in Martineau and those in the wall on Sugar Island. You'll never guess."

"They're not the same?"

"Man, Karen you should be a cop!" the lieutenant said jokingly. "There's a vacancy in Greenville, how about working here?"

"Thanks but no thanks, even if you're the one, I imagine, who will be the new Chief of Police pretty soon?"

"That's what they're saying. I'm the highest-ranking officer, so I'll logically be the new chief. I'm already filling in until Greenville elects a new mayor."

"Congratulations. So, what about this ballistics thing?"

"It's strange, you'll see. I would imagine that you already have a few notions in this field because of your job, but I'll just quickly sum it up for you. You must know that each firearm, just like everyone on earth, has its own print, one that's unique and identifiable, due to the many parts that are required to produce the weapon. Especially for the barrel. This one, the arm that we use in our jobs, has some small stripes. Without going into details, they allow the bullet to gain speed inside the barrel. So that means when the bullet is propelled through the barrel, it's covered with minute striations linked to those stripes. And these striations are also unique and identifiable and can be linked to the gun they were shot from. See where I'm going here?"

"The striations we saw from the bullets extracted from the mayor's chest weren't the same as those we saw on the bullet that Patterson shot in the Lake family's villa. So you can conclude that..."

"That it's probably not Patterson who shot Martineau. At least, the only certitude we have, is that he didn't shoot him with the same gun that he used when shooting at Virgil and Cynthia in the villa. So we'll have to check if he didn't have several guns to conclude. And if not, we'll have to answer the question of *who* shot the mayor of Greenville."

"The investigation goes on," I said, nodding. "But it'll be without me. As for Veronika Lake's disappearance, it's already been explained, and all the rest is collateral damage. But I'd love to know about your progress in the investigation."

"Of course, Karen. This investigation was also yours. We owe you a lot. Are you going back home?"

"That's what I usually do."

"Another investigation in the pipeline?"

"Maybe... Probably a more... personal investigation," I said evasively before finishing my cup of coffee.

CHAPTER 78
Giving fate a little nudge

I STILL HAD to say goodbye to one more person before leaving Piscataquis County. Barry Fenton probably already knew what Lieutenant Davidoff had just told me, but I wanted to get his opinion on this. I called him to say I'd be leaving soon and went over to his place.

When I walked into his yard, I saw him behind the windows in his veranda, where we'd discovered the photos on the USB flash drive, which now was incriminating evidence that the lieutenant had consigned in the thick file on the Lake family and their acquaintances.

He waved and came out.

"Karen, I'm glad you came over to say goodbye."

"We don't know each other very well, Barry, but I'm so happy I got to meet you. Because of you, I was able to make good progress in my investigations."

"Teamwork. I miss that," he said with a smile, inviting me to sit down. "Tea, coffee?"

"Thanks, but I just had one with Shana at the Dockside. I'll be too hyped up to drive if I have another one."

"Your Ranchero doesn't have an automatic pilot?" Barry joked.

"Just what's necessary: an engine, four wheels, a steering wheel and two pedals. Already not too bad. You want to know what else it has?"

"Sure."

"I love it. When I've got the steering wheel in my hands, I've got the impression of seeing my father driving, and me as a kid in the passenger seat, when he took me to my pony-club courses."

"Nostalgia..."

We both remained silent for a couple of seconds. I saw Barry's wife in the hall, waved to her, and she disappeared into the living room, on the other side of the house. A discrete wife.

"You know about the ballistics expertise?" I asked.

"Shana told me, yes."

"What do you think?"

Barry frowned mysteriously and I didn't know how to interpret it. Then he finally answered.

"You know that forensics has made a huge amount of progress. Every TV spectator is now overjoyed and an expert. *The Experts* here, *The Experts* there. Pretty soon they'll be a series with *The Experts in Greenville*," said Fenton ironically. "I suppose it'll take a while for

Shana to find out who the murderer was. She'll have to contact everyone who has a Sig-Sauer P226 around here, or even in the entire county. Or dismiss the case because of lack of proof. Lots of work for Greenville's new chief of police."

"You'll help her out though?"

"Of course, if she needs it. Once a cop, always a cop!"

"Do all the cops in Greenville have the same type of pistol?"

"For the past couple of decades, yeah. Already when I was working, and I'd say for over twenty years here. Wait a sec."

Barry got up and disappeared down the hall. I saw him go into a room, where he stayed a couple of minutes. He came back to the veranda, put his hand behind him, and in a Shakespearian gesture, put a shiny pistol on the table, one that looked like he'd just polished it.

"One of those?"

The former Chief of Police nodded several times.

"You have a permit?"

"Of course I did when I was working, and I just renewed it when I retired. I like to practice at the shooting range sometimes. So I won't forget how."

"And is this the pistol you had when you worked? I would imagine that you had to turn in your service gun when you retired?"

"Our administration isn't foolproof," Barry said, raising an eyebrow and making a strange face.

"You mean... this pistol..."

"That's right Karen."

"Can I?" I asked, getting ready to pick the pistol up. "I never held one in my life."

"If I were you, I'd avoid leaving any fingerprints on it... You could get in trouble."

I opened my flabbergasted eyes when I began to understand what this retired cop was insinuating.

"Barry... I'm afraid to understand... Are you the one who...?"

There was a moment of embarrassing silence between us.

"I suppose," he finally answered, "that if ballistics analyzed the striations on the bullets fired by this arm..."

"Barry, that can't be true. But why?"

"Sometimes you have to know how to give fate a little nudge..."

I looked him right in the eyes, challenging his steel-blue regard.

"Are you going to turn me in?"

I shook my head, sighed, got up, got ready to leave the veranda and turned around.

"Let's just say you worked for the public good. Goodbye, Barry. You're a good man."

...for such a long time.

There were three of them.
    Three guilty men.
    They had to pay for their crime.
    Did they?

I left Greenville yesterday, leaving a story and lives that were broken or repaired behind me.
    A new chapter in the book of my life was completed, waiting for the next one.
    Upon leaving Piscataquis County, I had to and will continue my life, progressing step by step.
    Up until I solve the huge riddle of my existence. That question mark that has been hanging over my head ever since that terrible day. The night of the tragedy that has impacted me ad vitam aeternam.
    Now I know a bit more about my past. I'd found out some details about that unfortunate child I'd been forced to abandon, because he wasn't desired, because he had

been marked with the seal of shame, because I was too young, too alone, too much everything and so much nothing to be a mother at that time.

The date, sex, and place seem to correspond. I'd finally located the point of departure, point zero, the end of this ball of yarn that I'd have to unravel. I hope it will lead me to him... to my child who is now twenty-four. If he's still alive...

I'd searched, investigated, dug, and I'd found something.

All these years have not been in vain, nor have these past months where I wrote all of this down.

Nothing better than...

... words... to help... healing... my fault... this crap that has been eating away me... for such a long time.

Back at home, I closed my black notebook on these hope-filled words.

These words that have helped me cope, that I write some nights before going to bed to evacuate my apprehension and my doubts, between the time I take my pills and the time I turn off my lamp.

For me, the Veronika Lake affair is over. Now I can devote my time to another case, that Myrtille Fairbanks, my favorite boss, and I will define. It's easy, I've only got one boss, but she's the best! *Right, sweetie?*

And then, of course, take time to investigate *my* story, *my disappearance*, the one that has touched me in my heart and in my body for the past twenty-four years.

The search for Karen Blackstone's lost son...

What a great title for an article in True Crime Mysteries!

But that's another story.

THE END

Acknowledgments

The last pages of this story have been closed, for you and for me.

I've entrusted them to you, take good care of them.

One I write THE END, I no longer control the story. These 83,000 words are yours and yours only! Perhaps you loved them. But you've also got the right to have detested them. Whatever your opinion, I thank you so much for having read them. This will be my first "thank you" in the list. Thank you for having discovered me in English with this novel or thank you for your loyalty over the past years, novel after novel. Our shared history is written title after title.

I'd like to thank Sacha, he knows who he is, and thanks to him *transidentity* no longer has any secrets for me. His story was priceless for me, and I'd like to apologize if I incorrectly interpreted his advice sometimes, but it was to be in line with fiction, and often with fiction you have to twist or tweak reality. As the old saying goes, *the author takes full responsibility for any inadvertent errors.*

Special thanks to Ludovic Metzker, Zedole, for his graphic work on the book's cover. He knows that I'm probably his most demanding, picky and undecided client. The hours we spent on the phone just go to prove this.

Thank you, Jacquie Bridonneau for your translation of my novel into English. We've worked together now on three novels, if I've counted correctly, with more to come!

So, there you go. I'm not going to spend hours on my acknowledgements that most people don't read whereas others love them, trying to find indiscretions or allusions.

I'd just like to invite you, if you please, to comment on this novel on platforms or shared sites or on the site where you purchased it. That always makes other readers want to discover my novels. The best publicity for a novel is always by word-of-mouth.

Click here for more information (including a few surprises!):
https://linktr.ee/sebastien_theveny

About the Author

What now?

If you liked this book, my dear Readers, and the troubled past of Karen Blackstone, our journalist, still remains a mystery for you, I'd like to invite you to discover what comes next in this American series.

A new investigation, one that's both scorching and freezing, a brainteaser for our heroin...

Volume II, published on May 12, 2023, is entitled *<u>I WANT MOMMY</u>*.

You can read the prologue on next page and purchase the book here: I Want Mommy

Also by Nino S. Theveny

DISCOVER « I WANT MOMMY », A KAREN BLACKSTONE THRILLER, VOLUME II

"Shoot! I'm going to be late with this lousy weather," grumbled Rebecca, her hands gripping the steering wheel of her old Ford Taurus. Its tires were having trouble finding purchase on that snowy road in the countryside, weaving through two softwood forests.

The young lady had been complaining ever since she left the Village of Four Seasons, when after having done her hair and makeup at home, she saw that it had started to snow again. There were already a couple of inches of immaculate white snowflakes on her doorstep and she knew that the snow would just make things more complicated. She was on the brink of phoning Gavin to cancel their date, but she wanted to see him so badly that her stomach was twisting with desire. She'd been waiting for this date for days now and it wasn't four inches of light snow that would come between her and a good time! She'd even thought of phoning him to ask him to come and pick her up, but a bit of Jewish prudishness had stopped her. She couldn't have one of her office colleagues in her house for a formal first date! Things like that just weren't kosher! Rebecca knew herself well: should she let him in, she would be the one dragging him to her bedroom to keep him there until daybreak. Meeting up in a neutral venue was the best idea for their first love date.

She thus braved the freezing cold, snow and mist, and put her key in the car to start it up. She carefully put her foot on the accelerator to see how her Ford reacted on the snow and slid down her driveway about thirty feet before reaching the road, that luckily had been plowed not too long ago.

Right after that though she began to swear like a soldier.

Night had fallen on Morgan County over two hours ago and the cold weather had morphed into frigid weather, making it difficult to drive. Rebecca encouraged herself by thinking that Gavin would be waiting for her. She turned the radio on. Creedence Clearwater Revival was asking "*Have you ever seen the rain?*".

"The rain?" Rebecca answered. "No rain, but too much damn snow, for sure!"

She glanced at the clock on the dashboard. Already fifteen minutes late. Better to arrive late than not at all, she thought to herself.

The snow was falling harder now and large white snowflakes were making it difficult for her to see more than ten feet ahead of the Ford and the windshield wipers barely helped. She was afraid to go over fifteen miles an hour.

And luckily so.

Otherwise the accident would have been inevitable.

Though she wouldn't have been judged as guilty, Rebecca would never have been able to forget the death of that little girl all alone on the side of the road who appeared suddenly, like a phantom, in her headlights…

Other titles translated into English

THE BASTARO TRILOGY

KAREN BLACKSTONE THRILLERS
Sugar Island (2023)
I Want Mommy (2023)
The Lost Son (2024)
Alone (2024)

OTHER NOVELS
French Riviera (One Too Many Brothers) (2022)
Perfect Crime (2024)
True Blood Never Lies (2021)
Thirty Seconds Before Dying (2020)
Eight More Minutes of Sunshine (2019)

In His Eyes (short story, 2021)

Printed in Dunstable, United Kingdom